# The Malefactors

*By*
*Anne Haw Holt &*
*Richardson Wallace Haw, Jr.*

Paperback
ISBN-13: 978-0-9983877-2-7
ISBN-10: 099838772X

Kindle
ASIN: B075J8RHZ5

Library of Congress
LCCN: 2017917486

Published by Old Atlanta Publishing

Edited by Mark Sherfy

Cover art by Jamie H. Sherfy

Dedicated to my father,
Richardson Wallace Haw, Jr.

Other Books by Anne Haw Holt

*Fiction*

High Plains Fort
Ten in Texas
Silver Creek
Blanco Sol
Riding Fence
Kendrick
Blood Redemption

*Nonfiction*

Grant Writing Step by Step
From Writer to Author
Beautiful Places:
Monticello & Jefferson County Florida

# Preface

Josias' head sagged, his chin almost touching his chest. The pain had stopped. He could no longer feel his hands and feet, but his chest hurt -- he could hardly breathe. Hours passed. Occasionally, as from a distance, he heard Lucius' bitter voice, cursing and railing against his fate.

Forcing his eyes open, he squinted against the hot sun. Most of the crowds were gone. Several groups of people knelt or sat on the sand at the bottom of the hill. The soldiers allowed only a few to climb close to the crosses. Two women sat together near the brow of the hill. Forcing his eyes to focus, Josias recognized the scarf his mother wore and the tendrils of dark hair touching Sarah's brow.

*Sarah, oh Sarah, my beloved wife.*

He closed his eyes on the tears that blinded him and slipped into unconsciousness. Hours later he awakened again. There was no sound from Lucius. Straining, Josias finally opened his eyes a little way. The sun was gone. The cool night of the desert was falling. The two women still sat on the sand.

I wonder if they're thirsty—if they will soon leave—they should go home. They know they should not be here alone. They should find Barabbas--he will protect them. I did not see Barabbas. He wasn't here— he should have been here—Argubus should have been here—.

# The Malefactors

# Chapter 1

The hot, high sun of late afternoon beat relentlessly against the craggy rock cliffs overlooking the empty Roman road west of Jerusalem. Argubus the cripple seemed barely alive. He lay snuggled into a niche under a wide-overhanging cliff, high above the north side of the highway.

Many, many hours the old man spent sitting quietly, watching the road below, ever on the lookout for travelers. His lot, among the many followers of Barabbas, was to watch for some victim for the small robber band hiding in the bush filled wadi below. It was a trying, tiresome task, but one that him paid well. For Barabbas was generous in the division of spoils.

As he lay half-dozing in him as Argubus the Prophet. He the hot shade, Argubus' thoughts were of the clever ways of his life. In the teeming city, people knew forever warned anyone who would stop to listen to his tirades of the anger God felt for his chosen people. They committed many sins.

Most mornings found him at the entrance of David Street. He marched up and down before the gate, waved his arms about and loudly prophesied the forthcoming curses that would soon be visited upon all Jewry by a vengeful God. He told his listeners of a God angered with his people for collaborating with the Romans—for allowing graven images to be displayed in the Holy City and for their many, many sins.

After his harangue, Argubus would go through the crowd holding out his beggar's cup, seeking coins—coins he loudly proclaimed he would use to help the poor. He stared into the face of each person, a wild look of madness in his yellowish-brown eyes. The grim and fearsome expression on his sun-darkened face intimidated many out of at least one small coin.

When he gathered sufficient contributions, he would then leave the city, announcing to everyone in hearing distance that he was going into the desert to commune with God. He promised he would return the next morning to reveal his message to the people. Many scoffed at the old man's preaching of doom, yet others believed and were fearful.

Argubus chuckled to himself as he thought of the foolishness of the devout. Especially those who believed him and gave of their small possessions, for he was a wealthy man according to the standards of his followers. He thought gleefully of a small hoard of coins hidden in a rock cleft directly behind where he sat. It was only a small sample of his treasure. He started to reach for the coins, to know the joy of holding their round smoothness in his hands, when out of the corner of his eye he saw a small dust cloud rising far up the road.

Keeping his head down, he crawled to the far side of the overhanging rocks. Staying bent close to the ground, he scurried down the steep path to the ravine behind the cliffs.

"Josias, Josias, hurry to the lookout and see who comes."

Alarmed and excited, every member of the waiting band dropped what they were doing and rushed to gather around the old man. He waved one arm toward the lookout post.

"Go and see for yourselves."

Josias, leader of the band and Emilack, the youngest member, rushed to climb the cliff path to the spot overlooking the road. Josias pushed his long hair away from his face and held one hand over his eyes to shade them as he cautiously peered over the rocks. The caravan was hidden from his view by a bend in the road. He motioned for Emilack to drop down lower in the rocks to assure he could not be seen.

The two men chafed at the long wait. Finally, the approaching caravan came near enough so they could examine it. Made up of a string of pack asses following a richly dressed merchant, the train moved slowly. The man rode on a fat black mule with richly caparisoned harness. Six poorly armed guards marched on each side of the merchant. The men moved dispiritedly, as though they were exhausted from a long day's march.

Josias crowed with delight as he turned to Emilack. "Look, my friend. The caravan will be rich. Watch the way the guards walk—they're exhausted. They'll be no threat to us and there are no soldiers within miles. This could turn out to be an afternoon well spent."

Still keeping their heads low, he and Emilack rushed back down the path to the waiting men. Motioning for them to come close so he would not have to shout, Josias ordered, "You men see to your weapons and get mounted. We're going to take that caravan. It looks as if it was made for us."

After a great scurrying about, Josias and ten well-armed men mounted their small but sturdy horses and rode to the narrow pass west of camp. Argubus returned to his lookout—he knew his part well. The robber crew hid themselves in the rocks and brush and waited impatiently for the old man's signal to attack.

Argubus looked up and down the road again, to make sure no Roman Patrol rode within sight. As the caravan came abreast of the opening of the wadi that hid Josias' band, the old man screamed the signal to attack. The men swept down on the caravan guards, scimitars swinging. It was over in no more than an instant and the tired guards were dead.

Josias himself held the merchant with his sword point in his throat. He ordered his men to clear the road of all evidence of the raid. Working in tandem, the men dragged the bodies of the slain guards into the broken rocks and brush and tipped them over into the ravine.

When the bodies lay all piled together, Josias' men broke the rim of the ravine and pushed dirt over the dead guards. Finally, the robbers lead their own horses and the heavily laden mules through the mouth of the wadi and out of sight of the road.

Simon of Cyrenia sat his mount quietly, watching the eyes of the robber who still held his sword at his throat. Other members of the man's band rummaged through his merchandise. His chest swelled with anger to know that the robbers touched his possessions, but he was cautious. Wisely reasoning that if the robbers planned to kill him he would already lie dead, he kept silent. All he could do was wait and see what would happen.

Tired of the golden-haired bandit grinning at him, Simon finally said, "I shall inform Rome of Pilate's inability to make his province safe for honest merchants."

"And well you may someday, my fine merchant," Josias said, smiling at the anger so plain to hear in Simon's voice. "If it happens that our master sees fit to hold you for ransom instead of taking your life."

Simon of Cyrenia was one of the most successful traveling merchants in the Empire. He began his work young and seemed naturally shrewd to all those who dealt with him. Many named him a worthy descendant of Phoenician traders.

Usually he gathered costly items along the Southern Mediterranean Sea, conveyed them across the old Syrian caravan routes to Damascus and from there took them to Antioch and Corinth. He sold these goods to the wealthiest residents of those cities. Men and women demanded the best of the Empire's offerings. Everything Simon offered his customers was of great value. The robbers shouted with joy as they opened the packs and examined their loot.

When it was full dark and safe, the men set out on a familiar path, leading the laden animals around the city to Gihon. From that place they could smuggle goods into Jerusalem by a secret door in the side of Nehemiah's tunnel.

Moving everything in the packs took many trips by all members of the band that could be spared from guard duty. Carrying the heavy packs on their shoulders, the men splashed their way through the cold waters that flowed under the city's walls. As soon as the merchandise all lay safely hidden away, Josias turned Simon over to two of his most trusted men.

"Take this merchant to the hidden valley, Micah. You and Elias stay there to guard him. Keep careful watch as you turn west of Mount Guarantania and Jericho. There will surely be Roman patrols moving about in that area. Take care you do not ride into them. This man will bring us a rich ransom.

"Don't you dare forget to blindfold him when you get close to the mountain. He appears sharp and will probably remember everything he sees on the way. It wouldn't do for him to remember the road to our valley."

Barabbas watched Josias' face as he recounted step by step every minute of the successful raid and described the valuable merchandise the men hid in their secret place. The bandit leader tried to keep a scowl on his leathered face, but could not contain an occasional grin. He was undeniably pleased with the returns from the attack on Simon the Cyrenian's caravan.

He felt dismay however, when he learned that Josias decided to hold the merchant for ransom. It was Barabbas' policy to kill everyone in a caravan. That policy served him well and kept his band in safety for many years. Only Josias dared to resort to holding his victims for ransom.

"You will let your greed for gold be our downfall, man. You're a fool to hold men captive instead of killing them." Barabbas began to shout angrily to Josias as soon as he rode into the hidden camp.

Josias showed no fear of Barabbas. Dismounting, he dropped the reins of his horse and approached the bandit chief. "Master, please listen to me. This is a truly wealthy merchant. He is far different from the usual petty traveling peddlers we find. His family will pay well for his release."

"Yes, I suppose they will at that. But what of the day you hold a friend of Caesar or another official of the empire?"

Grinning impudently, Josias said, "That time Master, may be the day we have our fill of excitement."

Barabbas stared at Josias thoughtfully. He valued the man greatly, but feared that his shrewdness and lack of fear would someday take him too far. He could endanger the entire band.

"Meet me at the summit beyond Rimmon at dark tomorrow. We will ride to the valley and see this merchant. I, Barabbas, shall decide his fate."

A little after moonrise the next night, Josias and Barabbas heard the challenge of a guard as they made their cautious way along a steep, rocky defile afoot, leading their horses.

"Halt where you are."

"It is I, Barabbas, and one of my captains."

"Enter Master, and peace be unto you."

A small fire guided their way to a cave-like shelter. The opening was hollowed out from the limestone cliff by some ancient river. All the men of the band except the guard at the narrow entrance and one other man slept beyond the fire, rolled in their blankets.

Without a word of greeting to the man beside the fire Barabbas announced, "We will sleep the night out here, and tomorrow I will talk to the prisoner." Taking his own blanket from the back of his mount, he joined the men who lay around the fire and soon fell asleep.

There was a great stir in the camp when the men wakened and realized Barabbas joined them in the night. Lucius, the captain of the band, feared the bandit chief's visit. His band had found little luck in the last few weeks. He felt tremendous relief when after breakfast Barabbas covered his face with a scarf and called for Josias' prisoner to be brought before him. Lucius' heart swelled with pleasure when he noticed the serious look on Barabbas face.

*I hope he's so angry with that Josias he kills him as an example—right here before my men. If he does it here, it will make the cowards even more afraid not to obey my orders.*

Following a guard, the prisoner emerged from an adjacent cave to stand before Barabbas. Turning to Josias and speaking pleasantly, Barabbas said, "Tell me about this fine prisoner we have here."

"He calls himself Simon of Cyrene, Master. He is surely a merchant of great importance."

"Is this so?" Barabbas said, laughing a little. "We shall see. Were his possessions many, my friend?"

"Yes, his goods are on their way to the usual place to be sold. I am convinced they will bring a tremendous price. Here is a heavy pouch of gold I realized from selling the fine animals of his caravan."

Pulling a rolled sheepskin from a fold in his robe Barabbas said, "Good, let us write a demand to his steward for ransom. Here, use this fine sheepskin. To what relative shall we send our ransom demand, Simon of Cyrene?"

Simon's voice trembled with anger. He held himself proudly, and stared into Josias' eyes, "Write it to my son, James of Cyrene."

"You will be pleased at the high value we set upon you Simon of Cyrene." Barabbas turned to Josias, saying, "Captain, write the ransom for five hundred shekels." He laughed aloud when he turned back and saw the expression of smoldering anger on Simon's face.

Barabbas handed Simon his own business seal, stolen from the merchant's personal possessions. "Here Merchant," Barabbas said, "Stamp the demand at the bottom with this, so it will be recognized by your son."

When Simon finished placing his seal on the document and handed it back to Barabbas, the bandit chief asked, amusement apparent in his voice, "Are you sure your son will think you worth such a sum?"

Simon turned away, pretending interest in the fire and refused to respond to the man's crude humor.

Rolling the piece of skin tightly and tying it with a strip of rag, Barabbas summoned one of his men. "You will take this message to Cyrene. There you will find the house of Simon and give this to his son's hand. The man you seek is known as James."

Leaning forward, he stared into the man's eyes. "Do not fail me. If you do you know I will punish you and all those you love. Remember what I say, I know where your family lives."

Without another word, Barabbas stepped to the other side of the fire. Still masked, he confronted Lucius. "I am disappointed in you and your men, my friend. I will give you only a few more weeks to do your part."

He turned away from Lucius without waiting for an answer and joined Josias at the horses. The two men immediately set out for Jerusalem, leaving Simon of Cyrene to wait in captivity for the many months it would take the messenger to deliver the message and return with the ransom.

The eastern band of Barabbas' men, under control of Barsubus the Philistine, known to his men as Lucius the Hawk, because of his prominent nose and vicious ways, operated along the old King's Highway in Perea. This was a vast, thinly populated area of wild and desolate country. There were many places to hide and escape if chased by the Roman Legion. The country, filled with rocks and gorges, contributed more to the band's success than the wisdom of their leader, for although Lucius was noted for his savagery, he did not have the cunning of Josias.

After Barabbas and Josias left the camp, Lucius sat in the shade of an acacia tree, nursing his jealous anger over Josias' success. "He's got the best place to operate. Old Argubus advised it. Damn both of them any way.

"I'll show them, I'll pull the biggest robbery ever heard of, bigger than Josias ever dreamed. Salem has gone to Gadara to watch for the next large caravan coming in this direction. He'll have plenty of time to ride ahead and warn us so we can get set.

"We'll give Barabbas something to brag about of us. It will be a relief to stop him always talking of the exploits of that infernal Josias and his men."

Lucius' very jaws ached when he thought of the insult he suffered when Barabbas chided him for his poor showing with his men looking on.

*Josias and Argubus throw it up to me every time I see them. That Josias might not brag much, but he has a lofty air. He walks around with his head up in the air as though he thinks he's better than anyone else—that's worse yet—I'll find a way to get even with him someday.*

Far into the night Lucius schemed and plotted future deeds. He planned how he would execute the biggest robbery the Empire ever experienced. It would be so big it would bring out a whole legion from Rome. Then he, Lucius the Hawk, bandit leader, would have followers of his own. He would be able to get out from under the heavy thumb of Barabbas.

Lucius schemed on, completely unaware of his shortcomings. He never knew that Barabbas only kept him around because of his murderous ferocity. His activities often kept Pilate's Legion searching the hills east of Jerusalem, leaving the road between Joppa and

Jerusalem clear and enabling Josias to overcome many travelers.

It chafed Lucius greatly that he must await Barabbas' orders as to what caravan he

might raid, and what merchant he might attack. He shook his head in bitterness as he thought of the ignominy. He could feel the shame in his gut, pressing, pressing against him.

*Attack this one, it is poorly guarded. Do not attack that one--that one is a favorite of Rome or do not dare touch this other one, or this man is owed a favor. He did not need this rigid control, he could decide for himself. He could decide just as the upstart Josias did—and he would do it soon.*

The headquarters of Lucius' band lay well hidden in the foothills east of the Jordan River. The camp was in a small clearing amidst a jumble of rocks, locust trees and wild grapevines. It gave the band almost impenetrable cover. A spring furnished unlimited sweet water and some small caves in the stone wall more than filled the need for shelter during falling weather.

A merciless leader, the men of the band and their women feared Lucius' unpredictability. Oftentimes he got the idea that one of his men may have complained to Barabbas of his cruelty. The thought didn't bother him overmuch. He knew Barabbas had grown soft and would have little heart if it ever came to a fight between them. Lucius believed he would easily kill the bandit chief in hand to hand combat.

Late one morning, after dreaming into the night how he would glorify himself, Lucius was awakened by the high sun reflected on mica flecks in stones at the cave's entrance. It was much later in the day than he usually rose.

Throwing aside his blankets and moving closer to the small campfire, Lucius chuckled as the women scurried to prepare his breakfast, thinking he was still in the bad mood of the previous night. He looked around the camp. Men were posted at the valley entrance and atop a high pinnacle of rock. Without instruction, they watched the road.

"Are there travelers on the road?" he cupped his hands around his mouth and shouted to the man on lookout.

"I see no one, Master."

The man's answer greatly amused Lucius. He required his men to call him master whenever Barabbas wasn't about to hear them. It helped somewhat to overcome his feeling of inferiority to the man who owned him, for Lucius was a slave.

Early in the afternoon, one of the lookouts rode into the camp with news of a large caravan heading to Jerusalem from Damascus. He described the caravan as well laden with goods and heavily guarded.

Jumping up to face the man, Lucius shouted, "Did you count the guards?"

"Yes Master—I counted twelve. They were well armed with spears and swords. Each of them carry one of those huge Damascus shields."

"Were they mounted?"

"No Master, they are not. Only the merchant was mounted. He rides like a Samaritan. Two guards walked ahead of the caravan and the rest followed behind.

Those men drove twenty heavily-laden pack asses before them."

Turning to his men, Lucius raised his voice to say, "Prepare for an attack at first light. I will ride ahead and spy out their camp."

Salem, the lookout that brought the message, stepped out of Lucius' reach and spoke softly, "Master, it would be better for us to ride now and attack as they make camp. Those guards are all tired to exhaustion from their long march. We would have a great advantage over them. Also, we would have the entire night to escape."

"You would give orders as Barabbas?" Lucius jerked around to face the man, yelling in his anger and astonishment at such temerity.

Cringing farther away, Salem said nothing more. He hurried to join the men who were busily stuffing food into their saddlebags. When they finished they brought the hobbled horses closer to camp, and made ready to ride. There was none of the normal jesting and laughter. Few of the men relished the idea of attacking so strong a force.

It took only a few minutes for the men to lead their horses away from the camp far enough to reach a flat area. Once the reached the plain and all were mounted, they spurred their horses to a gallop and headed for a hill several miles to the west.

When he reached the brow of the hill, Salem held his hand high, signaling for the men behind him to stop. Stretching out his arm, he pointed to the group of animals, off to the side of the roadway. A large fire revealed the outline of men huddled close together partly within the circle of light. Another, smaller fire glowed nearby. It undoubtedly provided warmth for the merchant.

Without dismounting, Lucius leaned forward to speak softly, "Withdraw out of sight in that hollow to the right. That's well out of sight of the merchant's camp. We can't risk a fire. Even if they didn't see it, they would smell it. You can sit close together to keep warm. Get some sleep if you can, and be ready to attack at first light.

"I'm going to check the area and make ready for a surprise attack at dawn."

The men sat huddled together in the darkness of their hiding place, glumly muttering about "lambs led to the slaughter."

Raising his head, Salem spoke softly, but loud enough for all to hear, "Surely Lucius is demented. He is planning for us to attack a caravan with more guards than he has followers."

"I wonder about him of late," Aaron of Judah muttered, "He has done some strange things since we were sent here from the Joppa road."

A deep voice from the shadows said, "We were only sent here because Barabbas trusts Josias more that he does Lucius."

"Shh—keep your voice down—he comes." Salem cautioned.

Lucius dismounted and thrust the reins of his horse to the nearest man without looking at him. In a harsh whisper, he demanded, "Are all of your weapons sharpened? Have you checked your shield bucklers? You know a loose buckler can cost you your life—check them now—all of you."

"All is in readiness, Master." One of the men answered for the group.

In the semi-dark and cold of the early morning, ten reluctant highwaymen mounted their horses to follow Lucius as he rode over the hill and onto the sandy edge of the highway. Holding their animals in to move quietly, they headed for the camp of the Samaritan.

Lucius, overbold and dreaming of his forthcoming triumph, allowed his horse to wander from the sandy roadside onto the main track. The animal's shod hooves struck the stones of the road. The sharp sound awakened one of the soldiers who guarded the camp.

The man jumped up and screamed a warning to the rest of the guards as he grabbed for his weapons. "We're attacked. Prepare to defend the camp."

All surprise was lost. Lucius spurred his horse over the rocks and into the camp shouting for his men to attack.

"Kill them, kill them all."

His men, lacking confidence from the start, followed him to the edge of the camp, but once there, most of them turned aside, urging their horses into the rocks and trees away from the road, desperate to escape what appeared to be certain death. A tall Syrian slammed the side of his spear against Lucius' head, unhorsing him.

Much later, Lucius stirred and tried to move. His head hurt as if it would split. His arms were bound behind his back. The shaft of a broken spear passed though the bend of his elbows. Groaning, he opened his eyes. Three of his men lay dead. Their bodies still sprawling where they fell. He could see no other prisoners.

Bitterly, he swore to himself. "The rest of the cowards ran away."

The tall Syrian, evidently the leader of the guards, was shouting at the merchant. "Let us kill the vicious scum and have done with it. That will surely be his fate if we take him to Jerusalem."

"No," the white bearded Samaritan ordered in a soft but stern voice. "That is the way of the ungodly. We will turn him over to Pilate's jailers when we reach Jerusalem. If there will be blood shed let it be on their hands."

"It would be better to kill him now."

The old man still shook his head. "No. I'll hear no more of it."

Much to the disgust of the guards he ordered, "Get shovels, you men. We'll bury these souls here."

The merchant stood by until the three dead highwaymen were well covered in a common grave. He added greatly to the chagrin of the guards by bowing his head to say some sort of prayer to his strange god.

The Syrians muttered among themselves about the strangeness of Jews. The tall guard said to the others, "They're always praying to some god men cannot see— a spirit they call their Lord. I'm convinced they are fools—they're all fools."

That night, the caravan camped near another that traveled north, in a smooth flat area hard by the sweet wells of Jericho. Still bound, Lucius leaned against the rough trunk of a palm tree, unable to sleep for the torture of the tight ropes and the hard spear shaft pulling against his back.

"Shh--." A voice whispered close behind him.

Lucius felt a hand on his bare forearm. Almost immediately, he heard the whisper of a sharp knife against the rope and his bonds fell away. His savior touched his arm again and motioned for him to follow. After crawling some distance away from the sleeping guards, his liberator rose and ran ahead of him. Lucius ran at the man's heels.

Soon the man stopped beside two saddled horses waiting in the dense blackness of a vineyard. Once mounted, he and Lucius whipped their horses so that they ran wildly between the rows of vines. Soon they emerged onto a deserted roadway and turned south to race through hidden paths. Finally, they reached the safety of the hideout, in the rocks west of Guarantania.

Obed, one of the newest and youngest of Lucius' followers, sat beside a small fire. The rest of the band sat in a group behind him, their heads hanging dolefully, refusing to meet Lucius' eyes.

Lucius said nothing, but his eyes and expression clearly expressed the disgust he felt for men who would desert him. Wordlessly, he leaned from the saddle to grab a sword and spear from the nearest man. Strapping the sword around his waist he looked over the men's heads and barked an order in a voice that dared anyone to disobey him, "Get ready to ride."

Turning his horse, he spurred away, leading the band west. After a series of long night marches they finally reached a remote hideout in the desolate hills west of Gennesaret in Galilee. Lucius was afraid of returning to Jerusalem. He knew the guards and the Samaritan they attacked could give the Romans a good description of him and probably of several of his men.

He was even more afraid when he thought of the anger of Barabbas. He dreaded their next meeting. He knew Barabbas would rage over the abortive robbery attempt. He would be furious over the loss of men, and more than furious at Lucius' failure to gain control of the rich train. Lucius brooded; knowing his failure would do nothing but increase Barabbas' confidence in Josias.

*He is Barabbas pet—the perfect Josias of Bethany—he will be even more the pet now. It is Barabbas fault. He should not have given me such cowards as followers. This was not my fault. We would have won the train if the fools had not run away. But I will be blamed—I know I will be blamed. Then he will think Josias is even more perfect.*

# The Malefactors

# Chapter 2

Mattathah, the mother of Josias, was born in Bethany. She was the only child of an old scribe, Cyrus of Bethany, and born late in his life. Overjoyed at his daughter's birth, he named her Mattathah, a gift from the true God in the old tongue. As she grew into maturity, the girl was beautiful, with small features, great dark eyes and glossy black hair. She was as sweet as she was beautiful and her father could deny her nothing.

At her insistence, he taught her the scribes' trade, contrary to the custom of the day. Oftentimes she sat under the scribe's tree, hard by the inn of Bethany, earning the fees of her trade. She wrote letters and contracts for the people of the town and merchants contracting their business.

"A woman scribe. What is the world coming to?" men asked.

She and her father often suffered crude jests from the other scribes because of her work, but the jests deterred neither in the pursuit of their trade. Mattathah gloried in being the only woman scribe in Bethany and her old father smiled when he saw her pride. He believed his beloved daughter could do no wrong.

Mattathah sat quietly near sunset, as she often did, knowing her workday was probably over. It was rare that anyone came to ask for her services after the evening meal. Suddenly, a young giant stepped through the door of the inn yard and approached her. "Good scribe," he asked, "wouldst thou write out a message for me?"

Mattathah smiled sweetly as she answered. "Of course I will sir, for the usual two sesterces."

She resettled her table and straightened the horn stand with its reed styluses, bowls of ink and sand, and stick of sealing wax. The man came close and stood near the table. Mattathah raised her eyes to look into the face of the stranger who spoke with the tongue of a Galilean.

Their eyes met, and she almost gasped aloud. Never had meeting anyone affected her so. Many men asked her to write out letters and documents for them. Some were young and several good to look upon. Some interested her, but never had meeting a man affected her as looking into the eyes of this handsome, golden-haired stranger did.

Quiet for a moment, Mattathah struggled to regain her composure and her ability to speak. Finally she asked, in her sweetest voice, "What would you have me write, please?"

"I would have you write for me a letter to Ruth of Bethsaida. Tell her that her son is well. That I completed my apprenticeship and the Mason's Guild sets me to work on Herod's new palace. I start on the morrow. Also, please tell her I am to be a finish stonemason at full wages. I shall see her and my brothers at the next Passover.

"When that is done, tell her also that I pray every day that she and my brothers may keep well. Say that the bearer of this message will give her a pouch of coins. She will know they were saved from my earnings. Please close the letter with these words. "May God watch over you."

"Sign the letter simply Ammon. When you are finished I will affix my mark beneath my name."

Mattathah handed Ammon the completed letter and held out her hands for the two copper coins. She could not resist saying, "It is good that you remember your duty to your mother and send her of your gain."

"She gave of herself for me these many years, and freely." Ammon smiled as he continued, "Please tell me your name, little scribe."

Shyly, Mattathah whispered her name and ducked her head as she gathered her tools to leave her work for the day. As soon as the man turned his back to leave, she stopped her work to watch him walk away.

Ammon lived in Bethany in the house of a cousin. He preferred to walk the few miles between the village and Jerusalem each day rather than dwell in the crowded city. The teeming population and the unending noise of the town made him nervous. He was used to the quiet of the country.

Each evening as he returned to the quiet village and his room, he walked by the scribe's tree in hopes of seeing the beautiful girl. On the days he found Mattathah sitting under the tree working, he entered the courtyard and greeted her.

She always smiled on him and they would spend a few minutes talking of their day. Soon, he noticed, she began to work every day, and seemed to be pleased when he stopped to talk to her.

As they left the synagogue one morning, Mattathah pointed out the tall Galilean to her father, remarking on how handsome he was.

"Handsome is as handsome does." Her father growled. His heart pounded with fear when he turned to see the look on his daughter's face as she stared at the man.

Months passed. One evening after nightfall, Ammon knocked at the door of Mattathah's home. She was surprised, but delighted to see him and greeted him with a smile. Inviting him in, she escorted him through the house to the small garden. There she introduced him to her father.

Cyrus invited him to sit. The two men chatted for a few minutes about the weather and Herod's plans for his new palace. Suddenly the old man leaned forward and stared into Ammon's face.

"Come man, what is it you want of me? Surely it is more than my opinion of the weather and that crazy man's plans for yet another palace."

Ammon rose to his full height. Standing before his chair and looking at Mattathah he blurted out, "I want your daughter to wife, good Sir."

"Hah," Cyrus of Bethany cried in a voice that almost sounded angry. He stood up as well. "I suspected as much. I've seen you two exchanging coy looks and sighing like sheep. Do you think me blind? What say you to this man, daughter?"

Mattathah hung her head modestly and spoke in a low voice. "Ammon is of a good devout family, Father. I have often read letters from his mother for him. I would not frown on the match."

Cyrus turned away in thought, humming and sighing. Finally, he turned to face Ammon again, a look of mingled joy and sadness on his face.

"It is well with me, my son, if it is you my daughter wants. Mattathah is my only child and will receive this house and garden as her dowry, but I must dwell here with you until I go to God."

At Ammon's urging Cyrus set an early wedding date. After drinking a cup of wine to celebrate, the two men discussed the wedding feast, arguing over how many guests would be invited and other details. They disagreed and finally agreed on how the wedding and celebration would be conducted.

Mattathah smiled and held her face up for Ammon's kiss when he left the house. Elated, he walked along the dirt lane, feeling more in the mood to leap and shout than to walk quietly back to his room in the house of his cousin, counting the days until the wedding.

Ammon and Mattathah knew great happiness in the little house with Cyrus. She stopped going to the scribe's tree when she grew great with child, and remained at home, happy in her garden. They were married almost two years when their son was born. Mattathah named him Josias, and was overjoyed that he was as golden haired and handsome as her beloved Ammon.

The little family knew a peaceful, joyful life, secure in the sleepy village. But in the city of Jerusalem and throughout the country, times were troubled in the last years of King Herod's rule. Sometimes word of these troubles came to the couple. Beyond that, Cyrus, Mattathah's beloved father, failed rapidly. He grew weaker each day until she knew his death was near.

On a warm sunny day in late fall, Mattathah worked in the garden, spreading clean clothes over the vineyard poles to dry. She heard a shout from the street. A stranger stood at the front gate. She hurried around the house, holding Josias by his hand, and opened the gate.

"Is this the home of Ammon, the stonemason?" a small man dressed as a craftsman, demanded in a loud voice.

Alarm stabbed her heart. Unable to speak, she nodded.

"I was sent to inform you, good mother, there was an accident at the palace today. A great capstone broke its lashings and fell to the ground. It crushed four men. Your husband Ammon was one of them."

Sick with fear, Mattathah finally managed to speak, "Wait please, Sir. Let me make ready to go with you and see to him."

"There is no use for it, woman. Only the good God can help him now, for your man's body is crushed. He is dead. Mercifully, he died the instant the great stone struck him."

Mattathah turned away and stumbled back to the front door of the house. The boy toddled behind her, frightened by the sound of his mother sobbing. He grabbed her skirt and held on with one hand, whimpering in his fear.

After many days passed, Mattathah tried to remember the details of her husband's funeral. Every time she remembered, her anger at the words of the priest returned like a dark wave across her heart.

"Gallileans can bring only bad luck," he said in his unctuous voice. Every time she remembered it she thought of the look of hurt on the face of Ammon's mother. Ignored by the priest, she stood beside the grave. She thought of her kind neighbors. Many things were jumbled and unreal in her mind. In an instant, the accident tore her world asunder.

Before the pain of Mattathah's grief began to ease, her father's many prayers were answered and he was called to God. She stood dry eyed beside his grave, listening as the priest read the service. She could not help but worry about her future.

*Surely God has placed a great burden on my shoulders. I have this boy to raise alone. After I pay to bury father here in this his chosen spot, overlooking the brook Kidron, I will have but little left for us to live on.*

She was much relieved the next week when a representative of the Masons' Guild came to the door and presented her with a small leather pouch of silver coins. The man assured her she would receive a like pouch regularly during the customary seven years of mourning.

Mattathah was devout. She spent much time in the Synagogue, helping the priests' wives complete the many tasks that fell to their hands. The boy Josias required a great deal of her time as well. She started to teach him the duties of a scribe each morning. Each afternoon she taught him as many of the blessed scriptures as she knew. Keeping busy seemed to make the grief of losing Ammon and her father a little easier for her to bear.

Her dreams of the future included her Josias studying at the Rabbinical College. Mattathah told no one of her dreams, but she desired her son to be great among men. Finally, her season of mourning passed. As the growing boy demanded more and better food, Mattathah again took up the scribes' trade. As she sat waiting for customers, she often heard men discussing changes in the land.

Great unrest followed the death of Herod the Great throughout the country. The turmoil so curtailed business in Bethany that she traveled to Jerusalem to find enough work to support them. Taking her place among the scribes gathered north of the city, Mattathah soon grew busy.

The novelty of a woman scribe caused many customers to come to her at first, but she quickly earned their loyalty with the deftness of her writing, and the beauty of her clear, well formed characters. Added to this, unlike many scribes, she had a pleasant way of dealing with everyone.

It became more difficult each day to find someone to keep Josias safe while she worked. His mischievous ways, often misconstrued as disobedience, gradually eliminated everyone who was willing to care for him. The only course she could take was to have him go to work with her every day. She told the boy she needed him to carry her table and case of tools.

It became a near impossibility for her to do her work and keep track of a nine-year-old boy amidst the many sights around the market. Each caravan that arrived was a new wonder. Josias examined and questioned every child who passed by, asking about his home, his parents, and his life. The boy avidly watched every quarrel, and participated in many, occasionally returning to his mother with bruises and his clothes dirty and torn from fighting.

After a few days, the boy began absenting himself from his mother for long periods. He made friends with a group of street urchins. Wearily, Mattathah admonished the boy to stay with her. When he would not change, she became distraught, and begged him to change.

Every evening he promised her he would stay by her side the next day, but after an hour, or even less, he would disappear into the city and not be seen again until the time arrived for them to return home.

Josias soon learned the ways of street children. He joined the groups of boys in stealing from shopkeepers and quickly learned to lose anyone who pursued him in the teeming crowds. He also learned the trick of attracting the attention of a caravan driver while a companion stole from his wares.

He became one of the most accomplished of the young thieves, for he was the cleverest of them. It was Josias who stole the most valuable items. Because of his shrewd bargaining with the shady merchants who sought the goods offered by the young thieves, he always obtained the best prices for his plunder.

Mattathah grieved and prayed over this beloved but uncontrollable son, but to no effect. On the first day of the fourth month of their going to Jerusalem, Josias left her for the whole day as usual, but did not return when the workday was over. She hunted frantically through the market, but he was nowhere to be found. When darkness fell she finally was forced to give up and return home.

The next day and for weeks afterward, she did not work, but wandered about the city, constantly questioning bazaar keepers and caravan drivers. They all answered her kindly, saying they knew nothing, but they were only elated at the disappearance of so clever a thief. None told her, but each supposed the Legion captured the boy and sent him to Rome as a slave. The honest merchants in the market constantly begged the Legion to do this with all of the young thieves.

What really happened on the day Josias disappeared was simple. He lounged beside the entrance to David Street awaiting his companions in crime when Argubus the Prophet approached him. The boy was much in awe and supposed this was a Prophet like those his mother told him stories about. Josias trembled in anticipation of the punishment he deserved, now that a man of God knew his every sin.

Moving close, the old man glared down at him. His voice sounded like thunder. "Follow me and be quick about it boy, for you are in much trouble."

Full of fear, Josias obeyed. He followed Argubus through the city and out of the Joppa gate. The boy constantly looked about him, ready to run if soldiers or temple guards approached.

Argubus led the way across the clearing surrounding the city's walls and into the sparse growth of brown grass and brambles. Sorely frightened, the child came out in Josias. He shed tears of sorrow and remorse for not obeying his mother. He suppressed sobs, almost overcome with fear.

Finally, he and the old man left the brush to enter a camp. A small group of people sat around a tiny fire. The camp lay hard by the Joppa road, hidden in the foothills, several dusty miles from Jerusalem.

When they came into view, a younger man called out to the prophet, "Argubus, who is this boy you have brought here?"

"Ahh--Master, you may well ask. Meet a small but clever thief who has been about the city but a short while, Barabbas. This is one with great promise.

"As I sat beside the bazaar entrance yesterday I heard the Centurion make a promise to a merchant—a fat whining pig of a merchant. The man complained of this boy stealing his wares. The Centurion promised the man he would capture the boy and send him to Rome as a slave, and rid the city of him. Such has never set well with me, as you know, so I thought he might be a good addition to our band. See? I have brought him to you."

"Fool. Of what use is a child to our band." Barabbas turned away to flop back down on his blanket, obviously angry.

"I vow he will not be much use now Master, you are right. But of all of your men I've seen of late, this boy is the only one clever enough to become a leader if we will someday have two bands as you say you wish. If you train him carefully as he grows, he will do well for us someday."

Josias felt only amazement to learn that this man—one he thought a holy man was only one of a gang of highwaymen. He stood there without speaking, his mouth agape, unable to comprehend what he heard.

As Josias stared at the two men, Barabbas turned to face them again and ordered, "Argubus, get to your nest. Take your new pet with you. Maybe his eyes are sharp enough so he can see a quarry approaching while you sleep."

Nodding his assent, the old man motioned for Josias to come with him and turned to follow a faint track into nearby rocks. The old man's nest lay high above the valley where the road could be seen for miles. As night came on, Josias spotted travelers in the distance and yanked on Argubus' sleeve. Rising from his blanket, the old man studied the approaching train.

"That's a slave trader boy, see the two rows of men moving together? It's not worth stopping. Slavers who come to this city are a motley crew, hardly worth bothering about. There's no need to tell Barabbas of this."

As they watched the column below, a tall young man who appeared chained near the center of twenty mixed slaves, suddenly sprang to the side of the road, his arm free of the heavy chain. He ran headlong toward the rocks of a narrow pass in the rugged hills north of the road.

One guard set out running after man as the leader shouted invective, waved his arms and cursed vilely. None of this affected the escaping man except perhaps to make him run faster.

When it became evident the guard would not catch the man; Argubus ordered Josias to run down to the camp to inform Barabbas of what happened. Two members of the band rushed to capture the escaped slave while everyone else made ready to break camp. The men feared discovery if the Legionnaires were ordered out of the city to search for the escaped slave.

Lucius fairly flew over the rocky ground as he ran away from the slave train. He did not know that he ran into the arms of Barabbas or that the bandit chief was a harsher master than any slaver. The men who served Barabbas lived in fear of his displeasure. They had good reason to know that once they joined, they could never leave the band. Any who ever tried was hunted down and murdered in some horrible way. If he was unfortunate enough to have a wife and children, they were murdered with them.

Barsubus, or Lucius the Hawk as he now called himself, proud of the harsh sound of his new name, knew only a life of struggle. He learned early to lie, fight, steal—do whatever it took to survive. Ever since his unwelcome birth in a forgotten hovel of Joppa he fought to live, and learned to be bitter.

# Chapter 3

In a row of ancient houses located at street level, below the soldiers' quarters in the old part of Joppa, a harlot gave birth to a scrawny boy. She must have felt at least a small spark of motherly love, for instead of drowning the infant in the sea, as most of her sisters did their newborns, she took the baby to a cousin whose child was stillborn the same week.

The baby's foster mother exclaimed her great delight in so fine a son, but he suffered neglect. She often left the apartment not to return to feed the child until the pain of over-filled breasts forced her. Being lusty, the baby then nursed more than was good for him and fell sick. He grew into a tough street urchin, always large for his age, and before he was ten, earned the reputation of the meanest boy and the slickest thief in the town's market place.

Barsubus spent his days among the crowds of the market place, forever on the lookout for something to steal. He always offered to carry a burden for some small coin or help a caravan driver with animals frightened by the noisy crowds. Many times he was in trouble. Sometimes he was whipped. Other times a merchant turned him over to one of the legionnaires who patrolled the city. He learned early though, that favors done for the soldiers or small gifts given to members of the patrols served him well whenever he was caught.

He went often to the quarters of Caesar's legions, that crumbling pile of stone built by Antiochus III, the Seleucid king who wrested the city from the Egyptians two centuries earlier. When there, he worked hard, cleaning and polishing shields and running errands. Sometimes he just lounged about and listened to the men talk. What he heard taught him many of the tricks he used throughout his life as a bandit.

As Barsubus grew into manhood he was very quick and strong. His strength was much in demand at the city's docks. This made him the most popular of those men hired to help load and unload the constant stream of ships that called at the city's port. Chaffing under the necessity of slaving in the hot sun day after day while he watched others walking about in their wealth, he dreamed of a way that he too might live as they did. He yearned to command others to do his bidding, carry a pouch filled with gold and travel about the Empire with a brace of guards at his back.

One morning when no ships eased against the ancient docks, he met a short, heavy-set Phoenician of Tyre. Barsubus had long despised this man. Several years before, the Phoenician ordered him severely whipped for stealing some trifle from one of his shipments. This same merchant named him Lucius, the Hawk. It was a name Barsubus at first hated, but now used instead of his birth name, for he liked the harsh sound.

Burning with hatred, he noticed the man swinging a coin pouch as he stopped to talk to another fat merchant. Lucius' eyes, the sharp eyes that helped to earn him the name Lucius the Hawk, fell on the heavy leather pouch.

He muttered to himself, "If I grab that pouch as he swings it behind him mayhap I can out run the old scoundrel."

Without another thought he raced by his victim, nearly upsetting the man as he jerked at the thong that held the pouch to his wrist. The Phoenician set up a great howl and clumsily gave chase, but Lucius easily outdistanced him. Elated at his success, he climbed to a rooftop where he could watch the street. There he opened the fat pouch to count the gold.

"That will treat the fat stoat to what he deserves for ordering me whipped."

He carefully hid most of his gains in a place only he knew, taking with him enough gold to pay for a wild night at a waterfront brothel.

Early the next morning Lucius hurried toward the docks to see if any ships arrived in the night. Suddenly, two men rushed out of a narrow alley and grabbed him in iron hands. They twisted his arms behind him and tied them securely with leather thongs. One man held tight to one of Lucius' arms, and the other rushed away up the street. In a short time he returned, leading the Phoenician.

The man holding Lucius arm asked, "Is this the man who robbed you, Master?"

"It is he, and I will square several accounts with him this day."

When the man reached Lucius, he raised his fat right hand and slapped him roughly first on one cheek and then the other. Turning to the guards he ordered, "Search him for my pouch of gold."

"We already searched him Master. He has only this one silver coin in his purse."

Lucius whined, trying to ingratiate himself with the irate man. "He lies, good merchant. These dogs took the gold from me before coming for you."

The merchant ignored Lucius' plea and turned to motion to one of his men to apply a large camel whip to his captive's back. Lucius clenched his teeth to keep from screaming aloud in his pain. He steadfastly blamed the two guards for the disappearance of the man's gold.

Finally the merchant stopped the whipping. "We are wasting our time. Tyree, go rent a cart and driver. Gag this thief and haul him out of the city to our camp. He will bring enough on the Damascus slave market to repay me for my losses. We will see how that pleases this piece of trash that likes to fancy himself a hawk. Once you get him in the cart, cover him over with straw, he may have friends in this scurvy town."

Lucius felt every bump as the cart rolled over the rough stone of the streets and then lurched along a rutted road. He could see nothing when the cart finally stopped. Wherever they were, he could tell it was much cooler than inside the sultry city and eerily quiet. The stench of the city was gone. One of the guards brushed the straw aside and grabbed Lucius' arms to jerk him out of the cart and onto his feet.

The camp lay near a small spring located not too far from the Jerusalem road. Lucius knew the spot. Over to his right he saw a mixed group of slaves. About twenty men, women and boys were chained to the same long, heavy chain by a wrist cuff and a short, lighter chain. The guards immediately dragged Lucius over and chained him with the others, placing him near the center of the long line.

After a short wait, a servant led out a small black mule and strapped a comfortable looking saddle on its back. The handler threw a set of black leather breeching over the mules' hindquarters and attached it to hooks on the back of the saddle. One of the guards picked up one end of the slave chain and hooked it to a large ring hanging from the back of the leather harness.

The guards ordered the slaves to stand. Mounting, the merchant clucked to his mule and tapped the beast's hindquarters with a small whip. Followed by the chained slaves, his guards and the rest of the caravan, he entered the highway and turned east toward Jerusalem.

Strong and healthy, Lucius found no trouble keeping up. He was greatly amused by the merchant as well as his guards. He was pleased that he caused them great trouble and much delay. After a while he stopped laughing to himself and began to examine the chains, confident he would find a way to remove them.

Suddenly one of the guards turned his way and noticed the grin on Lucius' face. He reached across other slaves to swing his whip at the boy's shoulders. Missing Lucius entirely, the whip struck the shoulder of the slave in front of him. The man leapt forward and howled in pain.

The slave's sudden movement wrenched Lucius' wrist. He started to scream a complaint, but noticed that the end link, the one attaching his short chain to the communal chain, was loosened. The other man's mighty jerk away from the whip had pulled the link slightly open.

The day was almost over when they made dry camp in some rocks near the highway. After a poor meal of dried meat, stale bread, and a sip of warm water from an old wineskin, the guards ordered the slaves to lie down on the hard ground and go to sleep. Lucius positioned himself so he could pry at the weak link in his chain.

He might have freed himself that very night but for his great weariness. He planned to remain awake and make an escape attempt as soon as the guards were asleep, but he slept little the night before, spending most of his night in revelry. The excitement and stress of his capture and his near exhaustion from plodding miles throughout the day caused him to fall asleep.

For six nights Lucius lay awake much of the night, worrying and prying at the weak link in the chain. Shortly after the short noon rest, on the sixth day, he looked up to glimpse the walls of Jerusalem in the distance. His heart pounded in fear. He knew he was lost once he entered the gates of the city. Determined to try to escape, he gathered his nerve and looked about for a likely route to take if he succeeded in yanking his light wrist chain free of the heavy slave chain.

Several yards ahead he spotted a break in the stone cliffs on his left. He braced himself, as best he could, knowing he might even break his wrist rather than pull free. Suddenly, he exerted all his strength and pulled the broken link free of the communal chain.

A loud wail from another slave at the pain of the sudden jerk on his wrist cuff gained the attention of the guards. Lucius broke into a wild dodging run toward the break in the cliff. The merchant turned to see what was happening. He screamed and shouted at the guards to catch Lucius. The slaves wailed. Several spears narrowly missed Lucius as he ran pell-mell for the rocks.

He hesitated when he reached the gap, and turned to laugh aloud at the guards, fallen far behind. Lucius the Hawk wore the brand of slave on his shoulder, but he was free. Free to join Barabbas the golden son of the tribe of Dan.

***

An old woman lived beside the road a dusty road in the far north of Galilee, near the city of Dan. The only bright spot in her poor life was pride in her ancestry. She claimed to all that she was a direct descendant of the warrior Caleb, of the tribe of Dan. This pride she instilled in her son Barabbas. She could not tell him who his father was. Like Lucius, and Josias' fathers, the men were undoubtedly, at least in part, northern Greeks. They all endowed their sons with their fair coloring and large size.

As a boy, Barabbas was inclined to study, but was forced to labor that he and his mother might live. He grew up filled with disdain for the people around him, knowing himself to be far above their best.

The young man joined a savage group of zealots—Jews who called themselves Herodians. Like them, he was fiercely determined to find a way to defeat the Romans and again place a Herod on the throne of Israel. The work of the group required time Barabbas, could not spare from working for a living, so seeking an easier way to live, he began to rob travelers on the lonely roads near his home.

Over time, Barabbas became important in the group. His affluence and ability pushed him above his fellows. The leader of a band of highwaymen Barabbas occasionally rode with, imprudently attacked a merchant caravan protected by a hidden patrol of Roman soldiers. The leader and many of his men lost their lives. Barabbas and Argubus escaped, riding furiously into the foothills near Mount Herman. They took little known trails to the safety of a remote hideout.

Barabbas sat without speaking, staring into the fire, a determined expression on his face. He was not willing to take so small a place in the affairs of men as offered to a young man of his station. He knew himself too able to be forced to live as a laborer or a herder of animals.

Finally, he turned to Argubus. "Old man, let us leave here and go down to Jerusalem. Mayhap we can start a band there. We are not known by those patrols as we are here."

"I've gotten too old for this mad riding about, Barabbas. I'll go along with you. I certainly can't stay here any longer and neither can you. Everyone hereabouts knows of my past and it is impossible to hide in safety when so many will turn you in to the guard for a small reward."

"Disguise yourself as a prophet from the wilderness, Argubus. Remember Elijah, the great prophet in the ancient scrolls of the Synagogue? You could claim God sent you to chastise the people for accepting the rule of the heathen Romans. Why think of it old man, you'll be believed as quickly as any of those prophets were. I'll wager all of them were frauds and started their preaching to cover up some crime."

Shortly before dawn the next morning the two men crossed over the Dan to enter their home village. Quickly, furtively, they gathered up their few belongings, and fled into the nearby desert.

Many days later, after a succession of night rides to avoid Roman patrols, the two men topped a rise in the rough hills and stopped to study the view. Before them lay the walled city of Jerusalem. As they approached the northeastern corner of the city, they marveled at the vast buildings and walls before them. The thick wall around the temple and its gigantic gates built by the great King Herod were much larger than any buildings they had ever seen.

They decided to wait until morning to find a way to sneak into the city. They were getting ready to make their camp just outside the city walls when they noticed a caravan driver having a great deal of trouble controlling his camels. Barabbus approached the driver, offering to help with the animals in return for the privilege of entering the city as members of his party.

He knew it was impossible for them to simply enter the city openly, and he and Argubus carried no permits to travel. Caesar Augustus made it the law of the land that all men must register and be taxed. That registration was the only way to obtain travel permits.

Contemptuous of all authority, Barabbas began an immediate search for a place in some local band of thieves. He was successful when he found a buyer for a few stolen jewels he brought with him from his home. That man recommended him and sent him to meet an unnamed man by the Joppa Gate.

When he named himself a Herodian he was immediately accepted in the man's band. Soon, by his forceful personality and the recommendation of another thief who left Galilee a year earlier and knew his reputation, Barabbas was elected captain of a band that operated from the hills adjacent to the Roman road.

The utter ruthlessness of his attacks on traveling merchants made him immediately successful. He left no witnesses alive, and sold his spoils in secret by sending them by caravan to Damascus. He also found a way to avoid paying duty to the Legate of the city.

When Barabbas' men rescued the slave Lucius, the man immediately became a staunch follower of the bandit chief and after several months of training, was made a leader in the attacks. This left Barabbas free to lounge about in the taverns of the city, seeking information about rich travelers.

While drinking in a bazaar on David Street one day an expensively dressed stranger approached him and asked if he was a merchant.

"Me a merchant? Hah," Barabbas laughed as he answered and shook his head vigorously. "No my friend, my idleness is paid for by flocks and herds in the hills of Galilee—they were left to me by my father. What of you then—you appear a scribe, or perhaps you are a scholar?"

"I am Sylvanius." the man said, "I am a scribe, assigned by Rome to serve Pilate, the Procurator of Palestine."

"Quite impressive, I am sure. I am known as Barabbas, and as you see, I am an idler."

"You are certainly the most fortunate of men." Sylvanius said, stepping closer and lowering his voice. "This will be of great interest to the Procurator, we must tell him of one so blessed by the Gods."

Barabbas long suspected Pilate somehow obtained more knowledge of his activities than he liked. During a past robbery, one of his men was captured by the Legion and carried before Pilate for trial. Pilate delayed the man's sentence and while he waited, the man mysteriously escaped and disappeared.

Common gossip throughout the town said that Pilate was hard pressed for money. His wife Claudia, a former member of Tiberius' court, made great demands on him for fine furnishings, clothing, and entertainments. These things cost much more than the Procurator's percentages of Palestinian taxes should yield, and forced him to obtain money in other ways than through the Empire's allotment.

Barabbas correctly thought Sylvanius' approach was a prelude to an agreement with Pilate. He fully expected such an agreement would enable him to gain valuable information on wealthy travelers visiting Jerusalem. He speculated that it would also afford him some protection from the new Legate recently sent by Caesar to investigate the many complaints of lawlessness near the city.

The following day he entered the same bazaar and was immediately greeted by Sylvanius. "Barabbas, I would speak to you before you order your wine."

"What is it you want of me?"

"Pilate wishes to see you immediately."

Barabbas nodded. Hiding a smile, he followed Sylvanius out of the shop. They walked together to the building where Pilate gave audiences while in Jerusalem. As they entered a large room, Sylvanius raised his right hand and pointed to a small door beside the raised dais.

Barabbas ducked his head as they passed through the opening. When he straightened to look about the place he saw only a small dingy room without furniture. Telling Barabbas to wait, Sylvanius left by another door. After a short time, the door opened again and Pilate entered the room. He was alone.

"Your living is from flocks and herds, is it?"

"Yes, your majesty, that is true." Barabbas dropped his eyes, a small smile playing on his lips.

"Don't "your majesty" me, you rogue. I know of your occupation. Argubus, that loud mouth who pretends to be a prophet, is your spy. You give orders to rob travelers all over this cursed country.

"If that were not enough, your activities cause Tiberius to send all manner of messengers to me with threats of what he will do to me if I don't stop your marauding. You have made my life miserable for a long time."

Barabbus crossed his arms and looked into Pilate's eyes, his face serene. "What will you do, Master?"

"You will pay over to Sylvanius twenty-five percent of your future gains."

Burning with anger at the man's greed, Barabbus forced himself to speak softly. "Twenty-five percent is a large part, your honor. Mayhap you will reconsider and only demand a fifth."

Pilate smiled and hesitated a moment. Then he answered in a pleasant voice, "Mayhap you will be the one to reconsider. Think of the cross on the hill of the skull. That is your only alternative."

Before Barabbus could answer, Pilate turned and left through the same door he entered. In a few moments, Sylvanius came back in the room and without a word, motioned for Barabbas to follow him out of the building.

The bandit chief clenched his jaws on the curses he wanted to send to Pontius Pilate. Lowering his head to hide the fury showing plainly on his face, he walked behind the scribe.

# The Malefactors

# Chapter 4

Pontius Pilate was a citizen of Rome. He was born in the lower city near the Coliseum, where he was a sturdy but unruly child. His parents gave him little guidance, busy with their own pursuits. His father served as a soldier of Caesar's famous Gallic Legions and was away from home for most of his son's young life. His mother was a daughter of one of the old Etruscan families, the learned ones who first settled Rome. She spent her time in study.

They lived with Pilate's maternal grandfather, a soothsayer who practiced the ancient arts. Oft times the old man studied the entrails of chickens, sheep, cattle or any animal available to assist him in prophecies for the greatest citizens of the city. He even used the entrails of freshly killed slaves in truly important cases.

As Pontius grew to manhood his antics attracted the attention of the city patrols. Warnings made no difference to the young man. The youth's trouble with the patrols increased. He was forever breaking some law. His final and worst crime, was the theft of a Senator's horse—he nearly rode the animal to death before the patrol caught him.

The judge at his hearing gave him the choice of joining a company of legionnaires or being sent to row in the galley of a ship. He chose service in the legion, of course, and was sent to Gaul under the General Tiberius. It was a busy and exciting life that suited him. He served Tiberius well while they fought in the Gallic Wars.

An excellent if cruel soldier, Pilate grew large and strong as he reached his full manhood. He could march the day through in heavy armor while carrying a full complement of weapons. He was rewarded for his service with the title of Centurion when Tiberius gained the office of Caesar at the death of Augustus. Lounging about the palace in Rome however, Pilate became a great worry to Tiberius, always seeking another favor.

Old Tiberius became infatuated with Claudia, a member of the Empress Julia's court. Julia found this out, and was determined to rid herself of the woman. She went to the Emperor and offered to help him with his problem of Pontius Pilate, suggesting that the man be appointed Procurator of Judea. It was a fitting reward for his services in the Gallic wars and a way to send him far away.

She also strongly suggested that Pilate be given the hand of Claudia in marriage. This told the Emperor that his wife knew of his affair. The last thing he wanted was to alienate Julia or her family and followers. It could mean the end of his rule. Tiberius delayed as long as he dared, but finally agreed to his wife's plan. Thus Pilate became the possessor of an attractive highborn wife, the Procurator of Israel and owner of a large baggage wagon filled with expensive gifts.

Like all emperors of Rome, Tiberius practiced rewarding faithful followers by naming them Procurators or Governors of their provinces. As Governor, a man could garner enough gold to retire in ten years and live in ease the remainder of his life. Except for Julia's insistence, Tiberius would never have rewarded Pilate so. His wife was the daughter of Caesar Augustus and strong politically. He knew she and her father could do him great harm if he angered her beyond forgiveness.

Pilate's rule of Israel was tempestuous from the first day. His first insult to the people he would rule was when he ordered his bodyguard to show the garlanded image of Caesar Tiberius on their staffs when he traveled from Caesera to Jerusalem. Leaders of the Jews raised a great tirade when they saw the images. They screamed that the display was contrary to the laws of Moses.

Later, Pilate confiscated a huge sum of money from the holy treasury to build an aqueduct. The project was to bring flowing water to Caesera, and please his wife. Claudia wanted to add extensive gardens and bathing pools to their home.

Worse yet, he ordered his guards to disperse a group of Galilieans while they were making a holy sacrifice. When they failed to move at once, he ordered his legions to attack, and most of the Galilieans were killed.

This and many other incidents were reported to Rome. The man's entire tenure as Procurator of Judea became a ceaseless trouble to Tiberius. Just as various leaders of the Jews complained to Rome of Pilate's actions, Pilate in turn complained to Rome of the lawlessness of the Jews. He begged Tiberius to send more legions to help him keep peace in the province.

The beautiful Claudia was also a trial to her husband. She continuously complained that she hated the filthy country and demanded that they leave Palatine and return to Rome. She yearned loudly for court life, and constantly coaxed for more slaves, new gardens, or finer garments.

Pontius Pilate was soon to get the help he demanded from Rome. It came in the form of an entire legion and a new legate, but first, he received a visit by an emissary of Tiberius, Marcus Aurelius.

Weeks earlier, Marcus Aurelius made his way through the crowds of the Via Appia toward his home. His thoughts were full of Sejunas, prefect of the Praetorian Guard and chief advisor of Tiberius. He feared greatly that this Sejunas set his own welfare above that of the Empire. Aurelius himself spent almost a lifetime working selflessly for the crown of Rome. He became wealthy from his efforts, with just rewards well earned.

Aurelius' campaign against the Phoenicians of Tripoli resulted in the capture of several wanted leaders of this rebellious people. He also recovered huge stores of stolen goods. For this the Emperor heaped rich rewards on him. Sejunas, although an excellent soldier, apparently wanted wealth without the great effort of earning it in the Empire's service. Rumor said he routinely accepted bribes from persons seeking audiences with the Emperor.

Others charged that he shared in the profits from favors he influenced Tiberius to grant. Aurelius objected to this and complained to Tiberius, but his complaints had no effect. Sejunas found ways to make himself so valuable to the court that the Emperor refused to hear any wrong against him, believing he could do no wrong.

This very day, Aurelius was ordered to Palestine. His orders were to investigate Pilate's governing of the Jews. He knew he owed the orders to the machinations of Sejunas. Tiberius also announced that Aurelius would be freed from the crown's service when this last duty was completed.

"By the Gods, I'll be ready to retire. The Empire is getting too rotten for my liking." Aurelius muttered to himself.

His thoughts turned to Corsica and the pleasant valley he purchased for his retirement. It was a quiet place. A place to grow oranges and other fruits, with the foothills of Rotondo to escape to when the weather grew too hot.

*Yes, yes, I will be glad to leave all of this turmoil, this constant fight for place and favor, to live in the peace of my valley.*

There were many posts Aurelius would prefer over Palestine, but at the moment, he preferred any place other than Rome. His orders were to investigate the growing litany of complaints by merchants who reported being robbed on the country's roadways. Many families sent letters to the Emperor saying their fathers, uncles or sons disappeared with all their goods, or the robbers held them for ransom.

He was ordered also to find out why Pilate clamored endlessly for more troops. On his return to Rome he was to advise Tiberius of the advisability of sending enough troops to effect the forced dispersal of the Jewish people so he could resettle Palestine with others who might be more tractable.

Aurelius could not help but feel this was a total waste of his time. He believed all that was needed to govern these people of Palestine was a stronger procurator—a procurator with some character, instead of one such as Pilate. He had known the man for years and knew him to be lacking in intelligence, a man who oftentimes resorted to violence when he was unable to immediately find a sensible solution to a problem.

He knew Pilate served Tiberius for many years in the Gallic wars. It was possible the Emperor remembered him as an excellent soldier. The Emperor probably thought that with a small secondary force, Pilate would be able to govern the backward people of his province.

Aurelius knew from experience that Jews were exceedingly shrewd people who bitterly resented Rome's authority. He also knew it would take a stronger and better man than Pilate to govern them.

In the semi-darkness of morning he rode into the street of his home. A trusted slave ran alongside his mount. The man was to accompany him to Portus Ostea so he could lead his favorite Arabian horse Jaffa, back to his stable. Aurelius knew it would be foolhardy for him to leave so fine an animal in the care of the Legionnaires stationed in the seaport town. They would ruin the horse in a week.

He would have liked to take the horse with him, but the mean and filthy ship he was to travel on did not have accommodations for the animal. His humor was foul. He caught himself grumbling at Jaffa for his prancing about, a show of spirit he normally loved.

Under his breath Aurelius cursed, "A pox on Sejunas, mayhap someone will assassinate him before I return. Had I been wise, I would have retired long ago and this would not have happened to me."

When he arrived in Ostia, Aurelius found that the ship would not sail until the following dawn. He went aboard, showed the captain his papers, found his quarters and left his bags inside. Returning to the dock he ordered the slave to return home with the horse.

He planned to rest in his stateroom, but the tiny space was impossibly stuffy. He could not sleep, so he left the ship, spending the rest of the day and most of the evening ashore, visiting successive wine shops. It was late when he finally returned to his stateroom and to bed. After a restless night, he watched at the rail as the ship sailed on the morning tide for the port of Caesarea.

They made the trip across the sea without incident. Aurelius amused himself by hanging over the rail, watching the turbulent blue waters of the Mediterranean. He never ceased to wonder at the continuous movement of the water. He also enjoyed watching the ever-changing marine life the sea contained. Fish swam near the ship and leaped high above the waves.

He slept soundly each night. He hated for the pleasant days of the crossing to end when the ship sailed into the beautiful harbor at Caesarea and anchored safely behind the great man-made sea wall.

Securing his possessions, Aurelius left the docks and made his way across the enormous parade ground to the quarters of the centurion in charge of the garrison. He presented his official papers under the seal of the Emperor and was immediately assigned comfortable quarters.

He ate in the officers' mess, his meal typical of the food of Palestine. A waiter served him a dish made of mutton or goat, he wasn't sure which and some sort of hard bread with raw vegetables and sour wine. He always found the wine of Semitic peoples, wherever he traveled sour on his tongue.

When he finished eating Aurelius walked about the garrison. The sound of music attracted him to a large veranda on the opposite side of the parade ground. He found a seat and spent several pleasant hours watching the dancing of three almost naked girls. He drank a full bottle of the sour wine and watched the revelry of the soldiers and the people of the seaport.

At dawn he left the city by its main gate. He followed the coast road to the city of Joppa. From thence he would take the new Roman road directly to Jerusalem. This road was said to be much safer for a lone traveler than the shorter one that ran through the hill country of Samaria.

He rode a big, ugly, rough-coated brute of a horse. The animal was more fitting for pulling a loaded dray than bearing an emissary of Caesar. He almost laughed aloud as he imagined the picture he must make. Aurelius saw the humor, but knew the horse didn't matter. It was more urgent for him to finish this business than to waste time arguing with petty officials for a better horse.

To his eyes, the country appeared peaceful enough. He saw no highwaymen; neither did he know that he was carefully watched several different times. Mainly because of his ordinary looking mount, he was deemed unworthy of attack.

Several days passed before he rode through the Joppa gate into the walled city of Jerusalem. The city, due to its troubled times and Pilate's constant whining to Tiberius, now boasted a Legate in command of its Legion. Far more men were assigned to the city than could be commanded by a Centurion. Aurelius showed his papers to the guard and was taken before the Legate. He requested a patrol, as befitted his position, to accompany him when he went before Pilate.

Once his business of properly announcing his arrival to the authorities was taken care of, Aurelius sought the area's finest inn. He took the establishment's best room and rested the remainder of the day. The Legate contacted him the next morning to lead him to his audience before the Procurator.

He strode into the audience chamber and nodded to Pilate, "Good Morrow, Pontius Pilate, I bring you greetings from Caesar Tiberius."

Pilate hesitated before he answered. His voice was gruff, but held no tone that revealed the irritation he felt at Tiberius sending this man as his emissary.

"Greetings, good Marcus. What brings you to this fair land?"

"I carry the commission of the Emperor to investigate the many complaints emanating from your province. His highness has received a host of messages filled with complaints from citizens and travelers. They tell of robberies, disappearances and holdings for ransom.

"There is a particular complaint made by one Simon of Cyrene. This man is an old friend of Tiberius. He came to the court and told the Emperor a terrible story of being accosted and robbed by a band of these highwaymen.

"This man said that all his attendants were murdered, and he was held captive for months until his son could gather and pay a huge ransom for his safe release. As you can easily understand, Tiberius was truly furious to hear this. Throughout Caesar's campaigns in Gaul, this Simon was with him as supplier for his troops. They became great friends.

"Tiberius demands that these people be governed without incidents of this nature. If they cannot be governed he vows he will command that they be dispersed and the country resettled with people from other lands who will be more tractable. "

Marcus Aurelius stopped speaking for a full moment, and looked directly into Pilate's eyes. Finally he spoke again, saying, "Is it your wish that we discuss this problem now or shall we set another time?"

Anger flashed across Pilate's face, but he controlled himself enough not to speak his fury. He watched Aurelius as he thought.

*This Aurelius has Tiberius' ear and could influence him greatly, all to my disfavor. Mayhap I best press for time to think.*

Clearing his throat, Pilate said, "I have many petitions that must be heard today. I also must hear the reports of campaigns against the highwaymen from my patrols. It would be better to give more time to consider this. Is it agreeable that we discuss the Emperor's complaints in the early hours of tomorrow?"

Aurelius nodded his agreement and without further word, spun on his heel to leave the audience room. He went back to the Legate's quarters to learn what he could of the problems the man and his troops experienced.

Pilate sent a messenger to Aurelius' quarters early the next morning, claiming an emergency requiring his presence and canceling the planned meeting. As soon as the messenger left the audience chamber, Pilate went to a small audience room and sent a servant to summon Sylvanius the Scribe. The men spent an hour discussing how they could appease Aurelius and protect the respective positions they held.

Neither man wanted to return to Rome. Pilate's personal greed and his need to cater to the insatiable demands of his wife Claudia decreed that he remain. Sylvanius feared facing the victims of old crimes he committed in Rome years ago, before he was forced to flee to Jerusalem.

Pilate and Sylvanius finally agreed that Barabbas must be ordered to completely cease his activities until given further notice. They could wait. After a few months Tiberius would surely be in a better frame of mind. They would also caution Caiaphas, the high priest, to order the moneychangers and sellers of sacrificial animals in the Temple to be careful that no pilgrim was cheated. These two actions would stop the flow of citizen's complaints to Tiberius.

Pilate called Aurelius to a meeting in his great audience chamber the next morning. Aurelius was infuriated—insulted by the long delay. He stood proudly erect, refusing the honor of a proffered chair. His barely controlled anger could be heard in his voice. "It is plain to me that you have not properly enforced the laws of the Empire."

"You are hasty, sir—and making a judgment without full knowledge of the problems I must face in this strange land. "

Losing control of his temper, Aurelius took a step closer to Pilate and shouted, "Not since the rule of Valerius Gratus has this land been so poorly governed. It is a disgrace. There is no need to disperse these people. They only need a true procurator to govern them. Be warned Pontius Pilate. I, Marcus Aurelius, shall recommend to Caesar that you be immediately recalled."

Pilate dropped his head to hide his eyes. Employing his softest, most persuasive voice, he pleaded, "Aurelius, please, please give me more time and send me additional troops so that I may straighten out this problem."

Calming himself, Aurelius considered a moment before he grudgingly agreed. "I will recommend to Tiberius that an additional Legion be sent out to you. It will have a carefully chosen and experienced leader.

"Meanwhile Pilate, you must make every effort to capture those highwaymen who mistreated the Cyrenian, the Emperor's friend. Their capture would much appease Tiberius and weigh greatly in your favor. I shall remain here a short while longer to see some more of this land before I return to Rome. I advise you to be certain no further reports of robberies reach Rome."

Aurelius returned to his hotel and packed his belongings. Accompanied by a squad of soldiers, he left the city by the north road. He planned to spend another week wandering about the country before he went home. He had high hopes that on his return to Rome, Tiberius would release him from duty—that he would be able to retire to his beloved Corsica.

He knew the Emperor would want him to recommend someone to lead the new Legion for Palestine. He knew exactly the right person, a promising soldier, and the only son of his old friend Flauvius, now a senator. The boy would greatly benefit from a field appointment, it was Aurelius' firm belief that idling about the capitol would soon ruin any young man.

# The Malefactors

# Chapter 5

Flavius, a Senator of Rome, was greatly disappointed in his son Marcellus. The young man appeared more interested in reading his collection of scrolls or drawing pictures or chiseling crude statues of marble than charioteering or playing at war as his father did when he was a boy. Marcellus grew larger physically than the old Senator and attended the tribunes' academy where he became quite proficient in the use of weapons. He was highly praised by the scholars of the academy, for his knowledge of military strategy, yet it seemed he held small liking for it, preferring the pursuit of art to the more manly war games.

The boy puzzled Flavius, who was made Senator as a reward for his many years of military duty. He fought under Tiberius in Gaul and afterward served as Procurator of Syria. Later he returned to Rome and received this reward for his years of work for the Empire. No matter how hard he sought to understand, he could not fathom the mind of this son who was so quiet and studious.

Flavius was amazed when a messenger from Tiberius presented him with a scroll appointing Marcellus a Tribune and ordering him to immediately report for duty. When Marcellus returned from an audience with Galio, the Emperor's general, he told his father of his orders to train a Legion for duty in Palestine. Marcellus made no complaint, but the old man was furious.

"Why is my son being sent to that accursed place?" He almost screamed in indignation. "Have not my years of service warranted better than this for my only son? I shall see Galio and have these orders changed. No son of mine shall be forced to suffer this outrage."

Galio showed Flavius the orders he received. They bore the Emperor's seal. He advised that Flavius accept them without complaint. Everyone knew that Tiberius loved Flavius, but Galio himself angered Tiberius mightily by trying to get him to change the order the day before.

"Tell me why such an order was ever issued, Galio? It is an outrage."

"I know it is, my old friend. But your son brought it on himself."

"How so—how do you mean?"

"It is his courtship of Asinia. She openly prefers your Marcellus to Gaius, the stepson of Tiberius. He and Sejunas wrote the order and got Tiberius to sign it without knowing what he ordered."

"Then I shall seek audience and inform him what his stepson and that low-life Sejunas have done."

"It will do you no good. That was what I tried to do on your behalf. I know you fought with us in Gaul and you are an old friend of the Emperor, but it won't help you in this case.

"Nothing you can do or say will turn him against Gaius. He's afraid the boy and Julia will turn on him. They hold great political power, as you know. I argued long with him. Tiberius finally became so angry he ordered me to leave the court."

"It is such as these who will cause the Empire to fall. The efforts of those of us who built it and kept it will all be wasted if the Emperor continues on this path. May the Gods grant that such as you and I and even old Marcus Aurelius be given respite from living to see the fall."

On the appointed day, Marcellus reported to Galio to begin his mission among the Jews of Palestine. Galio explained that the plan was for Marcellus to proceed immediately to Jerusalem, accompanied only by a trusted slave. He would begin his investigation without the local representatives of the Empire knowing his true identity. In the mean time, Galio was having a full legion trained especially for duty under Marcellus. They would be sent on to meet him at a later date.

Marcellus made his preparations and said his farewells. He chose Leonidas, a trusted Greek slave to accompany him. Leonidas was born in his father's household and grew up with Marcellus—more his friend than his servant. The two men set sail for Caesarea. Marcellus assumed the guise of a rich young Roman idly traveling about the Empire as a sightseer before he assumed his life's work.

The port city was abuzz with activity. Little notice was taken of the two travelers as they went about Caesarea purchasing suitable mounts and a packhorse to carry their camping gear and food. Marcellus made sure many shoppers saw him with a large purse of gold. He hoped to be pointed out as a likely target for highwaymen—if he were, he could possibly end his quest as it began, but to his disappointment, his trip to Jerusalem was without incident.

The famed Holy City fascinated the young Roman. Its crowded streets were lined with innumerable bazaars, and jammed with vendors loudly hawking their wares. Its wine shops teemed with jostling, screaming and cursing shoppers. Each vied with the other for the best merchandise and haggled for the cheapest price.

Neither Marcellus nor Leonidas ever saw such activity. They were truly astonished. They both anticipated that the Semite people would be quite different from the people they knew from the northern side of the Mediterranean, and the streets of Jerusalem offered them ready and ample proof they were correct.

The city was so crowded with travelers that the two men found great difficulty finding suitable quarters. After a long search, they engaged rooms for themselves and quarters for their animals in a dilapidated old inn located far into the old city, close by the pool of Siloam.

They both carried fine arms and were proficient in their use. They were disappointed not to have some of the robbers reported to be so prevalent make an attempt to stop them. Of course, they could not know of Pilate's order to Barabbas that all robberies and attacks on travelers and caravans must cease until he gave him leave to order his men to resume their normal activities. After days of fruitless pretending to be the wastrel tourist, Marcellus went to the Tower of Antonia and sought out the Legate of the city.

Time passed swiftly and Marcellus became increasingly nervous. He knew Galio and Tiberius expected prompt reports of success against the highwaymen. He was determined to find a way to act— to make some real effort toward finding the criminals— an effort that would provide something concrete he could include in his first report to Rome.

After a mercifully short wait, he was ushered into the Legate's council room. He identified himself and presented his orders for the Tribunes' inspection. Marcellus watched the man's facial expression as he read, but if Legate Quintus was surprised to have someone of higher rank usurp his place, it did not show in his face.

Quintus stood and stepped around the desk to reach out and grasp Marcellus' arm in the traditional Roman greeting. "Welcome Marcellus. It is good that you have come to assist us in patrolling this forsaken land. There are endless miles of roads, probably hundreds of those infernal highwaymen and more than adequate hiding places for every one of them."

"Quintus, Leonidas and I have ridden the highways around the city and walked its streets all hours of the day and night. No one made any attempt to rob us. We have not even seen anyone being accosted. This place appears so safe and peaceful I find it hard to believe what I see."

"Had you been driving pack assess loaded with goods I vow you would not have fared so well. Your experience also speaks well of our patrols. A few months back you would certainly have experienced an attempt. More to the point, you might not be here to tell me of it, for these highwaymen are brutal murderers."

"Will you tell me of those men you suspect of these robberies and have a trusted person point them out to Leonidas and me so we can also watch them? I am in hopes of discovering who their leaders are."

Looking at the floor, Quintus raised his arms out from his sides, his palms upward. "There are no suspects, my friend. We have captured and executed all those who were known to ride with the highwaymen."

Marcellus did not allow his expression to change, nor make any answer, but quickly took his leave, thinking to himself. *It seems strange to me that a soldier who is assigned the safekeeping of merchants and traders would not have even one suspect—not know of even one person who would bear watching.*

His immediate reaction was regret that he identified himself to Quintus. He could not help but suspect that the soldier was in league with the robbers. He didn't know how the man could manage such a thing, but he suspected Quintus protected the highwaymen in some way.

Disgruntled with himself for having his mission known, possibly to a confederate of the highwaymen, he sent a message Rome, asking Galio to have the Legion assigned to him sent ahead immediately. He resolved to begin patrolling the roads of Palestine as soon as they arrived. He was determined to find a way to put a stop to the robberies if a way could be found.

Several days later, at Quintus' urging, Marcellus appeared before Pilate. The Procurator received him with apparent friendliness, but seemed extremely evasive, turning off every question Marcellus put to him without a clear answer.

When the audience was over, Marcellus was more convinced than ever that Quintus was involved with the highwaymen—and worse, he was almost certain Pilate was also.

*How can this be? Am I jumping at shadows? If I am right, there is no wonder the highwaymen cannot be controlled. If the very men who attack the caravans are being protected by the legions sent to find and eradicate them, I must wonder if Leonidas and I will be safe until our Legion arrives.*

Unknown to Marcellus, there was another sore festering in the Holy City of Judea. This was partly caused by the misrule of Pontius Pilate as well, but the trouble would come, without the Procurator stirring the dissent.

The Temple priests held great power over the people, but it was weakening. Ananias, Pilate's enemy and the power behind the high priest Caiaphas, did not worry about robbers, highwaymen, or even the Roman Procurator. He worried about a much more potent enemy.

Ananias grew old, fat and somewhat feeble physically, but his mind was still sharp. He sat in the garden of his palace, not taking his ease, as an old man should, but fuming to himself about the cursed Romans. He cursed them thus through all the years since he was disposed as high Priest by Valerius Gratus, the former Procurator of Judea.

He made the decisions of the priestly office still however, for his sons served as High Priest in turn and now his son-in-law held the office. Even so, he was still jealous of the title. Were it not for the cursed Romans, Ananias knew he would still hold the coveted title and sit in leadership of the Sanhedrin.

His thoughts turned to his son in law, Caiaphas, the present high priest. *What a fool the man is—an ineffective fool to let the cursed Galilean heretic go into the temple and cause trouble.*

The money changers and priest merchants all came whining to Ananias, filling his peaceful garden with their complaints. They almost screamed over their mistreatment. Caiaphas was warned to drive the demented preacher from the city before any of this happened, but he did not, not believing the man presented any danger.

As Ananias sat brooding, a servant entered the garden announcing that Caiaphas stood at the gate and asked to see him.

"I will see him here. Send him around to the side gate."

"Father," Caiaphas began without greetings. "The priests of the temple complain of not having enough money yet again. The temple treasury is empty. It has been empty ever since it was raided by that cursed Roman Procurator, that Pontius Pilate. There is nothing to give them. What shall I tell them?"

"I fear we may have to melt down some of the gold ornaments that adorn the Holy of Holies. We could easily sell the gold they would yield. We cannot have unrest among the priests. It would eventually bring about our downfall.

"While you go back to the temple and gather up some of the ornaments and bring them to me to sell, I have a few shekels you can distribute to them. They will be enough to quiet their complaints for a few days.

"I will need privacy to gather the money. Return to me as the sun sets today. Take care to hide the ornaments, wrap them well in some old rags."

Without another word the high priest turned on his heel and left. As soon as he heard the gate slam shut behind his son-in-law, the old man rose and went to a small stone sarcophagus in a corner of the garden. Grabbing a small carving in both hands, he pulled upwards to remove a portion of its top.

Reaching his right arm deep inside the cavity, Ananias picked up a leather bag of coins. Doling out coins when they would do the most good helped Ananias to avoid several crises in the temple over the years. He amassed this secret hoard of gold when he was high priest--when he controlled the people's offerings to God.

Taking a seat on a bench in the shade of an olive tree, the old man awaited the return of Caiaphas. He shook his head as he thought of the many troubles plaguing the priesthood of late.

*The main problem and the most intractable one is, there are simply too many priests. When Moses decreed that all men of the tribe of Levi become priests, he could not have foreseen the enormity of problems he created. Those priests all try to live on a portion of the tithe paid to the temple by devout members of the other eleven tribes of Israel.*

*Over the years, the numbers of priests have increased by unbelievable numbers. These men need not labor hard in order to live and none run the risks of being killed at work. Priests live cleanly and eat well. They are not as susceptible to disease as those who labor for their livelihood and in time of war none are called to bear arms.*

Ananias shook his head. He knew that thus protected, the priests would continue to increase in numbers much faster than the men who supported them. Roman tax levies were crushingly heavy and they grew steadily heavier. Every year, more and more Jews simply could not pay the temple tax after they paid the levies demanded by Caesar. Money had gotten so scarce in the temple that many of the priests turned to money changing. Others sold animals to the faithful for use in sacrifice.

Angry at their plight, many of them were involved in organizing a revolt against Rome. They all knew of the revolt organized by Judas Maccabeus against the Syrians some two hundred years before, and hoped to emulate it. As yet, no leader had come forth that might lead the revolt.

Added to the priests' money troubles was Pontius Pilate, Palestine's gift from the Romans. The Procurator reveled in any opportunity to bait the Jews, particularly the priests. He would periodically send a patrol through the Temple courts with an image of Caesar on their banner to draw their ire.

He even had his soldiers carry staffs emblazoned with images of bronze eagles. These acts never failed to send the priests into a frenzy of anger that the man should so disrespect their religion. They considered the face of Caesar and the outline of the eagles on the soldier's staffs as the graven images forbidden by Moses' law.

At times, Pilate forced Jewish prisoners to sweep the streets on the Sabbath or banned them from the cemeteries on their holy days of ancestral prayer. All of these things created political unrest and fed the priest's fear that Caesar would someday strip them of their religious rule.

Ananias foresaw other troubles. He feared the worst of all would be the strange Galilean. The man appeared to be building an enormous following among the northern tribes. Many of the people simply ceased to pay the tithe since the man began preaching his heresy.

"I will have Caiaphas go before the Sanhedrin and get a ruling. We must rid ourselves of this thorn." He said aloud, slamming his fist against the bench beside him. "That one is becoming even more dangerous since that fool Antipator, the Tetrarch of Galilee, beheaded the desert preacher, John—the one they called the Baptizer."

# The Malefactors

It was plain to the old man that the problem of this Jesus of Nazareth could only grow, for his followers were now speaking of him as the long awaited messiah.

*They are so foolish—the poor uneducated rabble--how could they think an event so great as the awaited Messiah could come from such a benighted place as Nazareth? Why, nothing good ever came from that lowly place. Why should it change now?*

Ananias knew the highwaymen were only dangerous to the Romans, and wished them well. He also knew about Pilate's order to Barabbas that he was to disband his followers and hold them idle until given word by Pilate that it was safe for them to again haunt the roadways of the province. He also knew that most of Barabbas followers lived and worked openly in the city.

One, the large man called Josias, the one with long golden hair, worked openly as a scribe as he awaited word from his leader to return to his true calling.

## Chapter 6

Josias rose from his bed to look out of the window of his room in the Shepherds' Inn. It was a sunny and beautiful spring morning in the month Nizan. Rain had fallen and flowers returned to the hills of Judea. It was the first day of Passover. Vast crowds of Pilgrims would be coming to the Holy City to celebrate this, the greatest of all Jewish feasts.

He dressed hurriedly, and gathering up his scribe's tools, set out for the Golden Gate to take his place among the other scribes who gathered there. He wanted to arrive early to get a good place to set up his desk. The scribes vied with each other for the business offered by travelers coming to the city.

As he smoothed the rough ground under the shade of an ancient acacia tree to settle himself for the day, Josias noticed a handsome young Roman and another man with the face and coloring of a southern Greek, climbing the steep ascent from the Valley of Kidron. He had noticed the two men walking about the city several times before. They seemed to have no set direction, but simply wandered about.

"I wonder where those two went this early in the day?" He muttered to himself. "It seems to me they act in a peculiar manner for tourists. I wonder if they could be spies for Caesar himself?"

His eyes followed Marcellus and Leonidas as they passed through the gate. After a moments thought, Josias decided that Barabbas should be informed of their actions. When Argubus came by, making his way to his favorite spot on David Street to preach to the gathering crowds, Josias motioned for him to come close.

Leaning close to the old man, he asked, "Look to your right, do you mind the tall Roman and his Greek companion? The same two men I pointed out to you yesterday?"

When Argubus nodded, Josias continued, "I fear they may be spies for Rome. Barabbas should be told about them as soon as possible."

Argubus said nothing in response. Turning away, he settled his bundle on his shoulder and traced his footsteps back through the gate.

Cursing the Romans under his breath, Josias settled down behind his low table. He thought of the boredom of the scribe's life—the quiet and simple life he led and would continue to lead until Barabbas resumed raiding. Barabbas had ordered the entire band to disperse a short time after the ransom money was paid and the merchant of Cyrene was released.

Barabbas promised to contact the men as soon as he felt it was safe to resume raiding, and ordered all of them to find work as honest men. The bandit chief knew Pilate was fearful of Caesar's wrath, and could offer them no help until all again grew calm in the province, and Caesar's attention turned elsewhere.

The Procurator explained to Barabbas that an emissary of Tiberius threatened him with dismissal if the robberies did not stop. That man had since returned to Rome to make a report to Tiberius on conditions in the province. He promised to send Pilate an additional Legion to help patrol the highways of Judea and protect travelers. Barabbas agreed that Pilate's obvious fear and the large quantity of gold each member of the band divided from the ransom justified this action.

Josias obeyed Barabbus' orders and took up the scribes' trade—the trade he learned many years before from his mother. Other members of the band made the trek into the mountains each day to cut firewood to sell in the streets. A few found work in the bazaars.

Old Argubus went about his preaching, gleefully collecting offerings from his listeners under the guise of collecting alms for the poor. As bored as he felt as he waited for his first customer, Josias was happy he learned the trade for it was a much better way to pass the time than most of the men of the band found.

Silently waiting for his first customer, Josias noticed an old man approaching. He held the hand of a small but well-formed young woman. Tendrils of dark hair blew about her temples, and her eyes were large and dark. The scribes who were not busy began to call out as they always did, telling the old man how well they wrote and offering their services.

Josias felt it beneath his dignity to do this, but nevertheless, he was often approached first. He was a large handsome man with his curly golden hair and beard and therefore very noticeable. People were also attracted to his welcoming smile.

He looked directly at the girl as the old man asked, "Good scribe, will you prepare a message for my sick wife?"

Abashed under Josias' stare, the girl dropped her head. Josias was so intent on the girl that the old man repeated his question.

"I asked sir, will you prepare a message for my wife?'

Dragging his eyes away from the girl, Josias bowed and said, "Of course I will, good sir. For the customary fee."

The other scribes howled in protest. They always charged three instead of two sesterces at feast times. Their indignant screams provided entertainment for the crowds milling about the area, and Josias grinned, delighted to torment them.

He stood up and shouted, "Begone from here, you cheats. The guild set two sesterces as the price for writing a letter. You overcharge when you ask more."

He turned to smile at the old man. "What would you have me write, good shepherd."

"The letter is to be addressed to Salome, the wife of Joel, of the village of Ramah. I would have you say greetings, Good Mother of our hours. We hope the God of Judah has taken away thy sickness as we asked of him in our prayers.

"The Chosen are a vast multitude in this great city. There are many strange sights to be seen. We grieve that thou were not fit to come with us, for we miss thee sorely. See that the laborers guard the flocks well and keep them safe against our return. Look well to thy health, and may the blessings of peace be thine until we are together again.

"Please sign the letter Joel, thy husband, and Sarah, your daughter. I shall wait for the letter if you please. I can send it by a Syrian merchant who goes that way this very day."

Josias made the letters slowly, raising his eyes occasionally to steal a glance at the beautiful girl. When the letter was finished, Josias stood up again to put it in Joel's hand. He turned to look in the girl's face again.

They both smiled when their eyes met.

Joel and his daughter turned and walked through the Golden Gate into the court of Gentiles. Partway through the gate, the girl turned to look back and smile at Josias. He stood unmoved, watching her walk away.

*Never before have I seen a woman that attracted me so. I have enjoyed women of the streets, camp followers, and a few decent women, but this shy girl intrigues me—she's only a quiet little girl from the northern hills. I do not know why she attracts me so, but I vow I will see her again.*

A dour looking merchant engaged the services of the scribe to Josias' left. Josias jerked out of his dreaming when he heard the man dictating a message to his supplier in Caesarea. He ordered that the supplier immediately rush a long list of merchandise to him. The merchant told the scribe to write that his stock ran dangerously low. He also had him add that the thoughts of not having all the goods on hand that could be sold were unbearable to him.

Josias felt this information might be worthwhile to Barabbas. He decided to pack up his table and tools and leave his post immediately. He would send a message to Barabbas of this opportunity.

As he thought of the attack, the thrill he knew in the highwayman's life caused him to smile and his heart began to beat a little faster. The profits of robbery were never of first importance to Josias. He loved the excitement. To swoop screaming out of the hills on a fast horse, overcome caravan guards, gather the spoils and elude the patrols over and over made his life exciting.

He often brooded over the future, asking himself. "What on earth will I do when I am forced to give up this way of life?"

*Possibly I will become so well known I will be forced to stop raiding. Other things could happen. A Roman patrol could cripple me in a failed raid. Or capture me and send me to the cross.*

*Perhaps fortune will smile and I will simply grow too old for such a dangerous way of life. However this thrilling life might end for me, I cannot help but dread the time of stopping. I know that spending the whole rest of his life as a lowly scribe, sitting beside a tree, at the beck and call of unctuous merchants and other travelers, will be more than I could bear.*

Shaking his head, Josias muttered under his breath, "I vow I will go to Bithynia or some far off land and start a new band before I will do this every day for the rest of my life."

Standing up with a sudden movement, he gathered up his table and toolbox to leave. One of the other scribes called out, "I see that Josias the wealthy one has no need to work as long and hard as the poor among us."

Josias laughed aloud. Turning to face the speaker he called back, "I go to write for a wealthy merchant I serve regularly. I only stopped here to pass the time until he was ready to begin."

Several of the scribes cursed and screamed dire threats—the first speaker stepped closer. "You have no feelings for ought but thyself. How can you take work here when you have contract work waiting for you? We shall all go before the guild and ask for your suspension."

Another pushed forward to say, "I shall have Argubus the Prophet cast a spell on thee that will cause everyone to turn against thee."

Settling his table and his box of tools under his arm, Josias ignored their threats. He waved a hand and laughed as he left the group.

He found Barabbas in the wine shop of Josef the Idumean, near the entrance to David Street. The bandit chief drank wine and shouted his base opinions of Pilate and all Romans to whoever would listen.

This Pilate encouraged him to do, for whoever would suspect such a critic to be his ally? His crudeness reinforced the Jews' reputation of unruliness Pilate so often complained of in his reports to Rome.

As Josias entered the shop Barabbas shouted, "Why do you seek me, good scribe. The hour has not yet come that we agreed upon."

"Good Master, I seek some of the good wine you speak of so often. Is this the very shop you frequent? Is this where you purchase the wine?"

"This is the very place, Josias. Nowhere in Jerusalem is there wine so good as Josef's."

A dark-skinned serving girl placed a flagon of wine and another cup on the table. Barabbas leaned across the table, placing his head near Josias' he whispered, "What is it? Why are you here?"

"I overheard a rich merchant writing a letter with another scribe. He ordered an extraordinary list of goods to be delivered immediately. I want to take my band and intercept it below the long curve in the road."

"No. Forget it." Barabbas whisper was almost a hiss.

"Have you forgotten I gave orders there would be no raids? Pilate ordered us to forgo all raids until he gave the word it was safe for us to start again. Besides, Argubus told me about those two suspicious looking Romans who are wandering around the city. I believe they may be spies sent here by Caesar to watch Pilate. I sent Emilak to follow them, but they may also be a danger to us."

Josias did not want to give up. "But Master, think of goods. This is such a good opportunity."

"You and your men have money do you not?" Barabbas began to sound thoroughly irritated.

"Yes Master, yes, of course we have, but we tire of this drab life in the cursed city."

"A little patience is better than the cross, Josias."

Josias drained his cup and stared into Barabbas' eyes a moment. Finally he jumped to his feet.

"I vow I must do something. I shall leave this day for Damascus. It may be that when I return we can start our work again."

"Take care you avoid trouble, my friend. We will want you to lead our men when we begin again." Barabbas deep whisper followed Josias as he left the table and exited the inn.

At dawn Josias approached the Roman patrol on duty at the Joppa gate. He showed his pass and spurred his horse out of the city. Some miles from the gate he left the road to follow a dim path into the jagged hills of central Judea. He stole along so quietly that he surprised Ibriham, the old slave who cared for Barabbas' herd of horses. His best animals were kept well hidden, but convenient to Jerusalem.

The old man nodded when he recognized Josias, but did not speak. Silent also, Josias motioned for him to take the reins of the horse he rode. He entered the enclosure and caught his favorite mount, a large bay with a white blaze. The horse moved with a smooth gait and could run all night.

Josias transferred his saddle, saddlebags and blanket to the new mount's back. Without a word to Ibriham, he mounted and rode away, waving one hand as he left the rocks of the hideout.

Josias took a circuitous route around Jerusalem and entered the Bethany Road beside Kidron, well east of the city. After he left Barabbas the night before, he decided to travel to Damascus by way of the old Kings highway. That route would take him through Philadelphia and other cities in the Greek Decapolis. He wanted to see as many new places as his time and money would afford.

Nearing Bethany, he met a group of people walking together. He assumed they were on the way to Jerusalem to celebrate the Passover. He pulled his horse aside as they passed and was astonished to see his mother among them. Suddenly saddened and ashamed, he realized she might be the reason he traveled this way. He had not seen her in many months. It was hard for him to face her, for he knew she hated his chosen profession and suffered because of him.

Mattathah smiled a sad smile and patted her son's face in greeting, but her words and her voice proclaimed her heartache. "My son, why do you travel in the time of the Passover? You should go to the Temple in Jerusalem for the observance."

"I came this way to bring you this gift, Mother."

Mattathah took the small olive wood box wrapped in costly red cloth Josias handed her. She said nothing. She knew the box would be filled with gold coins—coins she would never spend.

Josias dropped his eyes to avoid looking directly in his mother's face. His voice was full of guilty impatience.

"Urgent business carries me from the city, Mother. You should turn around and go home yourself. The city is a ferment of strange people and it is no fit or safe place for you to be. Why do you not worship in the Synagogue at Bethany?"

"The law requires the Passover be observed in the Temple of the Ark of the Covenant. No devout child of God can do otherwise."

Josias kept his head turned away and did not answer.

"Go if you must, my son. I know your business is not of the law."

There was nothing more to say. His mother had known of his true profession for years. With suppressed farewells they parted, Josias continuing on toward the Decapolis and his mother toward the Holy City.

True dark fell about the time Josias made camp near the ruins of Beth Holga. He planned an early start the next day in hopes of reaching Philadelphia before another night. Tired, he rolled up in his blanket and slept soundly.

Reaching Philadelphia late the next day, he presented his forged papers granting him Roman citizenship at the west gate, and was readily admitted by the bored guard. Too exhausted from his travel to explore the city, he found an inn with stable for his horse. There he bespoke a room and leaving his possessions beside his bed, went down to the taproom to eat a hot meal before retiring.

Josias woke early the next morning and hurried through breakfast to go out into the famed Greek city. He wandered about, amazed at the beauty of the long colonnaded center. The shining marble temples and attractive buildings were so different from the cities of Judea that it was hard for him to believe they were so near, yet so different. He spent the day roaming about the city, admiring.

Early the next day he left Decapolis by way of the old Kings highway, heading north toward Damascus. He ate his midday meal sitting beside a spring someone had shored up with rock to serve travelers.

In the late afternoon the monotonous clip-clop of the horses' hooves made him doze in the saddle. Some sound made him awaken suddenly. Travelers approached from the North.

There was a familiar look about the man who rode in front of two well-armed guards. Josias gasped aloud in shock as the man rode closer. "Surely my luck can't be so bad as to meet the merchant of Cyrene? The same Simon that I robbed and held for ransom."

*Almost in panic, Josias stared as he noticed that the man's black beard showed many more gray streaks in it, and he looked thinner, but there was no doubt in his mind. It was the same man.*

The merchant also stared hard as they passed. Josias expected to hear a great shout and pursuit as he rode on toward Damascus, but none came. Pushing his horse to a trot, Josias cursed himself for being so careless.

*Only an idiot and a fool would allow himself to go to sleep and not see approaching riders in time to turn aside. I could have easily hidden in the rocks near the roadway until they passed by— then I would not have to worry. If I truly value my life I will be more careful in the future.*

The rest of his trip was uneventful. He rode into Damascus quite late, found an inn near the city gate that opened on the street called Straight and immediately retired for the night. He rose early the next morning, ravenous after missing his supper the night before.

Angry with himself for his carelessness, Josias could not make himself stop worrying that the Cyrenian recognized him. He felt a great dissatisfaction with everything in his life. His nights became a sleepless torment. As soon as he closed his eyes, his mind filled with the image of his mother's sad face

He left the inn early every day to walk about the city, determined to see all there was to see in the great Damascus before Simon of Cyrene sent the authorities to arrest him for the ordeal he put him through the year before.

# The Malefactors

# Chapter 7

Simon of Cyrene was well known throughout the Empire. Rich and influential, he was used to commanding a large number of people. He sat in the shade of a rock overhang in a remote canyon somewhere in the hills of western Galilee, dressed in a ragged gray robe, heavy sandals and a turban. The rough clothing gave him an appearance so different from normal that few of his acquaintances would have recognized him.

He spent the long winter awaiting the ransom that would gain his release. At first he questioned each of the men who would talk with him about climbing the canyon walls and escaping. Thinking him friendly, he questioned Salem, the tough old bandit who was in charge of holding him. The man constantly rebuffed him. Finally, after several weeks, he accepted the futility of trying to bribe a guard to facilitate his escape.

Salem chuckled when Simon approached him. "Good merchant, all the gold you possess would not pay me to face the wrath of Barabbas of Dan. I have a wife, children, and grandchildren. I would not see them tortured and slain before my eyes for aiding you."

He settled himself against the bole of a tree and continued speaking. "I mind a member of our band who let a prisoner escape once. He accepted a large bribe for the act, but it did him little good. Barabbas reached out with his sword and took his head as he sat in the saddle.

"He sought the man's widowed mother and his young sister and murdered them as well. Finally, he turned to the rest of us and promised a like fate for all betrayers. You will find no one here to help you escape."

Reflecting on these things, Simon wondered if the great fortune that his years of hard work accumulated was worth the cost. He was only a boy when he began his career as a merchant. He traded as supplier of the armies of his friend Tiberius during the Gallic wars. That work cost him lonely months on the northern frontiers.

He endured the severely cold winters and faced many other trials with the army. It took hard work and toughness to supply five legions. But he returned to Cyrenia a rich man.

He rarely rested. From almost a far back as he could remember his days were full of effort. Forever moving to new places, he developed an impatience that refused to allow him the ease of a trading station in his quiet home city.

Not long after he came home from the Gallic wars, Simon put together a caravan of pack asses and took a heavily laden train to Cairo. After much exciting trading, the caravan, with the protection of extra guards hired in the Egyptian city, set out for Ascalon. From that city he went to the Philistine cities and finally to Joppa, trading with anyone with goods to barter.

After weeks of trading, Simon turned his caravan inland from Joppa, stopping at Jerusalem, the cities of the Greek Decapolis, Damascus, Antioch and westward between the Lebanon ranges to the ruined city of Tyre. When he reached the port he sold his goods and animals and took ship for home.

This trip became his regular routine over the years. It took him from the earliest spring until the beginning of a new winter to complete the route, allowing the bad months to prepare for his next journey. It was an exciting life, forever on the move, and made the inactivity of his captivity especially hard to bear.

To pass the long weary afternoons, Simon often played dice with one or more of his guards. Speaking to the whole group, he complained, "After I am freed, I shall object to Tiberius himself of the treatment I received from your Master."

Laughing, one of the camp women said, "What care we for Caesar, or Pilate either for that matter?"

"You will begin to care when the Empire turns its strength to ridding itself of you vermin."

All the guards began to laugh again when one of the women asked, "Are you then so important that an Empire will concern itself with us on your behalf?"

Simon ignored their jibes and laughter. He stood up and stretched, then returned to his shelter to fall down on his rough pallet to sleep. He awakened in the deep darkness of early morning by the sound of a great bustle in the little camp. Barabbas had arrived with news that the ransom was paid.

The bandit leader again wore a mask that completely hid his face. He approached Simon and tossed him a small purse of gold. "This was sent by your son to provide funds for your trip home.

"Get ready to ride, Cyrenian," Barabbas shouted. "You certainly are a fortunate fellow. Your family actually does value your life more than your gold."

Simon wrapped himself in the remnants of his cloak and mounted the horse a member of the band held for him. Another man rode close and reached out to tie a dirty rag around his head and over his eyes so he could not see. He was blinded this way when he entered the camp. Someone led his horse over a labyrinth of remote trails until they finally released him beside the Roman road to Damascus near the market route to Chorazin.

When they reached the place they chose to release Simon they ordered him to step down from the horse to stand in the road, the rag still tied over his eyes. Barabbas leaned down from his saddle to speak.

"Do not dare to touch the blindfold until you can no longer hear our horses hoof beats. I will not hesitate to ride back and use my sword."

When the riders were well gone and he could no longer hear their horses, Simon unwrapped the dirty rag from his head and looked around. Recognizing his direction from the position of the sun, he set out to walk into the city. Once there, he kept the gold for traveling, but using his credit with the leading merchants of the city he purchased a horse and saddle for his ride to

Damascus. Two days of travel with a miserable night spent at the only inn he could afford brought him to the city where he was well known.

Obtaining an advance of funds from another merchant, he entered Damascus' finest hostelry. Once in his room, he sent a worker of the inn out for fresh clothing, and a barber. Restored to his normal appearance, Simon stopped to write a long, bitter letter to his friend Tiberius, the Emperor.

He rested at the inn for a day, then purchased two slaves to guard him and fine horses to ride, he set out for Jerusalem to confront Pontius Pilate with the ill treatment he received in his province. Simon grew angrier as he rode.

He muttered to himself. "If that Pilate gets high and mighty with me, I'll not stop until he is one Procurator that is recalled to Rome in disgrace. He should be recalled immediately, allowing prominent citizens of the Empire to be treated this way by common thieves."

Old Pilate will learn who is powerful in the Empire. Why Adonijah Mekel, the richest merchant in Damascus, sold me these Greek slaves at half price and offered his entire fortune to see justice done.

A little after his noon rest on the third day of the journey Simon observed a lone rider approaching. He was astonished to find there was something familiar about the man. Even his horse seemed familiar.

The rider was larger than most men, and had long, golden hair. He sat his horse like a soldier. As he passed close by, Simon looked into the eyes of the stranger. He suddenly remembered the leader of the band of highwaymen who overcame his guards on the Joppa road more than a year ago.

Could he really be the same man? Is it possible? I can't be sure. Should I have my slaves go after him? Should I capture him and haul him before Pilate?

Afraid of making a mistake, Simon held his peace and traveled on, turning several times to look back at the man as he rode farther and farther away.

*I'm almost certain it is the same man. I can't do it though. Suppose he turned out to be someone else. It worries me.*

*If he were the bandit leader, would he ride past me so openly? He must be someone else. If he were innocent, it would cause a great furor for me to capture him. Such a mistake would certainly hurt my cause before Pilate and Tiberius.*

Simon found quarters for himself and his guards at the inn of his choice only because of his past business with the innkeeper, for the town was crowded for the celebration of Passover.

He was forced to wait several days before Pilate deigned to grant him an audience. When he protested angrily to the Procurator's lackeys, they gave him the excuse that there was much business the Procurator must complete due to the crowds attending the celebration.

By the time he was finally admitted to Pilate's council room Simon burned with anger over his cavalier treatment by the Procurator. That treatment, when added to the insult of the robbery and kidnapping, infuriated him almost beyond bearing. He was completely out of patience.

He stood before Pilate and addressed him in a harsh voice. "Pontius Pilate, I am Simon of Cyrenia. The indignities I have suffered in your province are many and great. I am here to complain of them and demand that the perpetrators be caught and punished."

Pilate stared at the red face of the angry merchant, a small smile on his face. When he finally spoke his voice was full of sarcasm. "Have you brought those who mistreated you before me that I may act?"

His tone and his words angered Simon further. "Am I a soldier, then? I, a friend of Tiberius, must arrest your cursed criminals for you?"

Pilate did not answer but continued to stare at Simon quite rudely.

His face growing redder, Simon shouted in his anger, "Tiberius shall hear of your negligence as quickly as I can get to Rome. Mayhap the right complaint will bring about your recall from this place since you are not interested in protecting the life and property of citizens of Rome."

Pilate immediately changed his expression. The knowledge of the old man's connection with the Emperor began to seep into his brain. He thought of the many complaints Tiberius received since the Emperor appointed him Procurator. Pilate suddenly knew it was imperative for him to placate this merchant.

Leaning forward, he said in an unctuous, sympathetic voice, "Good Simon, please, describe for me the men who wronged you and make your charges against them.

We have the Emperor's promise of more soldiers. They are soon to be sent out to us from Rome. With their help we will find these cursed highwaymen who so ill used you and punish them as they deserve."

Somewhat placated by the Procurator's change in attitude, Simon recounted the death of his guards and the loss of his goods. He related the story of his capture and long captivity, and the heavy ransom exacted for his release.

He carefully and fully described the men who participated, particularly the leaders. It was obvious to Pilate and his scribe Sylvanius that Simon described Josias of Bethany as the leader of the men who attacked and captured him, and the masked leader of the bandits could only be Barabbas.

Sylvanius wrote all this information down. Pilate turned to his scribe and asked, "Have we other complaints against men described in this way?"

"None, Master, none at all." the scribe lied without a change in his expression, shaking his head vigorously.

Pilate stroked his beard. Turning back to Simon he said, still in his placating voice, "There is a new tribune assigned to me here in Jerusalem. I shall give him these descriptions and set him to work on your case right away."

Simon calmed at the Procurator's words. "I would like to add that I am almost certain the leader of the band who attacked and captured me was a man I saw riding north on the Kings' Highway as I came toward the city.

"I only saw the bandit for a short while and at night, but I am almost sure it was the same man. Had I been completely certain, I would have had my guards capture him and bring him before thee."

"We will send a messenger to Damascus then, and have the wretch brought back here if you are certain he is the one. You must be sure of it though, good sir. I warn you, if he turns out to be another, we will have a great fuss to contend with.

"These Jews are mighty men with words and I have little liking of being accused of false arrest. Indemnity must be paid by law in such cases and these people cause me great trouble with their everlasting messages to Rome."

Early the next morning, Simon left the city by the Joppa gate on the first leg of his journey to Cyrenia. He knew full well that he accomplished nothing by reporting his grievance to Pilate. He looked into the Procurator's eyes as he spoke and knew the man simply mouthed words to stop his complaints.

His last words to Pilate were a warning and a promise. "I shall appeal to Caesar. The man responsible for my ordeal must be captured and punished."

# The Malefactors

## Chapter 8

Josias sat near the door of a small inn. He spent his days drinking wine and sorrowed for himself, lamenting over and over his poor lot in life.

*I miss the excitement, the wild rush that comes from riding with armed men to swoop down on a caravan, then escape into the desert. When we're idle I can't stop thinking of my mother's words. She said to me over and over, a man must have a mate and a family or the traditions of the Jewish people cannot be lived.*

*She always said that as a Jew and a child of God I must live in a community and fend for the common good. Her words fill me with unrest and self-loathing.*

His mind tumbled with confusing thoughts. The things his mother taught him as a child were alone in his experience in life. All other men and women he knew taught him to scoff at convention.

I know I feel no desire to be a part of the scurrying, screaming, and grasping masses of the Jewish people. It would be far better to die of a Roman spear or to be executed as a criminal than to live so commonplace a life.

The city of Damascus appeared to him much like Jerusalem. It wasn't quite so dirty, but it was dirty enough. Josias was disappointed. He had heard all of his life of the great Damascus and its many wonders.

I see little in this place for anyone to boast of so loudly. The great temple of Ommiado, where Aphrodite, the goddess of love is worshiped is not really so great, it's simply pretentious. Its magnificent beauty and architectural triumph is all but hidden under the accumulations of filth in the streets and heaped upon the wind-swept porches on its either side.

*He wandered about the city, stopping at the monument to Tiglathpileser the Third, that old Assyrian that Ahaz, when King of Judah, was forced to bow down before. The monument was worth looking at, but not exceptional.*

*Twice he passed a tall man in Arab dress who seemed to wander as he did, stopping to look up at the façades of buildings, and then disappearing around some corner. Once he saw him in the distance holding the leash of a great Saluki, one of the shaggy racing hounds of the desert.*

*His pulse quickened as he turned into a row of small shops. Here he found armorer's forges and booths where men sweated over hot steel, molding and hammering and shaping fine swords, daggers, spears and shields—fascination for a man who lived by violence.*

*Once he visited all the shops and still felt dissatisfied, Josias continued to wander about the city. He stood before the Roman Insula of the Procurator of Syria, an impressive building. It oozed strength, power and money. He turned his head and spat, then muttered venomously, "rich bastards."*

*Later that day, he hurried back to his inn. He spent the long afternoon just sitting, watching people walk about the bazaar, and it was almost dark. The Innkeeper warned him the first day to be sure to return to the inn before the sun went down. He said the city was full of footpads, desperate men who had no qualms about murdering a man for his purse.*

*As he turned to enter the entrance of the inn, Josias caught a glimpse of the tall Arab. He came around a corner several streets down, walking toward him. As the man moved past an open doorway, a figure dressed in dark clothes leaped out at him. His right hand held a knife raised high above his head, he reached out with his left hand to grasp the Arab's arm.*

*"Watch—watch out, "Josias called out to him. Drawing his short sword from under his cloak, he sprang into a run toward the two men. As he ran he screamed the wild undulating war cry he always used when he led his men to attack a caravan.*

*The Arab must have heard or sensed the attacker's movements, because he twisted around just in time and grabbed the man's wrist with both hands holding the knife away from him. The footpad tried to jerk away and overbalanced throwing both men down into the street.*

*Another footpad raced out of the doorway to join the attack. Josias saw the flash of a knife in the newcomer's hand. He raised his sword high and threw it, using all the power in his strong arm.*

*The blade flew straight, striking the second footpad full in the chest, knocking him down. He fell against the front of the building, the sword hilt protruding from the middle of his chest. He was dead before Josias reached him.*

*Josias placed his foot against the man's shoulder and pulled his sword free, whirling to do battle with the first attacker.*

*The Arab stood in the street, both hands on his hips, looking down at the first footpad. "These two were not very good at their job were they?"*

*"I must agree with you there Sir, they definitely were not very good at their job."*

*"What on earth was that hair-raising noise you made when you ran this way? You scared me so badly I felt weak in my knees."*

*"It's just a sound some friends and I make when we fight."*

*"Many could be frightened to death to hear it."*

*"It often gains just the second one needs to get the upper hand. Are you all right? Did the attacker hurt you?"*

*"I'm fine. The scurvy dogs did not touch me. I worked up a mighty thirst, though."*

*"My inn is just there, a few steps away," said Josias.*

*"I was turning to go in the door when I saw these two men jump out of that doorway. We could just leave the sorry villains where they lie unless you feel compelled to call the watch or the soldiers."*

*"I vote to let them lie. If we call the watch we'll be here half the night, as I said, I am powerfully thirsty. I'll soon be hungering for my evening meal."*

*"Come with me then. There's no one about to see us. We can be sitting in the inn taking our ease before anyone finds these two."*

*"Let's go."*

*Josias and the Arab walked to the inn and entered, taking a table in the back.*

*The Arab yelled to the innkeeper to bring him cool water. He leaned forward and grinned at Josias. "Look at that lazy lout. He moves like a snail. They beg for your business, then when you favor them they take the day to serve you. Damn Jews are all alike."*

*Stung, Josias leaned forward to answer him. "Yes, and only an ignorant Arab is so treated by all good Jews."*

*The Arab laughed aloud.*

*Josias grinned at the man. "I am Josias, a Jew of Bethany."*

*"Sir, I surmised you a Greek. You have the height and that golden hair and beard. No matter, though, I am Abdul Malis, a wanderer."*

*"My father was from Galilee. My mother speaks often of him. He has been dead these many years. He too was a large man. He was a stonemason who was killed while building Herod's palace. She tells me his hair was golden as mine is."*

*"It is often said we Arabs should hate you Jews, but is it worthwhile that we continue a fight Abram began?"*

*"Abram began? Remember that Ishmael swore revenge on all Jewry. This while we were yet Chaldeans."*

*"Come. Let us drink to another two thousand years of enmity, friend Josias."*

*"Agreed."*

*Malis raised his voice and announced to whomever would listen. "I find that Jews are most unpredictable. They have golden beards when you expect black ones. They are tall and comely against their tradition of growing short and mean. And finally, they are boisterously happy when you expect sniveling shrews. They amaze me to no end."*

*"Friend Arab, seeing your wealth by your dress and bearing you must undoubtedly be a member of the Arab royalty. Where is the traditional "Greater Than Thou attitude" of the leaders of your people?"*

"I find life a greater joy when that is left behind."

The two men passed several hours eating their meal and talking together. They probed and learned about each other and their traditions.

As the day darkened, Malis stopped smiling and stared at Josias. After a moment, he leaned forward and asked, "Friend Josias, do you boast the stomach for another adventure?"

Josias did not even stop to think. He was ready for anything to fill the hours and kill the boredom and guilt he felt of late.

He smiled as he answered, "I am ready for anything, my friend, anything."

"Lean close then, and listen."

Josias moved his stool nearer, his head almost touching Malis'.

"I have traveled about the world quite a lot and met some strange people. Several years ago, one man, an ancient Syrian of Corinth, told me of a lost city in the shadow of Mount Lebanon. His tale was of great interest to me—a tale too full of strange details to be wholly false."

Josias moved still closer, and tilted his head to hear Malis' soft words, whispered almost in his ear.

"As the slave of a rich merchant of Tyre, this man was sent with others to cut wood on Lebanon's lower slopes. The local villagers, a people who were a mixture of Jew, Syrian and Tyrean told him of a marvelous lost city near where they worked.

They said this place was in a valley a little south and east of Lebanon itself and guarded by many strange powers.

"This villager described the place and said a frightful skeleton lay in the narrow entrance to the valley and a pride of fierce lions guarded the opening. He swore these things to be true.

*He said he personally knew them to be true for he crept past the bones of some previous adventurer and entered the forest near the entrance.*

*"Once in the forest, he said he was attacked by a large cat that sprang on his back as he rode along the path. Badly mauled, he managed to escape and ran away as fast as his mule could run. When he finished his tale, he showed me double scars running from his shoulder to his wrist on his right arm as proof of the attack.*

*"The man went on to tell me of several men who ventured into the valley and were never seen again. He swore these things to be true. He also told me many tales he heard from the villagers describing the fabulous wealth of the mysterious people who once lived in the hidden city."*

*Malis leaned forward to look into Josias' eyes. "I have need of a courageous companion and you have proven your worth. You are not only strong and brave my friend; you are a lover of adventure.*

*"I want you to accompany me to this place. I owe you my life, and would repay you with a fortune if we are lucky.*

*"We may find only that the great treasure and even the fabled city are all old tales, told and retold—added to by all. But by my very eyes, I will never be satisfied until I try to find the place.*

*"Have you the heart to go with me?"*

*Josias turned his head and leaned back in his seat. Staring at the cup in his hand he thought,* there is nothing for me to lose other than my life. But what matter that? The excitement of adventure and danger is exactly what I have wished for. If I sit here much longer the same nagging memories will come back to haunt me and make my life miserable.

He turned back to Malis and said, "I have some small items of business to complete before I can leave the city. Can we meet here two days hence to make preparations for this adventure?"

"Agreed. I will roust you from your bed two days from now, before the sun is even awake."

It was too late in the day for Josias' business to be completed. He ate a small meal and retired to his room to sleep.

He rose early the next day and set out to find a saddle shop, determined to find a way to safeguard his small store of gold. After all, the Arab was a complete stranger and robbers infested the land. A man would be a fool not to take the most care of his belongings.

Josias never thought of depositing his small hoard of gold with a trustworthy merchant. He was yet primitive enough and poor enough to believe that a man only possessed the gold he could hold in his hand. In his entire life he never possessed more than he felt he could safeguard with his sword.

After a short search, he found what he was seeking near the banks of the river Baradah, at the outskirts of the city. An ancient Syrian, surrounded by leather goods, assured him he could do anything pertaining to saddles.

Josias instructed the man to remove the leather covering from his saddle frame and drill several large holes in the wooden cantle. Into these holes he fitted his gold coins, retaining only a few to buy the supplies he would need for the coming adventure.

The saddler then replaced the leather on the saddle as before, creating a perfect hiding place. Josias added a heavy bribe to the price the old man quoted for his work—hoping the coin would assure the secrecy of his hiding place.

*His business complete, Josias rode through the teeming streets of the lower city. Amusing himself with smiles at the younger women and occasionally offering a teasing word.*

*These tactics he often used in the past. Sometimes they led to fights with the woman's other admirers. Often they led to snubs and now and then, reciprocating smiles. Best of all, at times, they led to an enjoyable evening with an attractive companion. He soon found that Damascus' women only offered a few smiles to strangers.*

*Most of the women he saw were not to his taste, anyway. He kept seeing the face of Sarah—her beautiful dark eyes, her shining black hair and the grace of her small shoulders. He told himself he was a fool to let the girl's image interfere with his pleasures. She may have looked on him with favor once, but she was so respectable, her family would never let her speak to him.*

I have only a little gold hidden away—nowhere near enough to buy and furnish a proper home and care for such a woman. I must remove her image from my thoughts. Besides, when my gold runs low I will be forced to go back to Jerusalem and rejoin Barabbas to raid caravans for my living.

*The sun neared the summit of the distant mountains as Josias entered the side door of the inn of Camal the Syrian. A long and loud whoop proclaimed the presence of his new friend Malis. They enjoyed the evening eating the best the inn offered and talking. Josias drank deeply of the innkeeper's best wine although Malis drank only water.*

*Josias awakened early the following morning to a sick head, a foul taste in his mouth. He spent much time at his bath and dressing. He finally left his room to eat a small breakfast of wine and honeycakes.*

*He barely felt human when Malis entered the door of the inn. The Arab took a seat across from Josias, but refused food. Even without drinking alcohol, they stayed so long talking the night before that his eyes did not want to open either.*

*Leaving the inn about an hour later, the two men visited a trader of animals who set up his tent in a barren field at the outskirts of the city. Malis' efforts to bargain for pack donkeys resulted in a long harangue with the trader. After much shouting, cursing and uncomplimentary references to the ancestry of each by the other, he settled on the purchase of two pack donkeys from the trader.*

*Josias moved away from the noise of their bargaining to sit quietly beside the small stream running beside the field. When shouting and cursing stopped he marveled at the ability of both men to verbally attack each other as apparent enemies and then part as friends.*

*He and Malis made most of the purchases they would need on their trip and returned to their inns at nightfall.*

*The early light of dawn showed a bustle of preparation. Dressed for riding, Malis appeared more the swarthy Arab. His bearing, his garments and his horse were princely. He tied the leash of the great hound to his mount's stirrup and turned his hand to pack bundles of food and camp gear on a sleepy donkey.*

*Josias muttered curses at no one in particular as he cajoled a second donkey to accept a pack cradle. Both men could find little patience, but with effort and much time they were finally ready and the small caravan set out for the distant mountains west of the city.*

*Many days later, they sighted a woodcutter's camp near the southern tip of Mount Lebanon. Malis and Josias turned from the dusty road into the shade of huge cedars surrounding the peaceful park.*

*An old man stirred a pot over a small fire. He offered the travelers welcome and assured them the spring nearby would yield water enough for them and their animals as well as the woodcutters.*

*Pleased with the arrangement, Josias handed the man a coin.*

*Malis and Josias set up their camp for the night. When the evening meal was over Malis struck a bargain with the leader of the woodcutters to leave the donkeys and camp gear in the old man's keeping while they explored the forest for several days.*

*He showed the man his spear and sword, claiming he and Josias were hunters, seeking the skin of a lion as a trophy. He explained that he had heard stories of big cats roaming in the area. The presence of the hunting dog helped to make his story sound authentic.*

# The Malefactors

# Chapter 9

*Josias and Malis searched several days in that area, returning to the woodcutters' camp each evening. Finally, satisfied they would find nothing, they packed up their gear, sought and found a new location in a grove of tall cedars above a grassy glade. This camp lay near a spring where clear cold water trickled out of a fissure in a jumbled outcrop of rocks.*

*It was a beautiful place. Flowers carpeted the open area. Birds abounded. Small game trails crisscrossed under the trees.*

*Malis tied the dog near their beds at night, partly for protection and partly to keep the dog from chasing a passing fox or coney. Grass grew green and tall, abundant enough to keep the hobbled horses from wandering. Downed wood lay about, plenty for their small cooking fires.*

*Best of all, the place lay hidden and remote enough to please anyone seeking solitude. Working well together, Malis and Josias constructed a primitive lean-to of sheepskin to keep the morning dew from wetting them.*

*The next morning, Josias rose and walked for about five minutes to the east of the campsite to relieve himself. He decided to walk on a little higher on the hogback rising near the camp. He wanted to see the sun rising over rugged old Mount Herman and the large range of hills east of their camp.*

*Making his way upward through the pungent, but oddly pleasant smelling cedars, Josias thought,* I have missed a lot of life—growing up in the barren hill country of Judah instead of in forested land such as this. This wilderness makes me feel calmer than I can ever remember.

*After about thirty minutes of half-walking, half-climbing, he came out above the timberline onto a field of craggy granite. The rocky hogback and the softly curved swales on either side leveled into a line that lay almost straight. Josias turned north to study a magnificent panorama he knew that few were privileged to see. The timberline at its top was uneven, full of downward dips and an occasional spur of weathered trees pushing higher, but essentially straight as far as he could see. It ran northeast below the spine of the Lebanon range.*

*He stood and stared, his hand held over his eyes to shade them from the sun, admiring the grandeur of the view.* "Why," *he said aloud, almost laughing.* "A thousand cities could be lost in the vastness of these mountains. They keep on and on as far as a man can see."

*Lost in admiration, his eyes swept across the trees below him and over to the east. He suddenly realized there was a long valley in the treetops directly below him. It appeared to him that a fifty-foot-wide strip of trees grew shorter than the ones above or below the place. It looked as if some giant reached down and trimmed the tops of those few trees a little shorter, or Josias thought,* wait a bit—those trees must be—they definitely are younger than the great trees on either side of them.

*He stared a moment, then exclaimed aloud.* "It's a road. It has to be the ancient road."

*Surely this was the sign he and Malis sought. The place lay high enough above the valley not to be too muddy in the rainy season and far enough below the ridge of the mountain not to be too rocky for road building.*

*Staring intently, Josias searched the area again looking for landmarks. He finally settled on an ancient tree that was much taller than its fellows.*

*He would use the tree as a marker. It obviously died in maturity, possibly by a lightening strike. It stood stark and bare, making it easy to mark the lower patch of trees. After studying the area carefully to make sure he could find the place again, Josias turned to hurry back down hill to the camp.*

*As he rushed into camp the ever-jovial Malis shouted, "Where have you been, Josias? If it were not that your gear and your mount stood right here before my eyes I might have thought you deserted me."*

*"Stir yourself, man. Let's eat and get moving. I think I've found the ancient road we've been looking for."*

*"Don't you be building false hope in me man. I've about concluded this is a fool's errand and you and I are the prime fools."*

*"Wait until we get to the top and you see what I found, Arab—then conclude what you will."*

*The two men fairly gobbled their breakfast. Cleaning their camp gear enough so animals wouldn't find scraps of food to attract them, they set out to view the place where Josias saw the outline of the road. When they stood at the top, Josias pointed to the trace along the treetops and the ancient landmark cedar.*

*"Surely that must be the road to the lost valley. The very one we've been searching these woods for. Let's hurry back to camp, pack up our gear and see if we can't follow it."*

*Shaking his head, Malis placed his hands on his hips and said, "I am amazed at what I see. You're right. Mayhap you have found a way to our goal, Josias. It's possible we are not fools after all."*

*Throwing their things back into their packs, the two men caught up their animals and climbed westward along the hogback until they came to a place that leveled off and ran north and south near the crest. Small ridges cut from stone were piled on the lower side of the level strip. Faint ruts showed between the trees, as though heavy loads had once rolled over the road—sure evidence that man toiled there, fighting his battles against nature.*

*They turned north along this faint trace, almost breathless with excitement. The track soon curved westward as it came to an area cut by small ravines and then east again over the ridges in an attempt to maintain a level. There were no steep inclines. Malis and Josias walked their horses. Sometimes they were forced to dismount and lead their animals afoot through tangles of brambles, chokeberry and other native growth. Occasionally, they completely lost sight of the track, but kept going in the same direction and came upon the remains of the road again as it crossed the next ridge.*

*Darkness forced them to make a dry camp. Both men awakened in the semi-darkness of false dawn, much too excited to sleep any longer. They came upon a green sward in midmorning with a small brook along its side. Knowing it would be difficult to find a better camping place, they stopped for a few hours so the horses and pack-asses could drink and feed.*

*While the animals were grazing Malis and Josias worked together to prepare a large breakfast of flour cakes browned in the ashes of their fire. Both men added the sweetness of a handful of dried figs to their simple meal. Malis fed the dog bones from a small leather pouch he carried behind his saddle.*

*After two hours, the men rinsed their canteens and filled them afresh at the brook. Then they hurriedly prepared the animals to continue on their way. Late that afternoon, after following many false trails and cursing a great deal as barbs scratched their arms, they found the landmark tree. As tired as either of them could ever remember being, they made dry camp again.*

*From their camping place they could see a narrow pass in the distance, beckoning them on, but it was too late in the day to follow. The ancient road obviously went through the narrow pass they could see in the distance. It surely ran on over the crown of a small hillock that leveled off before reaching the mountain's summit.*

*Malis, Josias and the animals were exhausted. The way was difficult. In their excitement they had pushed themselves far too hard that day. They agreed to rest and follow on in the morning.*

*No matter their exhaustion, both men were full of excitement, and going to sleep was difficult. The talkative Malis, always interesting to Josias with his stories of strange lands, lounged against his saddle telling a long story of the land of the Pharaohs.*

*He told of the great Sphinx of Giza, lying east of the Nile and many leagues upriver from Alexandria. He described the great lion body, saying it was near one hundred twenty cubits long and its man head was forty-two cubits tall. He said the wonder was all made of stone and at least three thousand years old.*

*"You should see these wonders some day, Josias. This Sphinx sits facing the great Pyramid. The figure is higher than most mountains and the true wonder of it is that the entire thing is all man-made. There are also smaller Pyramids scattered over a large area around the strange man-lion."*

115

*Malis' voice droned on. He told tales of the rulers of Egypt and how they built great crypts while they yet lived, knowing their bodies would be sealed inside them after death. He continued to talk even when Josias fell asleep, dreaming of a beautiful girl. One so tiny and delicate that surely he could lift her with one hand. He remembered only confusing bits of Malis' account of the unrest among the present nomads living in that strange, far-away place.*

*Barely taking time to feed themselves and their animals, the two men set out at dawn to follow the track toward the narrow pass. In the late morning they turned aside from the ancient road to find a place with water and grass for the animals. The ever-narrowing pass became almost impenetrable—choked with a heavy growth of young trees and underbrush. In several places they stopped to marvel over grooves in the stone left by the marks of iron tools, clear evidence that whoever made the road quarried away part of the rocks to keep the track wide enough for the going and coming of wagons or carts.*

*The sun was low in the sky when the track made an abrupt turn. Before them lay a human skeleton—obviously the skeleton of the woodcutter's story. The bones were broken and scattered about. The man's skull leaned grotesquely against a stone and the late afternoon sun shone at an angle, making it appear he glared at them. Josias felt a momentary sense of intruding on a sacred place.*

*"This is what gave this place its reputation of evil, I vow. He looks as though he could rise up and chase us away from here, doesn't he?" Malis' stood looking down at the skull, his hands on his hips.*

*"I care not for the likes of that one. He's beyond committing any harm or meanness." Josias answered. "It's the live*

ones I worry about—the ones carrying sword and armor who give me trouble."

Both men gave the skeleton a wide berth, circling aside as they passed. The track widened, and they came into a forest of huge old cedars. It was a place so shaded there was little undergrowth, giving it a park-like appearance. They took only a few steps before the trees thinned. They could soon see in the distance and far below them, glimpses of white buildings set in straight rows.

"We have found it, Josias," Malis whispered. "Just look, will you? We've found it."

"Yes, my Arab friend. That is either your lost city of the woodcutter's tale or one that none in Judea knows anything about."

They moved together farther down slope. As the forest continued to thin they came to a large pool. It was cut by man from solid rock and filled with clear, fresh water. A three-foot wide flume or aqueduct made of stone with a water gate at its mouth ran over the hill and toward the city below. The watercourse stood on stone pillars. It was astonishingly well preserved—its structure a great wonder to Malis and Josias.

They decided to make camp beside the pool. It offered a place where the horses could water and plenty of grass for them to graze. Both men agreed that it might be safer to keep their gear and animals apart, for they had no way of knowing what or who might inhabit the city below. They had long ago concluded that the woodcutter's stories of wild tigers or some kind of big cats inhabiting the area must be a figment of fevered imaginations. They had seen only birds, squirrels and of course, the ever-present conies that were a plague on all the lands of the eastern Mediterranean.

When they started down hill toward the city, the Saluki refused to follow. He would not come running as he usually did when Malis called. He sat down on his haunches and whined loudly, refusing to move away from the horses.

"Come on, you fool dog. What is wrong with you?"

The dog refused to move. Malis called him several more times, shouting for him to obey, but he would not. Finally shrugging his shoulders in defeat, the Arab left the dog where he wanted to stay and turned to join Josias on the path.

Walking slowly and watching all about, the two men followed an ancient stone road from the pool down the hill into the city. They noticed in passing that the aqueduct running to one side of the road leaked but little. The stonemasons who built it did their work well. Its bottom was mortised into the sides and leaded against leaks. Josias commented that everything about its construction showed great skill and care.

When they left the trees they could see two rows of houses. Each house boasted a large front and side garden. A pedestrian's walk bordered the yards between the houses and the wide streets running on either side of a wide, park-like median. Without people, the layout gave the place the appearance of a drawing or perhaps a dream.

The houses and a colonnaded Pantheon sitting at the end of the street were all built of light-colored limestone that gleamed whitely in the bright sun. The buildings appeared remarkably clean. Aside from the great profusion of plant growth around the houses, from where the two men stood, the city appeared inhabited.

As they approached the level of the buildings, Josias said, "Malis, let us examine each house as we come to it. We can go along this side first and then come back on the other."

"That's fine with me. Any plan is better than none."

Excitement almost beyond enduring filled the two men. As they came closer to the first building an eerie feeling gripped

*Josias. He fancied that if they took another step, the dead must appear before them or at least hail them. He turned to hold his finger before his lips, signaling to Malis for quiet.*

*Speaking with hushed voices they carefully stepped around obstructions along the brush-filled walk to approach the front entrance of the house. Part of the way along the walk, they stopped to admire the way the colonnaded porch on its front and garden side shaded the house from the morning sun. They agreed that the columns were Corinthian, fashioned in white limestone after the fashion of the Greeks.*

*The roof was dull, red tile. The house boasted large windows with wooden shutters and a wide front door set between half-columns that were carved to match those of the colonnade. These features made the house seem similar to the temples and shrines of Hellenic cities.*

*Near the front porch steps stood a statue of Apollo, the god of perfection, beautifully carved in white marble with black veining. Malis commented that the stone was native to the mountains of Corinth. To the left of Apollo stood Zeus, father of the Gods—the Greeks revered both deities.*

*It took the strength of both men to push open the wide front door. Both of the doors bronze hinges were corroded from many years of disuse. Bright sunlight fell on a stone-floored entryway. A stairway of stone ran up on its left side, a doorway opened to the right and another at the far end. A magnificent old lounge, carved from a dark wood, sat against its inner wall.*

*One hand on the hilt of his sword, Josias stepped ahead of Malis and entered the room to the right of the hallway. A large fireplace stood on its opposite wall, its white stones blackened by smoke. Josias walked to the large front window and pulled at the shutters. They fell apart in his hands, flooding the room with light.*

*The inner wall of the room bore shelves that held rolled scrolls. Many showed the ravages of rodents and were pulled all ajumble.*

*A huge rectangular table stood in the room's center. Four chairs with high backs and arms were arranged around it. The table held two brass candlesticks and papyrus fragments.*

*A thick coating of dust lay over everything. Another rotting lounge stood against the wall beneath the window. On the far wall hung a tarnished shield and crossed spears.*

*Stepping to the window to look out, Malis said, "The sun is far down, Josias. The hour is growing late."*

*"We had better go back to camp then. This place feels odd to me," Josias said, shaking his head. "I don't wish to be caught inside this house or anywhere in this strange, empty city after darkness falls."*

*"Stop talking and come on then." Malis called over his shoulder as he left by the open front door.*

*Josias followed, stopping to force the door shut behind him. The two men hurried up the roadway to where they left their horses and gear. Everything was just as they left it. The great Saluki barked happily when they came in sight and leaped up to lick Malis' face.*

*They set up camp and after eating a small meal; both men fell into their blankets and slept the sleep of exhaustion. When they awoke at dawn they both were astonished at the shortness of the night.*

*Josias gathered some wood and started the fire while Malis tended the animals. While their camp bread was cooking they chattered with the excitement of actually finding the wonderful city.*

*"I have seem many of the most famous cities of this world, but never one to compare with this. The marble statues at the*

*entrance of the first house are the most beautiful I have ever seen. Such exquisite work must have been done by the greatest artist that ever lived."*

*"I will agree the whole of it is almost unreal," Josias almost sneered at the raptures of Malis the artist, schooled in the liberal arts and used to the finer things of life.*

*Josias, who counted life's gifts by the coin of the realm continued, "I saw little of value a man could use in the house we visited yesterday. It will interest me much more when we come upon the gold you said the old Syrian promised we would find."*

*Leaving the reluctant dog to guard the camp, Malis walked ahead of Josias as they returned to the flat bottom of the bowl-like valley. They argued as they walked down the hill and finally decided to look at the fountains and statuary in the median between the two rows of houses and streets before they finished exploring the house they had entered the day before.*

*Enormous shrubs covered in pink, red, and purple blossoms grew in profusion in the median between the two streets. They intermingled with chokeberry; mountain beech, other wild berries and many other species neither Malis nor Josias could give a name.*

*The thick growth made it nearly impossible to push through to get close enough to examine the two large fountains. Finally gaining a path near one of the fountains they could see that it too was beautifully formed. In addition, statues of the pantheon of Greek Gods surrounded it.*

*Malis stood without speaking and stared. He envisioned the park all cleaned and the shrubs properly trimmed. "This indeed must have been the world's most beautiful city when all was in good order."*

*"It must indeed have been quite beautiful. I wonder what manner of people lived here." Josias suddenly felt embarrassed for speaking so.*

*He felt he should have said he believed the beauty of the statuary and fountains a waste of time, a great foolishness that offered no benefit. He knew that was what he would have said to other friends and only a few weeks earlier.*

*After studying each image on the fountain, the ever-curious Malis led the way back across the roadway to finish exploring the house. This time they went directly through the little entry hall into a room at the rear of the house. It was a place for cooking and eating. The great fireplace on the back wall was equipped with a swinging hook on one side and a heavy piece of flat iron opposite it. The stone chimney shelf was filled with pottery jars of several sizes.*

*"These amphora must have held food supplies," Malis picked up a small jar and shook the dust out on the floor.*

*He opened a cupboard that rested against the outer-side wall. It was made of a dark soapstone and had a sink-like trough in its center. A terra cotta pipe ran through the wall and dumped a stream of water into the sink. The water flowed in turn through another terra cotta pipe to go out of the house. The men opened the rear door and followed the intricate water system into the yard.*

*Behind the house they found a small stone building. Opening the door, Malis and Josias found that the building was a privy. The water flowing from the house ran under a square box-like seat and into a large pipe. This ran into a larger pipe, which looked to run parallel to the street, behind all the houses.*

*"This is most unusual," Malis observed. "These people have piped water from the aqueduct into their kitchen, then the waste runs under the privy into a buried sewer. It is doubtful if*

another city exists as convenient or sanitary as this. I certainly never heard of one."

"'Tis truly doubtful, my friend. I thought every person of means had slaves who went about the house every morning collecting the household's human excrement and used it to enrich their gardens. The people of this city must have been truly wealthy as well as inventive." Josias frowned as he spoke, puzzling over the idea of living so cleanly.

They returned to the house and climbed the stairs to explore the upper rooms. Each one they entered was furnished simply with a low bed, a seat with no back and a small table.

Josias laughed aloud as they looked in the doorway of the last room. "It is certain no women lived in this house. There's no place for their fripperies."

Malis nodded and motioned for Josias to follow him to the next house. Their exploration revealed that every house on that side was similar. The statuary of different Gods or persons, many unrecognized by Malis, stood before each door. In several houses, a break in the water system had allowed water to flow out of its doors causing such a profusion of vegetation to grow up that it was impossible for them to force open a door to enter. As the sun waned, they returned to camp again.

Next morning, their simple breakfast over and the animals cared for, Malis and Josias again hurriedly descended the hill to the city. They set out to explore the houses on the far side of the broad avenue. It turned out that those buildings, although having the same outside appearance as the houses, were workshops instead of residences.

The one on the north end and the first one they entered held a complete Goldsmith's shop. When Josias pulled open the rotting shutters, the light revealed a large stone table covered with *exquisite vases, jewel boxes, chalices, candelabra and statuary. All were fashioned of gold and silver.*

*He spoke quietly, although he felt like shouting. "These things I can fully appreciate, Mali. Merchants in Damascus or Jerusalem will pay us well for them and beg for more."*

*Josias continued exploring. On a back shelf he found a pile of gold coins mixed with the dust of the leather bag that once held them. He rubbed one of the coins with his thumb so he could read the inscription. One didrachma was stamped on its face beneath the likeness of Pericles with the Olympiad torch over the date four hundred ninety. Mali reckoned that year to be almost two hundred and fifty years past.*

*"Malis, I will return to the woodcutter's camp for our pack asses. We must carry these treasures to Damascus and sell them. If we can do that safely, we will both be rich men."*

*"We'll do that, Josias, but wait at least a few hours. We should explore all the buildings before we leave. Someone else may find this place before we return. Besides, we've never yet found the reason for this city's reputation of evil."*

*Josias shook his head and muttered, "The place does feel strange."*

*"Aha, my skeptical friend. I believe you may be a little superstitious after all."*

*"No my learned friend, I'm not superstitious, I'm just a little cautious. You might think to be cautious too, considering it is your dog that refuses to come near the place."*

*As they entered the other buildings Mali and Josias found all manner of workshops. Some were used to make furniture, others brassware. In one they found a potters wheel and a supply of bowls and jars. There were several buildings where much writing had been done and great stores of rotting scrolls were shelved.*

*When they reached the end of the street again, Malis said he was curious as to how the wastewater escaped the bowl-like valley. They followed the elevated drain to where the two rows of drains from the houses came together. The pipes plunged underground through a large cave-like opening at the base of a sheer cliff forming the north end of the valley.*

*Malis shook his head. "If a rockslide should ever stop that opening this city will be at the bottom of a huge lake."*

*"Let's go." Josias insisted. "I've seen enough. There is only the gold and silver that is worth all this time."*

*"Have some patience, Josias, please. I want to explore some more. There must be some reason for this place to be deserted. I'm going back to that first house and see if I can find anything in some of the scrolls."*

*"Go ahead then, if that's what you want to do with your time. I'm going to explore the rest of the valley."*

*Josias wandered along, noticing there were few birds in the valley. The only ones he saw were vultures. The sight of the ugly black birds made him shiver. He turned his eyes away and continued exploring. When he reached the western side of the valley he found a large stone quarry. There was an ingeniously constructed slide that led from it to the valley floor. He saw great piles of cut, but obviously rejected, stone lying about.*

*South of the quarry, but on the same wall, he discovered a small cave. Smiling, he decided it would make an excellent place to hide the treasures they could not carry with them until they could come back for them.*

We'll never carry away but a small amount of the treasure in those buildings. I would not like to return someday and find some thief had made off with everything when they rightfully belong to my friend and I by right of discovery.

He returned to the first house and found Malis surrounded by a mound of open

scrolls. "Most of these scrolls are written in ancient Greek. I have found all manner of philosophical writings and mathematical equations, but there is nothing here that tells me anything of this city or its people."

"Well, let it be for tonight, anyway. The sun is low. We should go back to camp before dark. I'll get up early in the morning and ride out to get our donkeys. We'll need them. You can come down here and read all day while I'm gone if you wish."

Rising early, Josias left camp just as the sun rose and followed their back trail through the forest. Darkness was falling the next day when he returned, impatient to load the treasure and return to Damascus. Malis' had killed two coneys and a tasty stew simmered over the coals. He also made bread to compliment the stew. The men stuffed themselves on the hot meal and retired early, planning to again rise with the sun.

Malis helped Josias set aside as much treasure as he guessed the donkeys could carry. They took the choicest pieces left and piled them into large amphora and carried them to the cave Josias found, concealing the jars behind rocks. They filled the donkey's packs with the most precious pieces, covering the gold and silver with plain copper pots and hiding them under their camp gear.

The gold coins they divided so each might have an equal share if they were somehow separated. As Malis and Josias led the donkeys up to the cedars, ready to leave the mysterious place and return to their lives, both stopped and turned to look back at the beautiful city. Neither spoke.

*Malis was silent most of the way through the forest. He was obviously thinking about the strange city. It pleased Josias.*

*He felt unsettled, confused. His entire life had been spent striving for more. Now he had all any man could ever want. He was like a man newborn, his old life, his friends and even his beliefs, seemed only a burden.*

*The time spent in the wilderness calmed him. He felt excitement over finding the city and the treasure. But it was a new and different excitement, nothing like the wild ecstatic feeling he relished as he raised his sword and screamed when he rode at the head of a band of men to attack a pack train.*

*A week later Josias approached Abraham Mekal, the largest and most trusted merchant in Damascus. Mekal agreed to sell his treasures and gave him a receipt listing each item and his estimate of its value. His business done, Josias left the street called Straight and returned to the inn of Camel the Syrian where Malis waited. Long into the night they drank, and sang, telling stories.*

*Malis worked out an arrangement with an olive-skinned dancing girl, but Josias excused himself and returned to his room. The girl's soft voice and sweet smell reminded him too much of Sarah. He sought his bed to dream of her.*

*Both men slept late. After they bathed and dressed they enjoyed a breakfast of fruit and honeycakes. Josias noticed that Malis still said little.*

*"What is wrong with you, my friend? Are you angry about something or just sad that our adventure is over?"*

*"Josias, we must part this day, for I must return to Dedan. My father expects me soon and camels must be readied for the spring sale in Jerusalem."*

*When Malis left he kissed Josias cheeks. "Farewell, dear friend. I shall see you at the next Passover as agreed."*

*"I will be here in this inn waiting for you on the first day if I live. In the mean time, a small village called Ramah calls me. I have need to satisfy a great curiosity and know of nowhere else to do it." Josias stood in the inn doorway and watched as Malis rode out of sight.*

*He felt sad at parting with Malis, but deep inside he was filled with a great joy. He was going to Ramah to find Sarah, the daughter of Joel the Shepherd. He had something to offer her now.*

# Chapter 10

*Josias left Damascus by way of the Roman road. It brought him to Capernaum, on the northern end of the Sea of Galilee. When he reached there, he suddenly became doubtful of his welcome at Sarah's home. After all, met her only once, when he wrote the letter for them in Jerusalem. She saw him only that once, and it was just for a few minutes. She might not even remember.*

I'm probably a fool. It might be that it wasn't interest in me that made the girl turn and smile. Perhaps she will be insulted that I, almost a stranger, would presume to come to her home without invitation.

*Shaking his head, he took the road to Ramah, muttering to himself as he rode. "I have to find out. I cannot go on without knowing how she feels—if there is any hope for me."*

*Josias rode northwest over a hilly, ill kept road. He guided his horse carefully over deep ruts and around loose stones scattered about. Obviously, the road was little used.*

*It was late morning when he reached the village of Ramah. A small boy pointed the way to Joel's home. Josias rode to the gate and stopped to examine the house and grounds.*

*The place was clean and neat. Sitting well back from the road, a house built of fieldstone nestled in a grove of fig trees. A large arbor ran along its eastern side. Two rows of citron trees bordered a flagstone walk leading to the gate.*

*Near the house and around the trees grew clusters of Rose of Sharon, aglow with blooms of white, pink and violet, giving the place great beauty. As Josias dismounted he saw a girl come from under the arbor and enter the garden beside it. He tied his horse at the gate and opening it, walked to the house. An older woman, frail, with gray hair and a brow quite wrinkled, answered his knock.*

*"Good Master, seekest thou Joel the Shepherd?"*

*"Yes, Good Mother, it is to him I would speak."*

*"I fear you have come in vain. Joel is many leagues away from Ramah this day. He is somewhere in yonder hills tending his flocks. This is the season sheep graze the high country."*

*"Of that I am truly sorry, for I would see him."*

*"Why is't thou seekest Joel, a humble shepherd?" The woman's face showed her alarm. She feared something was amiss, that this stranger bore some threat.*

*"I see him in hopes he woulds't set me to work tending his flocks. Howbeit if he be absent I will put up at the inn until he returns." Josias amazed himself at how quickly he returned to the speech of his youth.*

*"What does this mean?" The woman drew herself up to her full height and spoke in an angry voice. "By your dress thou art a wealthy merchant or representative of those who govern. Why woulds't thou herd sheep? Surely you mock me."*

*Sarah suddenly spoke from behind the woman. "Mother, this man is a scribe. He is the same scribe my father engaged to write the letter he sent you from Jerusalem at the last Passover."*

*"Methinks it best for you to go to the kitchen with the leeks, girl and not be quite so bold."*

*Sarah's cheeks flamed. She felt mortified to be spoken to in such a way in the presence of the handsome scribe. She thought of him often since the trip to Jerusalem. Ducking her head to hide her face, she turned away and rushed out of the room.*

*"Are you truly a scribe?" her mother turned to ask Josias.*

*"Yes, Good Mother, I am."*

*"Then why do you come to my door seeking work as a shepherd from a poor man in these remote hills? The fine raiment thou wearest and yonder richly saddled mount give evidence that thou art a wealthy man."*

*"Forgive me, I come because there is no peace in the city. I merely seek a way to escape my many troubles."*

*"Troubles are the lot of all. Seek thee God, my son, for only he can cast out they troubles."*

*"I know not what I seek—to go into the mountains where it might be possible to think clearly perhaps. That is why I sought out Joel."*

*His heart sinking, Josias cursed himself for a fool to rattle on so.* Why don't I tell the woman I seek only to be with the daughter of this house?"

*"My husband shall know of thy desire to see him on his return, sir."*

*"Good day to thee and thine, kind lady. I will be stopping at the inn at Ramah. A message will find me there."*

*"The blessings of the Lord upon thee."*

*The woman returned to the kitchen. Sarah was standing beside a table cleaning the leeks. Tears flowed down her cheeks. Hesitating, Salome started to ask her more about the scribe, but decided to hold her peace. She could not be sure whether the child's tears were from the leeks or from her harsh rebuke.*

*Leaving the kitchen, Salome went to the arbor in the yard and sat on a bench thinking of her beautiful daughter.*

Are Joel and I too strict with the girl? I know she is lonely. She has always been. I never allowed her to play with the children of Ramah. She spent her time studying in the Synagogue or learning the many duties she will be required to know to make a good wife.

I have always been so fearful of the influence of the people of Samaria, Syria and Greece who have settled in this town. There are so many of them. I fear they may turn Sarah's head and damage her faith in the one true God. I have always shunned these people, but only to protect my child.

*Rubbing her forehead, she muttered aloud, "Maybe she would have married ere this if we were not so strict and allowed her to mingle with the youths of the village. There are several eligible ones near her age.*

*"What is to become of her? She nearly twenty-two and still has no husband."*

*She thought of their trip to Cana two years before. They went for the wedding of her Cousin Rebecca's daughter.*

*Of the many young men of good countenance at the wedding Sarah had eyes for the Nazarene only. It was true that Jesus was a great Rabbi, but he showed no interest in Sarah. He hardly noticed her other than to bless her as he did all those who believed.*

I will talk to Joel on his return. Mayhap we should encourage her to talk to the handsome young scribe. Surely I am not to be denied grandsons as I have been denied sons.

*Disheartened by his interview with Salome, Josias followed the dusty road through Ramah until he came to the public well. A* squat building across the way bore a large sign announcing that it was an inn.

He tied his horse to a rack under a gnarled old oak, and went through the open front door of the building into the main room. Several men sat about a table idly casting dice on its smooth top.

He could see no money. It appeared the men had little interest in their game. They showed much interest in him, however. He took no offence. This was a remote place and he was sure few strangers entered the inn.

Taking a table near the idlers Josias called out to the innkeeper, "A cup of cool wine, if you please."

The fat innkeeper hurried behind the bar and dipped a cup of his best wine from a pottery crock sitting in a tub of water. He brought the cup to Josias and whined a litany of complaints of poor business, the terrible heat, the oppression of the Jewish temple taxes and the depredations of the Romans.

Laying a gold denarius on the table, Josias asked, "Have you quarters and food for a weary traveler and his mount?"

Unable to take his eyes from the coin, the innkeeper answered, "Good sir, this humble inn has long awaited your coming. Travelers are but few these days and money scarce. You and your horse will receive the best care in this inn you will ever find, I promise you."

As he sat sipping his wine, Josias heard several remarks expressing great expectations of how things would be when "He is king" from the group gathered around the table.

He wondered to himself. Who could they be referring to? I have heard of no rebellion. Could anyone hope to overthrow Rome with its great power?

*He had heard talk of the Galilean who chased the moneychangers from the temple. Many thought him to be the long-awaited Messiah.* Josiah *wondered again,* are these people simple enough to think a mere prophet from these backward hills could defeat the might of Caesar and his Legions and become King. Surely they are all demented.

*He remembered how the Pharisees of Jerusalem and every temple priest screamed of the heresy the Galilean prophet preached. They demanded of the Romans that he be stopped. Josias cared little what the Pharisees and priests thought, for to him they were naught but hypocrites who stole from the poor, devout people by taking advantage of their ignorance.*

*He had been a robber, yes. But his robbery was by might and those of his victims who lived knew they were robbed. He thought the Romans should let the Galilean preach and the priests scream, for they let others alone when they were so engaged.*

*As he rose to accompany the innkeeper to attend the horse and secure his saddle and other possessions, he again heard the gossipers at the nearby table saying, "When he is king."*

*Shaking his head he muttered to himself as he stepped out of the door, "let the fools dream, nothing can come of it."*

*Once he secured his belongings under the bed he would sleep in that night,* Josias *again took the table beside the group of gamblers. The unrest, the anxiety that had so nearly driven him mad before his adventure with Malis seemed ready to take hold of him again.*

*He found that the only cure for the wild turmoil of feeling was activity, both physical and mental. He rose and left the inn, intending to walk about and explore the town.*

*He wandered through the market place, but found it small and mean. The wares offered were of little interest to him. There were no luxuries or any objects of beauty offered in any of the stalls.*

*"People in this town must be poor indeed." He said to no one in particular.*

*The village was so small he soon walked between the fields beyond the last house. He decided to walk into the nearby hills. There at least, he would be alone and perhaps he could think.*

*As he came abreast of a small shed sitting well back from the road, he heard the light taps of a silversmith's hammer. He decided to investigate. Ducking his head to enter the open door, he saw a small-featured, older man working at a table. He was holding a beautiful, intricately worked goblet.*

*Josias sat on a nearby stool and watched the man work. Finally, finishing something he was intent on, the man put down his tools and smiled in greeting.*

*"The Lord's blessing upon you, friend."*

*Josias was much taken aback by the greeting. The life he led for so many years had hardened him to where minor courtesies and the well wishes of a stranger all but ceased to be a part of it.*

*He stammered his reply, "Peace unto you also, friend. I judge from this shop and the chalice you work on that you are an accomplished silversmith, in fact, it appears to me you are truly an artist."*

*"I am fair. I will admit to that. But none of today's smiths do the quality work the ancients accomplished. If I were able to design these decorations as well as I can copy other's designs, I know my success would be much greater.*

*"A Greek slave of the Centurion of Capernaum drew the design from which I made these six goblets. Would I could do as well, great would be my joy."*

*"I have traveled a great deal and it has been my privilege to see some ancient work that was most beautiful. It may be that I can make an adequate drawing of a design for you."*

*The smith stared at Josias for a moment, half-smiling. "Please do try then Sir, if you would be so kind. You would have my gratitude."*

*Josias left the silversmith's shop to search the markets of the village. He found charcoal pencils, flax paper and a straight edge, everything he needed to make the drawings.*

*He returned to the smith's shop and sat on a low stool before a bench placed conveniently under the shade of a fig tree. Arranging his drawing tools in easy reach, he took up the charcoal and drew a design as near as he could remember to match the one he admired on several of the goblets he and Malis found in the lost city.*

*The old man was enthralled with the design. "Thou Sir, art indeed an artist and a fine draftsman. Would that I could design such as this. Pray thee, what is thy name and native country?"*

*"I am called Josias. I am but a poor scribe from Jerusalem. I come here seeking escape from my life and the cursed Romans that I might find some peace."*

*Taking a seat nearby, the silversmith said, "My name is Amos. I am a Samaritan. Many years ago I married Rachel, the daughter of a devout Jew of Ramah.*

*"The marriage was against his will. In his later years the man relented, my wife being his only child. He left us this shop and yonder house.*

*"Many generations of my people have been artisans of metal vessels. I began on bronze pots and after many years took up*

*working silver, now I make nothing but silver goblets, bowls and an occasional pitcher."*

*Josias visited the silversmith everyday. Sitting peacefully under the shade of the olive tree, he drew designs he remembered and devised new ones. Most of them he and Amos found beautiful. In the late afternoons, he put down his charcoal to take a long walk into the hills beyond Sarah's home.*

*Oftentimes, he saw Sarah in the distance as he passed. Sometimes she worked in the garden, others she sat under the shade of the arbor. Once she was at the gate and they exchanged greetings.*

*Josias nodded, unable to speak, as he returned her shy "Good Morning."*

Surely she is the most beautiful woman I have ever seen.

*Amos often sat under the tree and told Josias stories of people who lived in the area. He recounted the fame of ancient Ramah, telling the story of "Samuel, the great prophet of Kings, who was born here in Ramah. It was he who anointed Saul, the first king of Judea. Later he anointed David, Judea's greatest king. It was David who led the destruction of the Gods of Baal and the rout of the Philistines beyond Beth-Car.*

*"Here in our little Synagogue of Ramah lay the resting place of the Ark of the Covenant when the Philistines first returned our treasure to Israel.*

*"The Philistines wanted to get rid of it because of their great fear of its powers. Truly this poor place can boast an illustrious history to be so small and mean as it is this day."*

*It interested Josias greatly that this old man, a Samaritan, would know so well the history of a Jewish city. The two men spent many days together, Josias drawing and telling tales of those places* he had seen in his travels and Amos, casting and hammering out the designs in silver and telling of the glorious past of Ramah.

His most interesting stories were of David's camping in the hills around the village as he gathered his army prior to the defeat of Saul. No matter how many interesting tales the silversmith told, or how many drawings waited for completion, Josias still took his walk everyday, passing by the house of Joel, hoping to get a glimpse of Sarah.

Sarah soon noticed that the handsome golden-haired scribe walked the road by their gate about the same time each day. It was easy for her to find a reason to be near about the time he would pass.

She stood at the gate one morning when he passed by; pretending to be busy pulling away morning glory vines that had woven themselves around its slats.

"Good Morning." Josias said, "Have you been of good health since your return from Jerusalem, Sarah?"

"Yes Josias, I have. I trust you have been well also?"

"Quite well, thank you."

He started to leave, but hesitated. "Have you had word yet of your father?"

"Not yet, but he should return soon. It is necessary for him to return often for food supplies and to see all is well with my mother and me."

Josias smiled at her and touching his hand to his forehead, said, "I'll come by again."

After walking only a few steps Josias turned to look back. Sarah stood just as he left her. One hand rested on her hip. A lock of gleaming dark hair hung down on her forehead, having escaped the snow-white scarf around her head. She was staring after him with her wonderful brown eyes.

Surely she is the most beautiful woman in all Israel. Her face is creamiest white with a small flush of pink on each lovely cheek. Her lashes are long and full and her oval face exquisitely formed.

She is truly lovely. This is a mystery to me. She is the only woman I have ever felt this way about. I have heard all of my life of a man's love for a woman. I now believe I know its meaning. I will never be content again unless I can be near her.

*He began looking for Sarah each day as he came to the edge of the village. He was ever fearful she would not be at the gate and was filled with joy when he saw her standing there.*

*When she was in the arbor or far from the road they waved to each other. When she was at the gate, they spoke of all manner of things, no matter how trivial, so they could linger a few minutes.*

*Josias sat pondering over a new design for a wine pitcher one day. Raising his head he asked Amos. "Good friend, what manner of people are Joel the shepherd and his family?"*

*"They are Jews, true Galileans, and good people. I would judge them a devout family. They are always at the Synagogue on the Sabbath and making pilgrimages to Jerusalem for the Passover."*

*Amos chuckled as he added. "Beyond all that, methinks it's the lovely little daughter thou are most interested in."*

*Josias smiled and after a moment answered, "I admire Sarah greatly and will ask the shepherd for her hand when he comes down from his flocks in the hills."*

*"My wife and I have often speculated about her. Any other girl of sixteen in this village is usually married, yet here she is— still unmarried and past her twentieth year.*

"Be that as it may. She is good to look upon and well trained to run a man's home if she marries. I hope Joel looks on your proposal with favor."

A serious look came on his face and Amos said, "I promise you, my friend, this will not be spoken of until thy wishes are known."

"Thank you, Amos. I can't imagine Sarah's father would take it kindly if his daughter's betrothal was talked about before it was arranged."

Salome, Sarah's mother, watched the meetings of her daughter and Josias. She was somewhat amused at the girl for trying to make them appear accidental. She kept discreetly in the background.

It is not a proper courtship of course, but until Joel returns I will allow it. After all, Sarah is safe in her own yard and Josias is in the road. What could anyone say?

Only her desire that the girl marry persuaded Salome to allow the meetings to continue. She feared for a number of years the girl would not marry at all. She prayed that Joel would approve the courtship when he returned. Josias was the only man the girl ever seemed truly interested in meeting.

\*\*\*

The sun was low as Josias sat beside the silversmith's shop. He began to suffer from the same old turmoil and anxiety that punished him in the past. He drew all the designs he could remember, and created a few new ones. The peace he found in drawing the designs seemed to leave him more each day.

A stranger entered the shop and talked to Amos. At first their voices meant little to Josias, but he heard several references to *the man from Nazareth, the one called Jesus, that everyone talked about.*

This man everyone speaks of might be interesting. I don't know whether he's a charlatan or a prophet, but I'm going to find out more about this.

*When the stranger left Josias went inside. "Amos, who is this Jesus so many people speak about?"*

*"He is a Rabbi—a great man of God. He comes from Nazareth, and travels about our land preaching of the coming Kingdom of God. Many think him the promised Messiah.*

*"Some believe him to be Elias the Prophet, returned to us. Others say he is just a fake. I know not who he is myself, but there have been wondrous tales of many miracles he has performed.*

*"Sit down beside me, my son, I will tell you what I know about it.*

*"I saw no miracle with my own eyes. Malachi told a strange tale of a miracle this Jesus of Nazareth performed on the shores of Gennesaret. It went like this—hearing in advance of his coming, a great crowd of people gathered by the sea near Magdala. After Jesus preached of the glories of his Father's Kingdom, he healed many of the people who were sick and crippled.*

*"Seeking rest, he left the shore and boarding a boat, sailed to a place near Capernaum. When they saw this, the multitude walked around the lake to where he was. Jesus, seeing the people hungered and were weary from the long walk around the lake, commanded them to sit and told them more of the Kingdom.*

*"When this talk was finished Simon, the fisherman who is now called Peter, told Jesus to send the people away. Instead the Nazarene asked Andrew, another of his followers, to bring a small boy to him.*

"This boy carried a dinner basket that held eight barley loaves and five fish. Taking the basket in his hands, Jesus blessed it and breaking the food, he fed the multitude. Some have said the crowd was five thousand strong and when they had eaten their fill, several baskets of food were left."

Josias turned his head to the side and stared at Amos, "My friend, surely you can't believe this to be true?"

"I no longer know what to believe, friend Josias. The strangeness of the tales we hear are beyond belief, yet Malachi is an honorable man and swears to me that he saw this happen with his own eyes."

"But think of it—just think of it—to feed a multitude from one small basket is surely impossible."

"Somehow, I find it difficult to say what is possible. When I was in Capernaum last, the prophet restored life to the daughter of Jarius who is appointed to see that people attend the Synagogue and pay their tithe."

"Did you see him raise her from the dead?"

"No, Josias, I confess I did not. But I saw the girl as she lay dead and afterward I saw her walk and talk."

"Strange. I vow you must have been under a spell."

"I felt no different than I do now, except for the sadness I felt over one dying so young and the bitter grief of a friend."

"What were the circumstances of this so-called miracle?"

"All is not known to me, but I will tell you what I know. When I arrived at my friend's house, mourners howled at the door. I went around to the back to deliver a cup he ordered and a servant told me of the sudden death of Jarius' beloved daughter and the great grief of the house.

"The child's mother came to the door and invited me to where the child lay, awaiting the time of burial. As we stood beside *the bier, Jarius and the Nazarene came into the room. Jarius was very agitated. He asked that everyone leave. After a few minutes Jarius came out alone with tears on his checks. A short while later Jesus and the girl walked from the house to the stoop where we stood waiting.*

*"You have never seen such a joyous time. After much delay, I received the money for my work and left a house full of rejoicing people. All of this took such a time I returned to my home long after dark."*

*Josias shook his head. "Magic of some sort, I'll wager,"*

*"If it was magic Josias, it was a most clever and useful magic."*

*Josias paced up and down for several minutes, then returned to his seat under the tree and to ponder the strange tales.*

Maybe this is the long awaited messiah that Mother spoke of so often when I was a small boy. I almost forgot that. I thought it was just one of the stories all mothers tell small boys. But I remember her reading from the prophet Yeshayah or Isaiah. He forecast a messiah, but he said he would be out of Bethlehem. Everyone says this man is a Nazarene.

*He went to the door of the workshop. "Amos, the prophets of old said the Messiah would be a Bethlemite from the house of David."*

*"Jesus was born in Bethlehem in the first year of the Roman head tax—the year when every man went to the city of his ancestors to register. Joseph and Mary, the mother and father of Jesus, traveled from Nazareth to Bethlehem to register and while they were in that city Jesus was born. He is a Bethlemite."*

*Josias shook his head and returned to the bench, his mind full and whirling with questions.*

143

This just can't be true. I must go to the synagogue and read again the writings of Yeshayah. There must be a way to prove this man a fraud.

*A few days afterward, Josias sat in the shade of the fig tree drawing when he realized an old man was standing nearby watching him.*

*When he looked up, the man asked, "Art thou Josias, the scribe?"*

*He recognized the man as the shepherd, Sarah's father. "I am, sir. I came here seeking thee to talk of a private matter."*

*"Come to my home and we will discuss this matter."*

*Sarah showed the excitement she felt over Josias' visit with her father only in her shining eyes. She silently served the two men wine at a table under the arbor.*

*Joel spoke of his sheep and how well they did. He told Josias he was fortunate. His family was well and the weather was pleasant. Finally, he turned to Josias and looking directly into his face, fell silent, waiting for him to speak.*

*His voice strained with emotion, Josias said, "Sir, I favor the daughter of thy house greatly and ask thee her hand in marriage."*

*"Salome, my wife, and my daughter Sarah are much taken with thee, Josias. I know a marriage to be agreeable with them. Can you support a wife?"*

*"I have not yet a home for her, but that is no problem. I have enough gold to support her well."*

*"Was this gold earned as a scribe?"*

*"No, it was not. Another man and I came upon ancient treasure of great value. It was long lost and forgotten. The division provided me a small fortune. My money is deposited with the Mekel family of Damascus. They will vouch for this."*

"This is good to hear, for my daughter's dowry will be small. This house and the flocks are all I possess and my wife and I must live here in our lifetime. It will be hers when we are gone."

Joel looked beyond Josias, his eyes on the hills. After a moment he looked back at Josias. "Of what family are you, my son?"

"Ammon my father, was from Bethsaida. His mother was called Ruth. His father I knew not, but my mother, Mattathah of Bethany could tell you of him. She is a daughter of Andrew of Bethany from the tribe of Judah."

Joel shook his head and reached over to pat Josias on the shoulder, saying, "I find this astonishing. I knew Ruth and her sons well. Her husband died many years ago. They were truly devout people."

Joel excused himself and went into the house. Returning quickly, he said, "If you will return an hour before the noon meal tomorrow, there will be guests in my house and the engagement will be announced."

The two men drank another cup of wine to seal the agreement and Josias returned to the inn in a daze of happiness.

When he returned at the appointed hour, many guests were seated around a long trestle table. Cups of wine brimmed over. When Josias was seated and introduced to everyone, Joel rose and holding his cup high, he announced the betrothal of his daughter Sarah to Josias of Bethany.

Everyone around the table and stood and calling the blessing of God on the couple, drank from their cups and shouted their approval. Nearly every one of Sarah's parent's friends hoped the girl would marry, but when she passed her twentieth birthday with no suitor in sight, they had all but given up hope.

*Sarah blushed with embarrassment at the attention, but smiled her thanks. Her dark eyes sparkled with happiness. Josias nodded his thanks, never taking his eyes from Sarah.*

*He thought over and over, "This may not be real—I may wake up and find this is all an illusion. She is so beautiful—more beautiful than I ever dreamed."*

*When the meal was over, the men moved closer together to talk. The women busied themselves clearing the table.*

*A cousin told a strange story of a happening on the Sea of Galilee. He recounted how the man called Jesus and his disciples entered a ship and sailed toward Gadara, lying across the sea from where they were.*

*On the way across the water Jesus grew tired and fell asleep. As they approached the middle of the sea a great storm rose. Huge waves pounded the small ship. A great fear gripped the disciples.*

*Bartholomew, more fearful than the rest, awakened Jesus. "Master, carest thou not that we perish as thou sleep?"*

*Jesus rose and walked to the high foredeck of the small ship. The high wind whipped his robe about his legs and the rain poured against his head and shoulders. He stretched forth his hand and said,*

*'Peace, peace. Be still.' The raging storm ceased instantly, and the sea calmed.*

*"Andrew told me that the disciples were mystified. For moments, they stood mute, then James, the young brother of John, asked anyone who would listen, 'What manner of man is this, commanding the wind and the waves and they obeying?'*

*When he asked this, Jesus turned to him and said, 'Oh ye of little faith, knowest thee not that I am the son of the living God?'*

*Joel leaned forward in his seat and asked almost breathlessly, "Did Andrew, the brother of Simon, tell you this himself?"*

*"He did, Joel. Yes, he did.*

*"We met in the market place of Capernaum on the following day, and he told me this from his own mouth. When I shook my head and doubted him, he offered to accompany me to all those who saw it happen that they might tell me the story as well. I have known Andrew for many years and I know him to be a truthful man."*

*Others filled the afternoon with many tales about this Jesus of Nazareth. When darkness fell and the time of leaving came, all the guests agreed to return for the wedding that would be held in a fortnight. Josias joined several of the others to walk to his inn in Ramas.*

*He hardly slept at all that night. The excitement of his betrothal and the growing mystery of the Nazarene kept his mind in ferment.*

*He rose early the next morning, unable to sleep long, pondering the strange tales he heard at his betrothal dinner. Doubt drove him to the Synagogue. He read again every word of the writings of Yeshayah. In the book were many prophecies of a Messiah the Lord God would send to redeem his chosen people.*

Possibly this Jesus of Nazareth is the Messiah. Many of the things he is said to have done are such things as a Messiah might do. But if he is the promised Messiah, why is he so meek? Why has he not come to us as a mighty leader to drive out the hated Roman oppressor?

*Each day, as Josias walked far into the hills, he passed the gateway to Sarah's house. They waved to each other and she stood at the gate watching him until he walked out of her sight. But they did not speak. The custom of their day forbade them to speak from the day of their betrothal until the wedding. At times he was sure the day would never come.*

# Chapter 11

*The day of the wedding finally arrived. It began with breakfast in Joel's house—breakfast for a select few guests. They ate barley cakes fried in oil, with goat cheese and golden honey. All drank watered wine.*

*With a great scurrying about, everyone helped to ready the long tables in the orchard for the dinner preceding the wedding. Wide boards were placed on trestles set in long lines. This would make serving easier. Large earthenware jars of wine, cooled overnight in water, were placed in the shade. Side tables bore piled high trays of cakes and sweetmeats. Several large pots steamed and boiled over well-tended fires. The guests numbered more than the normal population of Ramah.*

*All the guests enjoyed a fine humor. Many came early just for the pleasure of the banter invariably included in a weddings. Amos the Smith sat among the guests, fondly watching his friend Josias smile in his happiness as Joel or Salome introduced him to more guests. He wondered at the man.*

Josias is truly an unusual man. My shop contains enough drawings to keep me busy for many years, all done by his hand. They are excellent ones too, delicately wrought and beautiful. Yet he has refused to take any pay for the many days he spent working to produce them.

A Jew who is willing to work without pay is truly unheard of in my experience. It is a strange thing and somehow, leaves me with uneasiness. It bothers me to know I owe him this great favor. Surely someday, soon or late, I will be called on to repay.

*The potter Hafia, loud and fat, but a good friend withal, interrupted his reverie to punch his shoulder. "My shop is very well represented here today, Amos. Look about you. The jars for wine, water and oil—the serving platters and covered bowls were all made by me."*

*"I see, my friend, and they are truly fine. But I notice that the brass cooking vessels, silver cups and most of the vases holding those beautiful flowers were made in my humble shop."*

*Joel stepped between them and placed a hand on each shoulder. "I am better represented than either of you. The bride is my handiwork. When have you ever seen better? I gain a fine son-in-law this day as well. Are your pots, jars and silver vases so fine as this?"*

*Merriment filled the air. The day was full of music, singing and dancing by the young. The older guests told many long and interesting tales, some caused much banter over their veracity, but it was all in good fun. As the evening drew near, many were heard to say this was the finest wedding feast ever, for none of the guests could remember a better one.*

*As the sun touched the hills, all came together for the wedding ceremony. The Rabbi of Ramah stood before the entrance to the bride's home. The bride and groom stood in the yard in front of him, surrounded by the crowd of guests. After the rites were said, the young men escorted Josias to his room at the inn. When darkness fell, the young women attending Sarah brought her to him.*

*Their days were spent in an ecstasy of love. Sometimes they walked hand in hand through the little town and into the hills beyond. Other days they visited their many friends in Ramah— many afternoons Sarah and Josias spent with Salome. Her loneliness without her beloved daughter was pitiful.*

*On a day that was cooler than most of the brassy summer days of Galilee, the couple took advantage of the pleasant weather to walk out of the city to visit the famous tower of Ramah. It was there a young David, before he became King, made his headquarters. This happened during the time when King Saul sought to slay him. The ancient stone walls of the tower were crumbled and broken. The ruined walls of the tower made them think of a fallen giant.*

*Sarah told Josias many legends of the past glories of Israel, especially those of David, the great king. The legends invariably led them to the Nazarene, his descendent. They talked long of this Jesus of Nazareth and his works. He created an endless amount of speculation among his people with the many miracles credited to him.*

*As they walked back to the inn one evening Josias turned to Sarah and said, "My dear, let us make a trip to the shores of Gennesaret that thou might see the beauty of the waters and perhaps see this Jesus and hear him speak."*

*Sarah stopped and smiled up at him, her sweet face glowing. "Oh Josias, I would delight in such a trip. Would it be that my father could go with us? He wants so much to hear the Nazarene speak."*

*"Of course he can accompany us, That would make the trip even more pleasant for us. Go thou to his house and tell him*

we will go as soon as he can leave. He will need some time to prepare. Tell him as well, that I will provide mules for all to ride and pack asses to carry our supplies. I intend to also hire a boy to attend the animals that we may be free to see what we will."

The following day, Sarah went alone to visit her parents. Josias spent most of the long hours with Amos. He enjoyed his friend's company, but felt lost without Sarah and watched the sun move across the sky as he counted the hours until she would return.

When she came into the inn Sarah said, "My father will be ready when we are, my husband. He sends thee word that he has no need to stay with the flocks. They are down from the mountains this time of year. His servant Eli can easily tend them without his help. He told me he was making a plan to travel out to see Jesus himself and is truly glad that we are to go and he can accompany us."

Early the next morning, Josias went to the trader of animals who was boarding his horse and bargained for two gentle mules and four pack-asses. After a great verbal brawl in which each man accused the other of all manner of terrible acts and even questioned each other's parentage, a bargain was agreed on to please them both.

As a token of respect, the Syrian trader offered to hire a stable boy in his employ to Josias for the trip. Once this agreement was sealed Josias, with the boys' help, went to different stalls in the market to purchase and assemble the camp gear and supplies they would need for the journey.

When all was in readiness for their departure, Josias and Sarah went to her parent's home to inform Joel they would be ready to leave on the morrow and to bid her mother goodbye.

Salome was saddened over the prospect of them leaving her, even for a short time, but she had lived with Joel for many years and knew it was useless to try to dissuade him from something he was set on doing. Without a word to her husband, she sent the servant Eli to her sister's house with a note asking her niece Rachel to come and stay during her husband's absence.

The next morning, Joel met Sarah and Josias at the city well. Many of Ramah's people gathered in the thin, early-morning chill to bid them Godspeed. They agreed to carry many messages that would be delivered along their way.

The large, chattering crowd, combined with the natural stubbornness of the donkeys, caused the stable boy Seth, much trouble getting the animals to form a line and begin the journey.

Josias had his own problems calming his mettlesome horse. The beast, not being ridden at all of late, felt fractious. It put on quite a show of tossing its head, bucking, and sun-fishing about before it accepted Josias' weight on its back.

The crowd was delighted; men and women shouted their encouragement for the show. Some cheered on the rider and some the wildly bucking horse. Josias and the boy finally got the animals calmed, and the little caravan set out along the dusty road toward the morning sun.

They made slow progress. The pace was set by the patient donkeys, working as they have since time began, ignoring man and his excitement. It was mid-morning of the fourth day before Gennesaret was sighted.

The lake rested on a large plain, below the craggy mountains northwest of the sea. The pear shaped sea, over twelve miles long and two-third as wide, lay gleaming like a magnificent sapphire. Small cities gathered close around it. From far away it appeared as if they paid homage to its beauty.

Choosing a grassy place to the side of the road, Josias and Seth circled the animals and hobbled them against their penchant *for wandering. The group stood long on the crest of the steep road looking at the lake below.*

*"Oh, it is so beautiful," Sarah said, sighing. "Father, do you know the names of the cities beside the lake?"*

*"Capernaum is the nearest one, my dear. There on its right side is Bethsaida with Magdala next. In the distance over the east-end of Mount Hattin you will see the white domes of Tiberias, the town that was built by the accursed Tetrarch Antipater. I know not the names of the places across the sea in the lands of the Gadarenes. It may be that Josias knows them."*

*"I fear I know but little of that country. I traveled this way but once in my life before this."*

*A man approached them. They noticed him earlier, sitting on a rock a few feet farther along the road, but hearing them speak, he rose and walked toward.*

*"Art thou strangers to the shores of Gennesaret?"*

*Wary of strangers, Josias placed his hand on the haft of his short-sword and examined the man closely. He finally decided he looked harmless and answered civilly, "Yes. We came from Ramah to the west."*

*"Then you know not of the spring that rests in the rock wall down yonder path." He motioned to a faint track that disappeared over the hill. "If you plan to camp here, it has cold, sweet water."*

*After the party found the spring and drank, they filled water bags for their animals. As they prepared camp they continued to chat to the stranger. Finally Joel said the name of Jesus of Nazareth.*

*"Hast thou come to see the Messiah? For if thou hast, I fear you will be disappointed. He left the sea and went up into Mount Herman. His leaving and the pressure of finishing the*

threshing of my grain before the season is over is my reason for returning to my home near Cabul."

Josias looked at the man thoughtfully for a moment then asked, "Dost thou believe this man is the true Messiah?"

"I saw him restore the sight of one born blind and cause the mother of a follower to be rid of a fever. Can anyone not a Son of God do such things?

"I know not what to make of this man." Josias shook his head.

"That's why we make this journey. We shall know the truth if we can see him first hand."

"Friends and strangers told me many tales of this man and I believed not. That's why I came to see for myself whether or not he was a faker."

"Do you believe he is the Messiah now that you have seen him?" Josias asked.

"Yes, my friend. I do believe."

The stranger looked directly into Josias eyes, his expression unreadable. "I believe the man is the promised Messiah—the true son of the living God."

After this saying this, the man expressed his regrets for leaving, saying, "I must be on my way. There is much work to be done on my land and I alone for the task. Farewell to all and may the Lord bless each of thee and let the light of his love shine upon thee."

With these words he shouldered his pack and trudged down the western side of the mountain. Josias stood without speaking, watching the man's back until he was out of his sight. All the while, he repeated over and over in his mind, the things the man said.

155

*Joel, Josias, Sarah and the boy spent the rest of the day looking at the ever changing scenes in the valley below. Fields of stubble left from the grain harvest reflected the bright, afternoon sunshine, making them appear carpeted in gold. A few of the fields still held round cocks of sheaves set in straight rows from one end to another. From their vantage point the stacked sheaves appeared more like a chessboard with men in place than ordinary grain fields.*

*Vineyards abounded. Some with rows laid out east and west, others opposite, all running straight and precise and reflecting their slate green color. Fig trees showed as jumbled piles of green, often with gray-green olive trees nearby.*

*Here and there they saw an occasional field of pasture grass, green and solid looking. Endless rows of dry stone fences divided fields one from another. All were criss-crossed with narrow ribbons of dusty roads.*

*In the distance they saw the houses of the seaside. Short and tall, they were made of many colors and strange shapes and from that distance appeared all ajumble. Here and there were gardens decorated with borders of bright flowers.*

*A tumbled profusion of green marked where the Jordan River came into and left the sea, meandering out of sight toward the Dead Sea. Looking to the south, they could see the new city called Tiberias, with the high tower of Herod's palace, built of white limestone and aglow with newness. Throughout the city they could see many small patches of green and borders of gloriously colored plantings.*

*Josias' sharp eyes caught sight of a small train of pack asses, plodding slowly along the road from Tiberias. The animal's feet sent up tiny puffs of yellow dust. A gray-robed man led the train, while a boy, naked from the waist up and shining with a copper hue, dawdled behind. A little closer he saw a lone figure* walking along a road. The man led a brown and white cow. A calf, an exact copy of the cow, gamboled about her.

They saw boats with sails apuffing, seeming to dance across the sea, and patient fishermen sitting still and quiet in small boats. Each vied with the other to point out some sight until long shadows began creeping close.

"Can it be possible the day is gone so soon?" Josias stood and stretched his arms over his head.

"It is indeed, dear son-in-law," Joel answered, "I have long known the passage of time is governed completely by one's interests. A day as unusual as this never fails to pass too quickly."

Always practical, Sarah turned to Seth. "Come boy, help me prepare the evening meal."

By full light the next morning, their tents struck and the donkeys loaded, the small caravan was on its way. Joel and Josias decided, in view of what the stranger told them, to go to Bethsaida, in hope of seeing Jesus there. The way proved much farther than it appeared from their viewpoint on the mountain. When they finally arrived, they found a place to camp in a grove beside the blue water.

Josias and Sarah went to the Rabbi of the village to learn what they could of his father's family. An empty sadness filled Josias when he learned that his uncles left the village after his grandmother's death. The Rabbi could not tell him whence they moved. The couple spent the remainder of the day exploring the village.

Early the next morning they noticed a number of people walking along the road from the village. Josias stopped a man to ask where so many were going. The man told him Jesus would preach on a small hill beside Gennesaret.

Excited, Josias, Sarah, Joel and Seth hurried to join the group. When they arrived, all seated themselves facing the hill.

*Suddenly a great stirring began. Someone whispered, then the entire crowd murmured, "He comes. The Master is here."*

*Josias watched closely as a group of men made their way through the crowd and to the top of the hillock. Their leader was tall and slender, yet strong looking. His hair and beard were dark, and he wore the gray, seamless robe of a Galilean. His thong sandals appeared worn and dusty. A pleasant smile illuminated his face—a smile seldom seen among the chosen during this troubled time.*

*All felt a powerful magnetism about the man. Everyone watched him closely as he prepared to speak. A man standing beside Josias whispered to identify the men accompanying Jesus.*

*"The tall, gray-bearded one is called Simon Peter. Behind him you can see James and John, sons of Zebedee. Seated close by him there, to his right, is James the son of Alphaeus, and the last one arriving is Bartholomew. As you can see, he walks with a stick and appears much older than the others."*

*Jesus raised his arms with his hands pointed out over the crowd and all fell silent. He began by praying to God his Father that all people be blessed with peace and salvation.*

*Josias thought it strange of a Jew to seek the blessing of God for all mankind, not even excepting Samaritans, Idumaeans, the cursed Romans, Nubians or lowly slaves.*

What manner of man is this, who thinks our God, the God of the Jews, cares for all those people. The Priests of Jerusalem all say he is the God of the Jews only, that he has no interest in those other people.

*Jesus began speaking. "My Father's house, which is in Heaven, is a place of peace and joy. Flowers lie about, the earth is green and birds sing always."*

He told them of God's great love and the grief he felt when he saw man's sin—the grief he felt when he saw the many creations of man all destroyed for their sins. He told how Noah and his family were spared because they loved and obeyed God.

He said that he, the only Son of God, was sent for the redemption of man's sins, eliminating the necessity of destroying the present family of man. He warned that unless they believed and were forgiven, they would not know eternal life. A life where all lived in peace, each working on some constructive project in Heaven, happy in his industry, never overtired, sick, too cold or too warm—living in a place where storms were beautiful and without fear, souls ruled without tyranny, servants living without slavery and all happy for eternity. These things, he said, God offers to man, but many, in their greed, refuse an eternity for a fleeting moment of false greatness.

All these things he told them, comparing the time on earth as a day in court, at the end of which the good and evil of man's life would be weighed and the sentenced served. This sentence could only be changed if a person sought forgiveness through himself—through Jesus—the Son of God.

He told them of the foolishness of men, comparing their lives to a fleeting moment in eternity or the time of the flight of a sparrow from sight. In this short time, he explained, many lived to exclude themselves from eternity, mostly for a few pieces of gold.

When he finished preaching, Jesus blessed the multitude and turned to a group gathered below him. Many in the group were sick, lame and afflicted in some way. They sought the miracle of cure.

The crowd surged forward to watch him cure the invalids. Their mass excluded all Jesus did from Josias' sight. He felt much *chagrined and determined to follow this strange man until he could see one of his miracles performed under his own eyes.*

*Pushing through the throng, Josias and his party made their way toward Bethsaida, walking a short distance behind Jesus. As they neared the village, a youth stepped from some bushes close to the path and said, "Master, my father is blind. We have traveled many leagues, seeking thee that he might be cured by thy miracles of mercy. We were not in time to come to thee and hear thy words this day. Wouldst thou heal my father's blindness? He is a devout man."*

*Josias was close enough to see the white film that covered the man's eyes and observe his clumsy actions when he was led before Jesus. He believed him to be truly blind. He watched closely as Jesus prayed, then reached to put spittle in the blind man's eyes.*

*"What seest thou?" Jesus asked.*

*The man stared in several directions, then said, "I see men faintly, as trees standing and walking about."*

*Jesus prayed again, then rubbed spittle in the man's eyes a second time.*

*The man jumped about in great joy and shouted, "I see. I see."*

*Josias was dumbfounded, for he plainly saw that the man's milky eyes were not clear before Jesus touched him, yet now—now he was healed.*

*He was lost in thought as he joined Joel, Sarah and Seth to walk back up the hill to their camp. Sarah chattered away happily, never noticing the puzzled look on Josias' face.*

*Sarah busied herself about the fire, fixing the evening meal. Her happiness was unbounded. The great love she knew with Josias was enough, but now there was more. Not only had she and her father found and accepted Jesus as the Savior, she was sure her beloved Josias believed, although he was obviously reluctant to admit it. She sang a psalm of the Temple as she worked, glancing now and again at Josias.*

*He sat at the outer edge of the campsite with his back against a tree, keeping his eyes down and his face pulled into a frown—pondering the things he saw and heard that day.*

*His head seemed to swim with questions. Several times he wondered if the events he witnessed would drive him out of his mind.*

Surely no mortal could do the things Jesus did— if the man really did the things at all. He must be a charlatan—he is surely a mountebank of great accomplishment in acts of duplicity and of magic.

Think of the tales he told. They must surely be made up dreams and falsehoods. Who is it that ever returned to this earth to tell of the hereafter?

*"No." Josias whispered to himself. "No, these things I cannot accept."*

*His mind teemed with the stories of this Jesus of Nazareth supposedly feeding five thousand souls with only a small basket of food, commanding the wild storm to cease and it obeying. People even told him tales of the man casting out demons, turning water into wine, and bringing the dead to life again.*

If this is the magic of a faker, it is a new magic. All the man did was for the good of others and no coin was demanded or taken. I actually saw him heal the blind man. Surely he didn't put some white substance in the man's eyes then rub it out to make a show.

This is all too much. I can find no answer. I must put it out of my mind and return to Ramah before the puzzle of this man causes me to lose my mind and need a miracle myself.

*Josias motioned for Sarah to leave him alone and refused to eat the meal she prepared for them. Distressed, she appealed, "But Husband, please, you must eat."*

*Joel caught her arm and pulling her away, leaned close to whisper, "Go to your blankets daughter. Leave the man to his thoughts. Your husband's great doubt must be overcome before he will know peace."*

*Josias dressed in the chill of the morning and started out to find Jesus. Within sight of their camp he met a woodsman leaving the village. Josias asked the man if he had seen the Nazarene, he answered, "The one called Jesus and all of his disciples left the city at first light. I heard the innkeeper telling other pilgrims that they were on their way to Caesarea Philippi."*

*Disappointed, Josias trudged back to the camp. "Let us stay here this day and rest before we return to Ramah. I for one am sorely tired."*

*Sarah, Joel and Josias lounged under the shade of a great oak and talked. Josias told them, "I never knew a father, mine was killed when I was yet a small boy, but as I listened to Jesus preach, my feeling was that he seemed what a father should be, protective, or wanting to care for me."*

*"I know," Joel said. "He makes me think of the quail of the fields that spreads both wings to cover its brood from the rains or flutters as though it is crippled to draw an enemy away from its young."*

*Sarah smiled at these descriptions. They exactly matched her feelings. She secretly hoped this trip would help Josias to put away his doubts and accept Jesus as the true savior.*

*As the sun rose high, a man approached the camp and introduced himself as Zechariah, a shopkeeper of Nazareth.*

"Good morrow. Do you know the whereabouts of a man named Jesus and his followers—the one many call the Messiah?"

"A man told us this morning that he and the twelve went to Caesarea Philippi." Josias answered.

The man dropped his head in sorrow. "I hoped to see him."

"Thou comest from Nazareth? Dost know Jesus?"

"Yes, I know him well. We lived near each other and played together as children."

"Has he always been so strange, so different from others?"

"At times it was difficult to tell a difference. Other times he was like a stranger. Nevertheless, I liked him well."

Joel moved to stand beside Josias and asked, "How was he so different?"

"Sometimes he seemed moody. He would go into the hills alone and stay for hours. Once I followed him, keeping from his sight. As he walked beside a gorge there lay the kid of a wild goat. It had fallen from a crag above and lay on the rocks, dead. He picked it up, closed his eyes for a moment and returned it to the ground alive. The kid lay there for a moment then gained its feet and trotted away. I saw this with my own eyes and know it to be true.

"Another told me of him molding birds of clay. He said Jesus gestured with his hands over them and they flew away. I did not see this with my eyes, nor did I think the teller trustworthy.

"As a boy, Jesus was loved by everyone in Nazareth. They did not regard his strangeness. Often times when one spoke to him they received no answer, for he always dreamed and might not hear them. This provoked me greatly at times and I would want to quarrel about it until he laughed at me. Then all would be well again."

*"Do you believe him to be the Son of the true God?" Josias asked in a soft voice. He held tightly to Sarah's hand.*

*"Do you know of another male child under the age of two who escaped the anger of Herod the great in Bethlehem? Do you know another who could discourse with the learned Rabbis of the temple at twelve? A boy who could cause a voice from the heavens to rise at his baptism or a man who could withstand the temptations of the devil for forty days?*

*"This man turned water into wine and chased the moneychangers and dealers in sacrifice from the temple. He heals the sick, and twelve responsible men chose to leave their homes and businesses to follow him.*

*"Who else can cause a net to fill with fishes with a wave of his hand? He preaches to the multitudes, blessing them and does not ask for money. He healed a leper and a Roman servant far away from him and he raised up a man's dead son.*

*"Think of it all, man. He raised his hand and stilled a wild storm, cast devils from men into swine, raised up a dead daughter, restored sight and fed five thousand from a small basket. If that is not enough, he was seen to walk on the surface of water by reliable men.*

*"Yes, I believe him the son of the living God. None other could do all these things."*

*Zechariah departed; leaving Josias with his emotions even more mixed. His mind was almost made up to accept Jesus, as the Son of God and the true Messiah, but this man's tales were fantastic.*

How could anyone believe ridiculous tales of clay birds flying and dead goats coming to life?

*"I shall be glad to return to the quietness of Ramah." He said aloud.*

## The Malefactors

*Once back in the village, Josias returned to his routine, spending happy hours with Sarah, visiting Salome and Joel and occasionally sitting an hour or two with his friend Amos. He lived as though he had known no other life, rarely thinking of the years he rode as a member of Barabbas robber band.*

# The Malefactors

# Chapter 12

*Barabbas seethed with anger. Rueben, his servant, informed him there was no more money.*

*"How can this be?" he shouted, as Rueben backed out of his reach.*

*"Master, we have lived well. The wine we drink, the money you lose gambling, and the gold given to the harlots of the upper city take all the coin you give me. Is there not more hidden away?"*

*"No. No--no more is hidden away. The money I gave you only a week ago was all of it. Go to Argubus, the prophet. Tell him I said to send me twenty denarius to last until I can get more."*

*Barabbas sank onto a bench to think, dropping his chin in his hand. Josef the innkeeper would give but little credit. He knew the habits of his life were expensive. He cringed when he thought of the laughter and ridicule that would come from the other loungers if they found out he had no money.*

*"This will not happen." He murmured under his breath.*

Perhaps Rueben robbed me. No, no, that could not be. He would have run away had he done such a thing. Damn Pilate and his fears, I will get my men together and rob a caravan. It is impossible to think of living with no money.

I will have to go slowly and act in secret. The new Legate of Judea, that self-important ass that rose above himself when Quintus was killed in a riot, flatly refuses to accept a share of the spoils. He says he will always uphold Roman law. Whatever I do, I must do it with great care.

*Across town, Rueben approached old Argubus. "Good prophet, Barabbas sends me to ask for twenty denarius from you."*

*Argubus waved Rueben away as he almost shouted in astonishment, "What? Barabbas, he who plays the wealthy idler would borrow from me, a poor beggar? I will not think of it."*

*Hidden away in the desert, Argubus had great quantities of money. But he was a miser. All he received from his store of gold was the pleasure of letting it run through fingers as he gloated. He dreamed of someday dressing in costly finery, with servants to wait on him. He would go about the city and people would point him out as the wealthy prophet God saw fit to reward greatly.*

*As Rueben turned away Argubus called him back. He feared reprisal from Barabbas, whom he knew to be ruthless, so he dug into his belt and pulled out the requested coins for Rueben to take back to his Master.*

*As soon as Rueben returned with the money, Barabbas sent him into the streets of Jerusalem to inform as many of his band that could be found to meet him in the secret room under the west wall of the city. Some men were found from each band, but all agreed that Josias and Lucius were nowhere in the city.*

*One of the men told Barabbas where Lucius could be found at an old hideout in Samaria. Given a fast horse to ride, he was sent on his way with orders to return as quickly as possible with the captain. Both men returned in time for a second meeting a few nights later, but Barabbas was bitterly disappointed when his men told him that Josias could not be found.*

*Barabbas sent Lucius, Argubus and five men, all of his band that could be found on such short notice, to the old hideout on the Caesarea road. Their orders were to take the first caravan they saw that was not well guarded by a Roman patrol.*

*In the meantime, he sent Rueben to learn of a better opportunity elsewhere. He also sought an opportunity by visiting the Insula and asking for an audience with the Procurator.*

*As he waited in the anteroom to be called before Pilate, Barabbas thought over his association with the Roman. Somehow, possibly through a spy in his band, Pilate learned that he was the leader of the highwaymen. In his greed, the filthy Roman took large shares of his proceeds over the years.*

I blame Pilate for my present financial straits. Not since he called me in here and threatened me with the cross have I failed to give him his full share of our take. I don't know how, but it seems the greedy Roman always knew to a denari how much each robbery netted.

I can't be sure, but it is possible that Sylvanius learned that Zerubbabel of the bazaar on David Street is the buyer of all my merchandise. It is possible that he threatened the old man with exposure if he failed to give Pilate a full account of all he received.

I may think Pilate is beneath my contempt, but I must admit he is shrewd. He gets ten percent of the Roman tax and a large share of all of my robberies. Mayhap he coerces others as well. I may be the greatest of the highwaymen, but I certainly am not the only one. I can only hope someone will assassinate the scoundrel, and soon.

After a long wait, Barabbas was called to the main audience chamber before Pilate. The Procurator was in a frightful mood. He had just given audience to several of the Sanhedrin, as well as Caiaphas, the high priest and they sorely tried his patience. All demanded he send out a patrol to arrest some Galilean preacher.

Pilate raved in his anger. "They accuse him of traveling around the whole province, preaching heresy against the Jewish law as well as against Rome. He also claims some king will come and rule this cursed land.

"It is my great hope this will occur. I would welcome a chance to leave this cursed place. Fighting wild Gauls was but child's play compared to ruling these people. Why are there so many who come to me demanding the arrest of this mountain preacher? What was the scoundrel's name, Sylvanius?"

"They say the man is called Jesus of Nazareth, Sir."

"Caiaphas brought word from Ananias demanding the arrest of this Jesus. They accuse him of blasphemy against the Jewish God and treason against the Empire. I counseled Caiaphas to make his own arrests, but no, the miserable wretch wants me to do his dirty work. I sent him out of here with a flea in his ear. "

As Barabbas approached his chair Pilate turned to glare at him. Still angry, he first looked to be sure the room lay empty and then almost shouted; "Now you come before me. Did I not tell you to stay away? What is it you want?" Moving closer so he could speak freely without being overheard, Barabbas answered, "Since the new Legate was appointed it is hard for a highwayman to live. I came to you in hope of learning the whereabouts of a rich prize. If there is one, you might arrange for the Legate to have his patrols elsewhere for the next few days. Surely you need funds as well?"

Pilate leaned forward and spoke softly, looking about to make sure no one was nearby to hear him. "I know of no prize, nor will this Legate run at my beck and call. I must wonder what manner of highwayman you are. Soon you will want me to ride into the hills and rob for you."

Turning to Sylvanius, Pilate asked, "Do you know of a likely prospect? It is true that my coffers are running low."

"There is a Greek merchant, Sire. He is called Siphos."

Sylvanius turned to Barabbas, speaking softly. "This man I speak of requested protection for a large caravan traveling from Caesarea to Damascus. His goods will be well guarded.

Generally, one or two smaller merchants will follow a large caravan like his closely, hoping to enjoy the protection of soldiers without paying the costs of a patrol. If you can contrive to hold these smaller merchants up a few hours, until the patrol is far ahead of them, you may find success."

Barabbas started to turn away. Pilate called him back, motioning him to come close to his chair, "Use great care in what you do, Barabbas. I fear the new Legate is suspicious the robbers get information only this court should know. I have no desire to go before Tiberius charged with treason."

Hurrying back to his inn, Barabbas sent Rueben to the hideout with orders for Lucius to have all in readiness for a long trip. Packing his own belongings, he sought his horse and followed Rueben. They arrived at the hideout after dark.

Barabbas rode into the glade at a gallop. Without dismounting, he began to bark out orders. "Lucius, you and the men ride quickly to the valley of Jezrell and hide in the foothills of Gilboa where you can see the Roman road. A merchant should pass in a few hours who is well guarded by a large patrol. Take care they do not see you.

*There should be one or two smaller caravans following close behind them. They will have no guard. See if you can scare their animals off at night to delay their leaving.*

*"If you can contrive to do that, the patrol will be far ahead and you can rob the smaller train in complete safety. Make no mistake, Lucius. This Legate means to exterminate us. He will spare no chance to do so.*

*"You must follow my orders regardless. I mean that. Even with all your ability to fight, you do not think well."*

*When he was sure Barabbas was out of hearing, Lucius turned to his followers, in an ugly mood. Barabbas criticizing him in their hearing galled him. His ire was directed to himself as well. His dissatisfaction grew almost daily over his poor showing of late and turned his naturally nasty moods worse.*

*He screamed curses at the slowness of the men and the poor horses they rode. Angry at everything, he was doubly angry that the band could not bring the camp women with them. There would be no one to wait on him when they stopped.*

*Taking torturous and little known mountain trails and pushing the horses over hard, the band arrived at a little known campsite hidden in the upheaval of rock and scanty brush near Mount Gilboa. There was enough daylight left after they set up camp for Lucius to send a rider in each direction on the Roman road to locate the caravan.*

*Jeptha, the man who rode west, returned after dark to report that a large and well-guarded caravan camped a few miles east of Megiddo. Another, much smaller caravan followed, just as Pilate predicted. It camped a mile west of the first, almost hidden beside an aqueduct, and well back from the road.*

*Lucius announced, "Get in your blankets, men. We must all have a few hours sleep. The guard will awaken us two hours before dawn."*

*A waning moon lighting the way, Jeptha led the band to a thicket, far enough from the unguarded camp that the horses would not give them away. Tying their mounts securely, the men crept near the camp, ready to drive off the caravan's animals. When the camels and one saddle horse were freed from their rope corral, the men drove them south from the camp into the rough hills overlooking the valley Jezrel.*

*Returning to the thicket for their own mounts, Lucius and his men heard a great shouting in the merchant's camp. The men of the caravan screamed curses on the thieves who drove off their animals.*

*The merchant berated his servants, "Hurry, you fools. Hurry. There were two of the filthy bandits. Their tracks show as plain as day in the sand of this dry wash. Look—here they are. They cannot be far. Sand is still trickling back into the tracks.*

*"Hurry yourselves, hurry and follow them, we must regain the animals soon. This country is infested with bandits. It is imperative that we stay near the soldiers who ride ahead of us."*

*The merchant and his servants retrieved the animals with ease. "This is not the work of highwaymen, but some cursed Jews, hoping the animals would be lost for them to find and sell later.*

*"Let us pack up and hurry on our way. The guards ahead left with the dawn and we are far behind. This is a truly dangerous stretch of road."*

*It was mid-morning when a lookout signaled Lucius that he sighted the approaching caravan. The one guarded by the patrol passed by them more than two hours earlier. A great bustle of activity filled the camp as the men prepared to attack.*

*Jeptha the scout, was usually a member of Josias' band. He watched Lucius prepare for the attack and thought of the difference in the two leaders.*

Why, if Josias was given a dozen good men, he could have defeated the patrol guarding the large caravan and we would not have to be satisfied with the smaller portion. There were enough goods in the first caravan to provide for all of us for a year.

This fool Lucius, all he knows is to run about shouting and waving his scimitar. He isn't a leader. He's nothing but a bully and a cursed loud-mouthed fool. He will lead us to our deaths.

*The band guided their horses into a fold in the land overlooking the road. When the small caravan came close, Lucius signaled the attack. Their swords made short work of the merchant and his four men. Lucius continued to scream orders. The men rounded up the animals and drove them toward the hideout.*

*Lucius personally searched the five bodies before ordering the men to drag them to a deep wash a small way from the road. Once the dead men dropped over the rim of the wash, the highwaymen caved in a portion of the bank to cover them.*

*The return trip to their hideout near Jerusalem took many days. The goods of the caravan were loaded on camels; camels that can only move with excruciating slowness. In addition, they are singularly ill fitted for traveling over mountain trails.*

*Barabbas glowed with appreciation for the success of the mission and ordered the men to bring the merchandise to the secret room hidden under the city wall near Golgotha. They would keep the goods there in safety until they could be sold.*

*"This is a fine lot of goods, men. You've done well."*
*Turning to Lucius he demanded, "What was taken from the*
*merchant's person?"*

*Avoiding Barabbas eyes, Lucius handed the bandit chief*
*a fat bag of gold coins. He failed to mention, however, a diamond*
*pendant hung on a gold chain he took from the neck of the dead*
*merchant.*

*Nodding his thanks, Barabbas tucked the bag of coins in*
*his belt and ordered, "Have three of the men take these animals*
*back into the hills where they cannot be seen until a proper buyer*
*can be found for them. Then take the men to the old camp and*
*wait to hear from me."*

*When the men with the animals were gone and Barabbas*
*closed the hidden door leading to the city, Lucius turned to the*
*remaining man and ordered, "Go over to the valley of Rephaim*
*and find Bella and the other women. Hurry to the big camp with*
*them. You should get there before dawn."*

*He followed the men out to their horses and mounting,*
*rode toward the old campsite Josias always used.* If I am to act
as leader of the band, I am entitled to the best. I'll show
that Josias who's the greatest robber.

*Early one morning, several days after the robbery, a great*
*turmoil occurred within the Insula. A Centurion escorting Siphos*
*the Greek sent a message to Marcellus from Damascus that a*
*small caravan following his own had failed to arrive in the city.*

*He reported that he knew Damascus was to be the*
*caravan's destination. Pilate, informed by Barabbas of his success*
*in the raid, turned the complaint aside with a shrug.*

*"I cannot sympathize. Were the merchant less stingy he*
*could have hired an escort. He would have fared better."*

*Marcellus stared at the Procurator. Filled with anger he shouted. "We are expected to keep the highways of the Empire safe, Sir. There should be no need of these hired soldiers to escort caravans."*

*"You were sent here by Caesar to apprehend the robbers, Legate." Pilate glared evilly down at Marcellus. "See that you do so."*

*Marcellus stepped closer to Pilate and stared back. "It appears to me that these robbers must be getting help from somewhere in the government. How else could they know of the movement of the caravans and their exact schedules?"*

*"What--what do you mean by this?" Pilate gripped the arms of his chair and almost stood as he shouted. "Do you dare to accuse me or one of my servants of this?"*

*Marcellus held his ground and said, "I accuse no one. I only know these bandits have information they should not."*

*Marcellus left, and Pilate remained in his chair. He repeated the Legates parting words over and over to him self, wondering if the Legate could possibly be suspicious of his own connection with Barabbas. He felt certain the man knew more than he wished him to know.*

*He finally thought,* I must find a way to protect myself. Perhaps there is a way I can have this Legate recalled.

*Grim faced, Marcellus marched into the barracks and shouted orders, "Second platoon, prepare to ride.*

*"Pack your camp and battle gear. Be prepared for a full month of field duty."*

*Turning on his heel, he went back to his office, appointed a Centurion as Legate pro tem and prepared to leave, seeing to his own weapons. He would lead this patrol himself.*

The patrol made a hurried trip to Caesarea where they learned the caravan took the northern route, going by Megiddo. Marcellus then led his men east to the Valley of Jezreel, across the Jordan, and north to Damascus. The messenger from Damascus reported the caravan was last seen near Megiddo. Marcellus put outriders on either side of the road, watching for signs of the victims.

Several miles east of the valley one of the soldiers found a jumble of camel and horse tracks near the road. The tracks finally straightened out and led into a desolate place of steep craggy hills. Here narrow valleys with steep walls and wadis twisted about aimlessly. Marcellus and his men searched until light failed and found nothing, finally calling a halt, they made camp for the night.

The next morning the patrol rode beside a dry wadi. Suddenly a vulture flew up from a cluster of small bones. At first Marcellus thought they were the bones of some dead animal.

When he moved closer, he could see the bones were the arm and hand of a man. They dug out the bodies of the servants with the S brand on their right shoulders and notched ears.

Under the slaves they found the badly decomposed body of the merchant. Soldiers rolled the bodies in blankets and began to load them on the backs of the mules. After almost an hour of cursing and fighting the animals that were terrified by the smell of the rotting flesh, they finally tied the bodies over the mules' backs and took them to the ancient city of Jezreel.

When this grim task was complete, Marcellus led his patrol along the main road, returning to Jerusalem. He knew something was wrong.

Whoever did this, or at least whoever planned it, was passing clever. The robbery was committed in such a remote place and all witnesses killed, it might have never been known. The carelessness in burying the victims was lucky for me.

It's going to be extremely difficult to catch these robbers. There are hundreds of excellent places to hide in this wild, broken country, and most of these people look amazingly alike. Nevertheless, I must do something.

I care naught for Pilate or his anger, but I can't help but dread recall to Rome if I should fail. Old Galio seems to enjoy making it difficult for a tribune who fails an assignment. I don't look forward to writing my next report.

*Pilate rose from his chair and shouted at Marcellus, "The merchant and his slaves were all murdered? Have you no control of these cursed highwaymen?"*

*"The men were not only chopped to pieces with swords when they were killed, but their bodies were further mangled from the robbers throwing large stones over them.*

*"The identity of the merchant or of those who killed him has not yet been learned. As for control of the highwaymen, who can control those who know every movement of caravans as well as those of my patrols?"*

*"Why have you not sent extra patrols along the roads, knowing there are many travelers between Caesarea and Damascus?*

*"Sir, you ordered that a large patrol sent to bring tax money from Galilee to Jerusalem be doubled. I must ask you Procurator, where would I find more soldiers to form extra patrols? I still must say it seems strange these robberies always occur when you have ordered extra patrols be sent out of the city for special duty, leaving me shorthanded."*

"Be careful what you say, Legate," Pilate stood up from his chair to glare at Marcellus. "I suggest you look to your soldiers for a traitor."

Marcellus glared back at the Procurator for a moment, then turned on his heel and left the room, speechless with anger.

Pilate sent Sylvanius to locate Barabbas, demanding he attend him post haste. Sylvanius found the slave Rueben on the Street of Camels and ordered him to find his Master. "Inform him that Pilate would speak to him immediately. Tell him to come to the private meeting room and do not delay."

Barabbas entered the Insula by a private door in the garden and awaited Pilate in the small private room below the public audience room. After a few moments, Pilate stormed into the room, slamming the door back against the wall.

"Why did your men kill that merchant and his slaves? The Legate is in a great rage, running about the province making all manner of threats. Your carelessness will have all of us in trouble."

"Your orders were to leave no witnesses or evidence to incriminate us, Pilate. How else can one eliminate witnesses?"

"Leave no evidence?" Pilate almost screamed. "Five bodies thrown in a ditch and a stadium of camel tracks to lead everyone to them isn't evidence?"

"What is this you say?"

"Marcellus the Legate and his men found the bodies of the merchant and his servants. How did this happen?"

Barabbas struck his left fist into the palm of his right hand and muttered, "Damn Lucius anyway. He spoils every plan I work out. I hope the Legate kills him. It would relieve me of doing so."

*"This whole business is getting too dangerous. If our association is found out the Legate will set up a great howl to Rome, causing me untold trouble. If this comes about, mark my words, Barabbas. It will mean the cross for you."*

*"Watch carefully for the assassin's dagger Pilate, if the cross is ever my sentence." Barabbas said over his shoulder as he left the room.*

*Argubus sat in one of his favorite haunts, under the covered turn in the Damascus gate. Barabbas found him there and leaned down to whisper in his ear, "Find Lucius and tell him to see me tonight in the regular meeting place. This is most important, see you do not fail me."*

*The old prophet kept silent as he watched two men pass through the gate. As soon as they were out of hearing he answered, "He may be hard to find. He left the city in a great hurry, fearing the Legate's anger."*

*"You and Lucius should both remember, the Legate's anger is but a psalm to mine. See he is at the meeting place tonight as I ask, or we will need a new spy."*

*Argubus grumbled mightily as he made way to an inn on David Street. He knew that Lucius returned to the city several days before and he knew where to find him. He almost trotted along the alleyways to an old inn.*

*The criminals of the city called the inn the thieves den, for there a bribe gained a place for a man to hide in the cellars. There was a system of caves under the old court behind the building that only criminals and those who helped them knew. A man could remain hidden there in safety, fed from the inn, until an opportunity afforded itself for him to escape the city.*

*The old man had known of the caves for many years. He used them on occasion to hide suspected criminals under the pretense of being guided by God to save them. He therefore was well known to the innkeeper and found no difficulty gaining admittance to the caves to search out Lucius. After almost an hour of effort he finally spotted him nestled deep into a side passage. He lay in a drunken stupor, resting on a vermin-infested pile of rags.*

*After much shouting, cursing, shaking and coaxing Argubus finally made Lucius understand he must meet their leader in a few hours. When he was satisfied the drunken captain understood what he must do, Argubus returned to his place under the Damascus gate.*

*He hoped to learn something more about the trouble Lucius was embroiled in or at least collect a few coins in his beggar's cup.*

*Meanwhile, Barabbas sought out Zerubbabel, the merchant who sold stolen goods for him. He obtained an advance in gold after describing the goods that were hidden. He knew he would have to give Lucius some money to make him agree to leave the city.*

*When he and Lucius met the session was stormy, but Barabbas convinced Lucius it was imperative for him to leave Jerusalem at once and stay away from the city until he told him to return.*

*He explained that one of the gang betrayed Lucius to Pilate, but refused to tell him which man, claiming he only had his suspicions, but would keep watch and eventually uncover the traitor.*

*Furious, Lucius shouted defiance of the edict. When noise did no good he resorted to whining, but finally agreed to leave.*

*Barabbas' slave Rueben accompanied him from the city. The man walked quickly into the hills, leading him to an unfamiliar hideout. From a corral near the hideout he provided*

*Lucius with a horse and gear, then guided him to the hill road leading north.*

*Barabbas returned to Josef's inn to order wine and spent the night brooding over his troubles.* I know that Lucius is a useful man, but I now realize he is too dangerous for me to use any longer. He's careless and refuses to obey my orders.

I need Josias, curse him. Where in the world can he be? It was Passover time when he went to Damascus and he's been gone long enough to be in Rome.

Josias is a good man—an excellent leader. Why hasn't he come back? Without him, there is no one left to lead. Unless he comes back soon I will be forced to lead the band myself—and everyone—even the Legate knows me by sight.

# Chapter 13

One evening, Sarah and Josias were settled in their rooms, when Joel knocked on their door. He called Josias outside the inn and led him to a seat near the fountain, where he turned to him, saying, "I must go into the mountains and see to my goat herd. The trip should take four days and three nights. Wouldst thou go with me?"

Josias rubbed his chin, puzzled and surprised. "What is this? I thought the flocks were all brought in before we left on our journey to see the Nazarene."

"Only the sheep are in. The goats stay out much later in the summer. They graze over the hills a second time, eating rough herbage that would starve the sheep. They also need less care, praise God."

"If Sarah will agree, I would like very much to go with you."

They left in the early morning, when the sky was still gray. Each wore a loose robe and sturdy sandals. Their only burden was a knapsack for food and a goatskin of watered wine. Joel led the way and walked quickly along the familiar paths. The fertile valley where he farmed was soon left behind and the high, arid plateau called Beth-Car lay before them.

*Joel stopped and waved his arm before him, "Imagine, Josias, this great desert was green with tufts of grass and covered with a carpet made of millions of flowers when I took our flocks across it early this past spring. The sheep and goats grazed along here and made their way north and up the side of those mountains you can see yonder in the distance."*

*It seemed impossible to Josias that this hot, barren land of sand, rocks and an occasional Sittah tree bristling with long thorns and clusters of reddish berries, could have borne greenery and flowers a mere few months earlier. It looked as though the land had been devoid of life for centuries.*

*Much later, the path led them into the foothills. The walking became difficult as the track ran through a deposit of loose shale. The place gave the impression of a huge dumping ground of waste stone garnered from some unknown quarry. They saw only an occasional stunted and wind-bent oak with clumps of laurel or acacia bush clinging to life in its shade.*

*As they moved higher, the path meandered between tall, sheer cliffs of stone. Polished by unceasing winds, the stone reflected the afternoon sun from the high walls, creating a prism of colors. They were first gray-green; then salmon, buff and ocher, as though painted by some artist to soften their stern lines. Here and there a cedar or stunted pine thrust out, twisted and gnarled from buffeting winds, clinging to the steep cliffs, its roots deep in small pockets of earth. The ever-present thorn bushes hung tenaciously from any crevice affording them sustenance.*

*Always alert, Josias began watching the sky. It seemed higher here than in the lowlands and a much deeper blue. Large puffy clouds idled along, gleaming white. Nothing could be truly urgent enough among man's small problems to cause them to hurry.*

He remembered watching such clouds as a child and finding pictures among them. Today he could see a fierce old Arab warrior in one, in another the battlements of a large city. He almost stumbled when he saw in the distance a large one holding a startling likeness to the Nazarene.

The man's words came back to him, 'Lo, I am with you always.'

Joel continued to lead the way, and Josias following, they walked steadily until they came to a fork in the trail where a small spring afforded cool water. There were signs about of many campsites.

Joel dropped his knapsack beside the spring. "Let's eat our evening meal here, Josias. We'll move along a ways after we eat and sleep elsewhere, for bandits often camp here and I fear them."

After they ate a simple meal and drank again from the spring, Joel led the way to a break in the canyon wall. Slanting slightly upward, the crevasse afforded a passageway into a small box canyon. The floor of the canyon was strewn with large and small stones from ancient rockslides. Wending his way through the stones, Joel went to the mouth of a well-concealed cave.

"I found this place many years ago when hunting strays. It was a fortunate find indeed. I've used it for my sleeping quarters every trip since. This area is riddled with bandits, and for a lone man to sleep out in the open is simply foolish. I would be asking to be murdered in my sleep."

Tired from the unaccustomed walking, Joel and Josias immediately wrapped themselves in their blankets and fell asleep. Both awakened at first light. Opening their knapsacks, they produced bread and dried dates and ate a quick meal. When breakfast was finished, they cautiously checked that no one, innocent or dangerous, camped nearby. Satisfied no one was about, they made another trip to the spring to drink and re-fill their waterskins.

The path through the barren gray highlands led ever upward. The vegetation became sparser, until Josias wondered how even a goat could find a living. Midday brought them to the goat herder's camp. The man's shelter was a small brown tent set close to a sheer rock wall. Its position defended it from winds and the afternoon sun. Behind the camp lay a shallow pool, filled by a trickle of water that ran down from cliff's edge.

As they entered the valley from the south, the goatherd came toward the camp for his noontime drink and rest. With the help of his dog and a small donkey, the man leisurely pushed his many-colored flock toward the pool of water.

Josias stopped and shaded his eyes to look on with envy at the high brassy sun shining down over the gray rolling hills and the herd lazily making its way to water and rest. This is a picture of true peace. I have rarely experienced such in my life.

Joel turned and called to him, smiling. "What is it you're thinking?"

"That surely men are fools. They build and live in such desolations as Jerusalem or Damascus when the peace and quiet of many places such as this can be theirs."

"Only those who are content with themselves know peace in loneliness."

Josias continued to stand and stare, thinking of the unrest he knew so often. He recalled how he could not abide the country—did not want to be away from crowds and noises--how discontented he felt most of his life, except during the wild excitement of a robbery.

I can hardly believe the tranquility I feel at this moment. It must be marriage to Sarah that brings this peace. I can think of nothing else.

*Walking ahead to meet the goatherd Joel asked. "Have wild animals been a problem of late?"*

*"Just a few days ago several wild dogs, running in a pack, attacked the herd. Our old dog made so fierce a defense that the dogs left without satisfying their hunger. Also, there is a large cat of some sort who screams in the hills at night. That one worries me, for he would kill the dog with one swipe of his paw. But the goats will fight to defend themselves, they are not as afraid as the sheep."*

*"What of the old dog when he hears those screams?"*

*"He runs wildly around the herd, nipping at their heels to make them close ranks. Then he puts himself between the goats and the direction of the scream, challenging the cat with his fierce barking."*

*"The herd is in good hands yet then. That old dog is a faithful servant—he has defended my herds for many years."*

*Joel and Josias passed the night in the goatherd's camp. They slept beside the pool, sheltered under a lean-to made of sticks and goatskin. The night was cool at that high altitude—cool to the point of discomfort that waked them early, before there was any color in the sky. They quickly prepared for the return trip, and Joel ordered the goatherd to begin the long trek to bring the animals to their home pasture.*

*"We'll go along ahead," Joel told the herder, "You graze the herd along easy. Food will be scant until you get to Beth-Car and there you will find nothing—nothing at all. Push them hard—force them across the plain to our home range. The grass is good there and the animals will gain weight quickly. They'll be fat and ready to sell at the fall market."*

*The trip home was one of many wonders for Josias. Walking quickly, they passed a small valley, all green and peaceful, nestled in rough hills. There he saw another sweet-water spring with willows and thorn bushes growing ajumble around it. Farther on, he stopped to marvel at a high jagged cliff that reflected the sun with its many hued sections of stone. The varicolored stone made a background for soaring flocks of birds. Stopping to look and admire, Josias often lagged behind the sturdy Joel, who had passed all these things so often they were commonplace.*

*Josias thought of his mother.* I wonder if she will accept Jesus as the Messiah. My Sarah has—she questions nothing about him. I doubt if Mother will accept him so readily. If she hears of him she will probably accuse the person who brings the tale of blasphemy. *A lump of emotion welled up in his throat as he thought of Mattathah and his eyes burned. He hadn't cried since he was a child.*

*Sarah and Salome met them in the courtyard, smiling and welcoming them home with joy. They saw them approaching in the distance and took time to prepare a fine meal. Sarah's hand on his arm and the comfort of her love eased Josias confused thoughts.*

*It was still dark the next morning when Joel pounded on their bedroom door. "It's almost light, Josias. I must be about breaking the land for barley and wheat. The time for planting grows near."*

*Throwing the cover aside and straightening his sleeping robe as he stumbled across the room, Josias opened the door and smiled down at Joel. "I am ready to help, though I must confess I know little of farming."*

"I knew you would be willing, my son. Your great strength is what I need. Come and eat. Salome and Sarah prepared some food."

Josias helped Joel as he hooked the plow to the great ox and followed him to the north field. He stood aside to watch as Joel positioned the ox at the end of the field and began the plowing.

Joel put both of his big hands on the plow handles and giving a tremendous heave, lifted the plow and slammed the metal point into the ground. At the same time, he slapped the leather reins on the ox's back. The beast strained against the harness and plodded forward. The point of the plow bit into the soil, turning a deep furrow. It took several minutes for the ox to reach the far end of the field and turn to throw another furrow as it came back to where Josias sat on the ground waiting.

"Is there another plow? I would like to harness our saddle mules and try turning some of the field myself."

"There's an old plow hanging in the barn. It's to the right just as you go in the main door. I cut it from a forked limb of an ancient oak that blew down years ago. It is passing heavy. Those mules will be hard put to pull the thing."

"Surely two strong mules can pull the same as that fat ox."

Joel laughed and wiped the sweat from his face with his sleeve. "You do have a lot to learn about farming, son. That ox can work those two mules to death and never even breathe hard."

"Well, I'd still like to try."

"Oh, the mules will pull the plow all right, you'll just have to be sure to give them a breather for about fifteen minutes out of each hour or you'll kill them the first day."

Josias spent the rest of the day working about the barn. He fashioned breast straps and lines to drive the mules with and rigged a double bar. Scratching around in a jumble of harness, he found trace chains to hitch the mules to the plow. The work was finished about the time Joel came in from the field. He was leading the ox. He turned the animal into the paddock where he could get water and fed him a large bait of grain.

"The beasts need fuel to keep going on, just as we do."

"I'll be ready to help you in the morning, Joel. I have everything I need."

"I hope the mules will stand for it." Joel called over his shoulder and chuckled as he left the barn.

When Joel hitched the mules to the plow early the next morning, they didn't hesitate to express their displeasure. The larger mule twisted his head around to bite his partner's neck. Then he tried to kick the trace chains and the rest of the hitch to pieces with both hind feet. The other mule reacted by braying loudly and jumping up and down on all four feet while holding his legs stiff.

Josias reacted by tapping their hindquarters with the end of a long slender pole and using some choice words to describe their temperament and their ancestry. When the mules were finally convinced there was nothing to do but cooperate, the plowing progressed extremely well. After the third turn around his section of the field, Josias found the knack of holding the plow in the earth at the proper depth and began to turn fairly straight furrows. Working with two plows, he and Joel finished the plowing two days earlier than expected.

"You had a fine idea, Josias," Joel wiped the sweat from his face, grinning in pleasure. "We've two extra days to gather firewood for winter and a fine team to help us haul it."

"The mules have finally learned to work together. If you have a stone boat we can haul the wood as fast as we can cut it."

"We'll finish early enough to go back to Capernaum if you wish."

"I would like to go back. There are many things bothering me, Joel. Perhaps I might find the opportunity to talk to this preacher from Nazareth. Sarah is so moved by his words, I want to understand."

"We will go. After we stack the wood, you can go to Ramah and make ready. That boy Seth was a great help with the animals, see if you can get him to go with us again."

Sarah, Joel and Josias made the trip three days later. They decided to stop at the inn at Capernaum, obtaining a suite of rooms for themselves and stabling their saddle stock, agreeing that Sarah should have a vacation from camp duties. They were also wary of camping out because several travelers told them harrowing tales of recent attacks by hill bandits on people following Jesus.

They thought at first the trip would be wasted. One group of travelers told them that the Galilean was seen last in the Decapolis, another said, "I heard he was seen leaving Caesarea Philippi and going to Knueitra."

The innkeeper insisted, "No. All of those stories are false. The man was on his way to Capernaum, traveling the Roman road."

Josias found the waiting hours tedious. With nothing to occupy his mind or hands his old ferment of thoughts returned. He began again to doubt the Galilean and the truth of what he preached.

He sat under an awning in a small bazaar, avoiding the sun and sipping from a small flagon of wine. He thought of the happiness he knew during his courtship and marriage to Sarah. He felt almost angry. The serenity of his life had been destroyed *ever since they left Ramah and traveled here to seek out the Nazarene.*

I knew real happiness before I set out to satisfy my curiosity about this strange man—be he God, faker, charlatan or whatever he might. I would like to return to Ramah—when I get there I would like to pack our possessions and leave for some far away place with Sarah. But where would I go? Why not the Decapolis?

*Josias poured the last of his wine in his mouth and slammed the flagon down on the table in exasperation.* Now why have I thought of this? I know why. It's because the Nazarene is said to be at the Decapolis. I thought of it because he is there. Is there no escape for me?

*He stood erect and stretched his arms and back. Dropping a coin on the table to pay for his refreshment, he left and walked back to the inn. Just as he reached the entrance he met Sarah running out to find him.*

*Her face glowed with happiness as she exclaimed in a breathless voice, "He is here. Oh, Josias. He returned and is resting. Down there, on the ship of the Zebedees. See the large one anchored just by the big wharf? Its sail is yellow. He promised to talk to the multitudes tomorrow morning."*

*Almost laughing aloud at her exuberance, Josias placed his hands on her shoulders and said, "Calm yourself, my beautiful wife. If he is here we will see him on the morrow. There's no need for you to jump up and down so."*

*Lying beside Sarah that night, Josias' thoughts filled with the stories Jesus told of his Father's kingdom. He remembered the look on the carpenter's gentle face as he spoke the wondrous words.*

*'My Father's Kingdom has many flowers that leave thee not for they are not of seasons but eternal and abound everywhere.'*

*He turned then, to point out the beauty of yellow and pink mustard—of rayed umbels, marigolds, poppy and lily of the valley. He reminded his listeners that they wore raiment finer even than Solomon in all his glory. He said all these they could see were not so beautiful as the least of the beauties of his Father's Kingdom.*

*'Is it meant that a man exchange this beauty throughout eternity for the greed of his sojourn here on earth? Acknowledge He is God, follow me and reap the promise of eternal peace and beauty.'*

*Those words haunted Josias. He was a practical man and saw a tremendous bargain in the offer. Think a minute, he admonished himself,* is it possible that Jesus could deliver all that he promised? A man could give up a lot. He could control his greed—his temper and his passions. He could even control his words for the span of his life. Suppose then, it happened that after a lifetime, he could not collect on this promise. Suppose there might not be an eternity after all? Surely no one has ever returned to guarantee it.

*These things Jesus demanded of him were little different from those his mother called the laws of Moses. He almost chuckled when he remembered her words.*

Maybe Jesus is right, only he just isn't so stiff necked about it. He always talks of joy and song, of birds and sunshine instead of sackcloth and ashes. Moses was big on fasting, long drawn-out prayers and dirges. They never did sound very attractive.

Josias' *wakefulness in the early part of the night caused him to sleep past his usual hour of awakening the next morning. When he rose and went to the common room of the inn, he found Sarah seated on a carved bench near an open window, weaving stockings, the bone shuttle flying in and out of the thread.*

193

"Surely we shall be forced to purchase a pack mule to carry home thy handiwork if we stay many more days."

She looked up at him and smiled. "Thee and my father must have warm stockings for winter, and I dislike idling time away."

Josias placed his hands on her shoulders and looked over her head at the gleaming lake for several moments without speaking. Finally he asked, "Sarah, what think thee of our returning to Ramah with Joel, then you and me making ready for a trip to Damascus, Cornith or some other great city? I can abide this idleness no longer."

"My father wants to follow Jesus, not return home."

"Surely we cannot follow him always, Sarah. I am so unsettled now with his preaching that I want only to escape him."

"Beloved, wouldst thou only go with us to hear him once again? Father and I believe he is the promised messiah and hope thee will accept him as well, if you will only hear him again."

"I will wait and hear him once again." Josias promised, telling himself he was doing this only to please Sarah, yet a great peace came to him when the decision was made. Smiling to himself, he returned to the great room of the inn and took a seat, whiling away time over his breakfast. A short time later he heard a man shouting frantically from the road in front of the inn.

"He is here. He is here. The Master has returned. He will speak on the knoll beside the sea. He will tell us again of his Kingdom."

Josias surprised himself with the urgency he felt as he quickly finished his breakfast. He hurried Sarah and Joel along, hoping they might find a good vantagepoint from which to see Jesus and hear him speak. As they hurried along the path he also *marveled at the behavior of other people who rushed along beside him.*

How can it be that this stolid, surly and quiet people are so affected by this Nazarene? Whenever they hear of him coming nearby, sensible, hardworking men leave their beasts standing to plows or carts and run after him. Women leave their kitchens, their weaving or whatever their work and merchants leave their bazaars with all their wares unattended. Smiths leave their shops and children their play. All go scurrying in a ferment of excitement to follow him.

They all seem to lose their reason, throw down whatever they were about and rush to hear him. Can it be he is the promised one? Or could it be only his dynamic personality. Who can tell?

Surely these Galileans are not all fools. I know they are burdened with the temple tithe and heavy Roman taxes—burdened enough to make them a woebegone and downtrodden lot, but they are not easily fooled. If this man is the messiah, their madness is justified, but if he is not, how can he fool so many?

*As they came to the foot of the knoll near the sea Josias heard the voice of a man who stood before Jesus. "Good Master, I begged of your followers that they heal my son. Since a child he has been afflicted of demons. They cast him upon the ground. He falls into the fire or against others in all manner of senseless ways. Your followers commanded the evil ones to leave him but the evil heeded them not. Will thou cast them out? I pray thee do, for he is my only son."*

*Jesus looked down at the men and women who followed him, his expression showing amazement that their faith was so small. Turning back to the man again he said, "If thou canst believe, all things are possible."*

*The man held his hands together in prayer, "Lord, I believe, help thee mine unbelief."*

*Jesus held out his hand to the son and commanded the evil spirits to depart. The boy lay upon the ground as one dead until Jesus raised his voice to command him to arise. Springing up, he leapt about with great joy.*

*These things Josias saw and heard and he felt greatly troubled.*

*Jesus turned to the multitude gathered on the plain overlooking Gennesaret. He spoke in a quiet, clear voice, without shouting, and yet all heard him, even the deaf and those who stood far back in the crowd. Peace came to all that heard his words. A quiet contentment and smiles of happiness lit their faces.*

*Josias made his way to a large stone rolled up beside the water, where he sat long after all the people but Sarah and Joel left. His mind was in a quandary. He felt perplexed, confused and unable to decide what to believe.*

"What can I believe? Surely I cannot accept this so called messiah as a reality. The boy's illness could have been a fake—part of an act arranged before he and his father met Jesus for the so-called healing. *More puzzled than ever and almost despondent over the unrelenting turmoil of his thoughts, he finally rose and without speaking, accompanied Sarah and Joel back to the inn.*

*As the reached the door Joel asked, "Can we not make ready to return home now? I must make a bower of willows to observe the ingathering and God's deliverance of His people from the wilderness."*

*Josias' answer sounded curt to the point of being rude. "Yes, I would leave, and hurry about it, for I wish to be away from that mountebank and his foolishness as soon as possible."*

*Sarah and Joel looked at each other without making an answer, but swiftly packed their things for leaving. Joel called the innkeeper and ordered their mounts readied so they could leave within the hour. They made no camp on the way, but traveled the night through, reaching Ramah near noon the following day.*

# The Malefactors

# Chapter 14

*Storm clouds rolled in over the mountains, pushed by a bustling westerly wind that heralded the arrival of the fall equinox. Josias and Joel finished sowing the barley and wheat fields. Joel strode forward and back across the field, swinging his arm in wide rhythmic arcs. Dipping into a basket held before him with one hand and balanced against his chest by a leather shoulder strap. Josias followed, his prized mules pulling a heavy log Joel called a "dead man," smoothing the seed into the ground.*

*When they finished planting the grain together they drove the sheep and goats from the valley pasture to a fenced in area with several stone shelters that lay near the house. They were barely finished when the first of the autumn rains began. Running to the shelter of the house, they found Amos the Smith waiting for them. His manner made it obvious he was fairly bursting with news.*

*"I followed Jesus and the twelve to Jerusalem when he left the hillside at Capernaum. As he and the twelve left there many followed them. He stopped a short way from Magdala and talked of the Kingdom to the followers and others who met them at that place. Afterward, he excused himself, saying he must hurry to the holy city to observe the feast of the Tabernacles.*

"When they heard this, most of the multitude returned to their own places. Jesus and the twelve made way again. A few who believed continued to follow, and I was one of them. We traveled quickly, stopping but for little rest, for the time of the feast was near.

"On the morning we entered Jerusalem, Jesus was nowhere to be seen. I swear I felt his presence with me, but I saw him not. Many Pharisees and spies of the Sanhedrin asked of us if he was with us, or if we had seen him, but none of us admitted we knew anything. We knew they sought only to arrest him for blasphemy and to be honest, we were fearful of our own fate if we admitted we knew him.

"On the second day, as we stood in the Temple before the veil covering the entrance to the Holy of Holies, Jesus suddenly appeared before us. He stood on the dais and looked over the crowd for several minutes. Then he began teaching.

"First, he upbraided the Jews who tried to kill him. He quoted much of the laws, answering those of the Sanhedrin who accused him of healing the lame on the Sabbath. He argued instances when Moses ordered circumcisions on the Sabbath and asked which was the more righteous. These things the Pharisees could not answer. They could only shake their heads and look about.

"Many in the crowd asked if he was the one they sought to kill. Several of the lesser priests answered, 'It is he.' We asked them in loud voices, 'Why isn't he taken now?' We received no answer, and many in the crowd accused the leaders, saying they knew the Nazarene to be the messiah and they feared to take him.

"When he heard these things Caiaphas ordered the temple guards to seize Jesus and imprison him, but the men stood *transfixed, unable to lay their hands on the man. Many of the people who saw this believed and became his followers."*

*Joel and Josias spoke at the same time, "Go on—go on please, tell us what happened then."*

*"Throughout the feast days we saw him not. Not even his disciples saw him—not even once. During the sacrifices of the eighth day he appeared before the temple again. He told of many things the prophets of old forecast and he prophesied, saying he saw the destruction of Jerusalem, with its mighty walls and temples all laid waste and the chosen scattered throughout the world.*

*"All who heard these things marveled, for it was known he was not a priest or one of the Rabbinical College. There rose a great confusion. Different ones in the crowd disputed back and forth over who he really was.*

*"Many quoted the prophecy of Malachi, arguing that the messiah would be of Bethlehem, and demanding of the crowd, 'is not this man of Nazareth?' After much argument and disquiet, the people left the temple, some believing, some scoffing and some greatly troubled by doubt."*

*Joel leaned forward anxiously. "All these things you heard and saw with your own eyes, Amos? This is truth?"*

*"Yes, my friend. It is the truth. I stood in the crowd and I saw and heard it all. I rejoiced throughout at the power of Jesus."*

*"Amos, let us gather at the Synagogue tomorrow. It is meet that all hear these things thou hast seen and heard. Thou canst tell them all of what thou hath told us today, then tell of any other things thee saw and heard. We will go about the village and inform the people that thou wilt do this."*

*Joel, Salome, Sarah and Josias sat late into the night, talking and marveling of Jesus and the miracles he performed.*

*Finally, Joel stood up and stretched his back as he said, "Let us retire to our beds. We have work to do tomorrow."*

*Many of the people of Ramah gathered in the aisles of the Synagogue the following morning. They listened raptly as Amos retold those things he told at the home of Joel. That complete, he continued his story.*

*"Caiaphas, the high priest seemed to be greatly troubled about Jesus, for each time the Nazarene appeared in the temple, a large company of guards came rushing in as though to arrest and carry him away. When he spoke to them however, they marveled at his words and left without accosting him.*

*"In the early morning, the day after the feast, Jesus came down from the Mount of Olives and stood beside the gate to the women's court. Speaking quietly, he taught all who would listen of God's Kingdom. Again a great multitude gather to hear him.*

*"In the midst of his teaching, a group of Scribes and Pharisees pushed their way to the front of the crowd to stop before him. They dragged a woman roughly by her arms. They loudly accused her, saying she was taken in adultery. They asked of the Master if she should be stoned to death as Moses commanded.*

*"Jesus stopped speaking. He stooped low and with his finger wrote in the dust at his feet. Then he raised his head and said in a loud, clear voice for all to hear, "He that is without sin among you, let him cast the first stone."*

*"On hearing this, the Scribes and Pharisees looked first to one and then another until they released the woman, without speaking and walked quickly away. When they were gone, Jesus turned to the woman and said, "Go thy way and sin no more."*

*"As he resumed teaching, the Pharisees came again to the front of the multitude and accused him, saying his record was not true.*

"He turned to them and said, "Ye know not mine nor my Father's record for ye do not believe." This speech angered the Pharisees, but they were afraid to lay hands on him before so many of his followers.

"He told us of his Father's Kingdom and many more believed in him, but those who believed not gathered up stones in their hands and began to cast them at him. They were so alarmed when none could cast true enough to hit him that they ran away in their fear. After that he turned to leave. When we followed him some distance from the city as though we would go to Bethel, he stopped beside a large fig tree and began speaking again.

'I shall always be as a shepherd to those who believe and shall lay before the door of the pen that if a robber comes he must first overcome me. If one of thee is lost I will hunt throughout the wilderness until thou art found and returned to the fold.'

Amos' eyes filled with tears. "I and all that stood nearby were greatly comforted when he promised to keep us from all danger."

Shaking his head, holding his hands out before him, Amos appealed to the crowd, "Now I must tell you that I am tired—I am tired, my brethren, in my heart and my body. May I return and complete this telling on the morrow? My friend Joel has offered to provide me a bed that I might rest."

The villagers left the synagogue, some believing and exultant, others skeptical, shaking their heads and greatly troubled. The people of Ramah did no work that day, but spent the hours until darkness standing about the village, collected in groups, discussing the strange things Amos related and arguing whether they could be true.

Those who believed, as Sarah and Joel did, felt no doubt. As they prepared for bed that night Sarah turned to Josias and asked, "Is it not wonderful that the messiah has come in our lifetime?"

"Yes it is wife, but never will the stiff-necked Jews of Jerusalem accept him. He is a Samaritan in the eyes of some and a Galilean to all. Only if he came from Judea would they believe him to be the true messiah."

Early the next morning the whole family made haste to return to the Synagogue. Josias looked about to see if those who heard Amos talk the day before had returned. He finally concluded that every one returned and brought with them villagers that were not there the day before. When everyone was seated and ready, Amos picked up his story where he left off the day before.

"When Jesus finished speaking of his care for us, we returned to the temple. He stood among the columns of Solomon's porch and taught again. Many Levites came asking of him, 'Why do you keep us in doubt? Say to us plainly whether or not thou art the Christ.'

"He again said he was the son of the living God, but they believed not, loudly accusing him of blasphemy. The low creatures rushed forward and attempted to seize him—they surely planned to imprison him and hold him for trial.

"To the amazement of all who saw it happen, he walked around a column of the temple and was no more to be seen. All who believed in him left the city in one accord and walked the entire night. We arrived the next day at a place beside the river Jordan near Jerico.

"I could find no one who knew why this happened. The people I spoke to could only say they felt within themselves a strong desire to go to that place. As we rested from the long walk Jesus appeared before us and again told of the peace and beauty of the Kingdom.

*'When he stopped speaking a man came forward and said, 'The sisters of thy friend Lazarus send word to hurry to their home for he is grievously sick and near unto death.'*

*"Yet withal, he tarried with us two days longer, fasting and praying. On the third day he rose to his feet and announced to the crowd, 'I must return to Bethany for Lazarus has need of me'"*

*"The disciples all implored him not to go, for they feared the Priests of the temple would hear of it and try again to arrest him. Thomas, one of the twelve, said to him, 'Lord, let us go with thee, for if thou be killed we will be also.' Jesus turned to the multitude, blessed them and bid them to leave him.*

*"He and the twelve went toward Bethany. I myself and many others from Galilee, returned to our homes."*

Amos bowed to the crowd, and exhausted by his emotional effort in retelling the extraordinary story, leaned on Joel's arm as they left the Synagogue. The crowd left the building as well, but again lingered in the street, separating into small groups, discussing what they had heard.

Josias spoke not a word as he walked beside Joel and Sarah returning to their home. His heart was greatly troubled. The talk of Jerusalem brought rushing back all the memories of his life as a captain of a robber band, serving Barabbas. He wondered if the bandit chief and any of his men were still alive. He wondered if he would still be alive had he stayed in the city.

Josias could not sleep that night and left his bed to sit on a bench under the arbor, holding his head in his hands, remembering every raid, wondering if he could ever be forgiven for the evil he lived for so many years. He cringed as he thought of how he once held himself so proud. He knew he was no better than the worst of them. Truly, he was as bad and perhaps worse than the one called Lucius the Hawk.

# The Malefactors

# Chapter 15

*Angrily striding back and forth between the campfire and the mouth of the cave where he slept, Lucius demanded of himself and the night sky, "Just who does Barabbas think himself, some sort of king or mighty Potentate? How can he cast me out of the band this way? I—I who worked harder for him than anyone else, and—just think of it—the nerve of that slave Rueben, telling me I could have my own horse, but to be sure never to show myself in Jerusalem again.*

*"I very nearly used my scimitar on him, the greasy little rat. His words sounded like something Argubus put him up to saying. He too should be killed--he is nothing but a liar and a sneak in addition to being a fake. I may be the one who will see it done."*

*Far gone in his cups, Lucius' temper boiled and he muttered vile curses—yet he was frightened. All the talk of Pilate, the Roman Legate and the danger of his ever being seen in Jerusalem again thoroughly disconcerted him. He gladly hurried from the city with the slave as Barabbas directed, but after he was on his horse and riding into the hills, it came to him that he would be lonely in the hideout without some company.*

After he thought about things for several miles, he decided he would return to the city for Bella if he could find her and while he was at it, he would lay in a store of supplies.

He turned his horse and riding into a bushy wadi in the valley of Kidron, near Mount Scopus, he carefully hid the animal. He walked back to the Damascus Gate, and finding it closed for the night, cast small stones against the wall of the gate tower where Argubus made his bed. Finally the old man finally awakened and answered him.

"What is it you want now, you fool. Were you not ordered by our leader to leave the city and not return?"

"Come, let me in the secret door beside Golgotha. By all that's holy, you old fool, you better hurry yourself if you know what's good for you."

Argubus started to ignore Lucius' orders and let him continue to rage, but after thinking about it a few moments he wrapped a cloak about his shoulders and went to the inn to awaken Barabbas.

Thoroughly angry that Lucius would disobey him so flagrantly, Barabbas stormed, "Go to the Legate and tell him the leader of the highwaymen is just outside the city walls and we will see a cross arise on Goliath hill tomorrow."

"I too thought of this as well, Master," Argubus said, "I vow it would be a joy to me, but after a moment's thought, I decided that such a thing would be most unwise. Lucius would tell the Legate of you, Josias and of me in seeking his revenge should we act against him in such a way."

"You are right old one, of course you are right. Go back, open the gate to him, and find out what he wants. But for the sake of us all, get rid of him as quickly as you can."

*Argubus made his way through the storeroom of Zerubbabel and opened the small, hidden door in the city's wall. Lucius stepped inside and barely waiting until the door was closed to hide the sound of his voice, he began to rage at Argubus, raising his voice almost to a shout.*

*"You call yourself a Prophet, you filthy old bag of bones? I'll prophesy an early death for you if I'm kept waiting like that again."*

*Undaunted by Lucius' bad temper Argues ignored the man's bluster and asked, "Why are you here again? Barabbas ordered you to go far away from the city and not return, under pain of death."*

*"Barabbas can find another to order about. I no longer take orders from him or from any man.*

*"Get me two skins of wine, some barley flour, a measure of salt and two cooking pots. I go into the city to find Bella. I will have someone to accompany me into the desert. See that all is in readiness when I return, and remember what I said about keeping me waiting."*

*Argubus worked his way to the back of the warehouse and entered the wine shop. Without waking the owner, he gathered the supplies from the storeroom and returned to the wall to await Lucius' return. It wasn't long before he arrived, followed by a slatternly woman. Without speaking, he motioned for her to help him pick up the bags of supplies. Ignoring Argubus, they left the city.*

*When they reached the place where he secreted his horse, Lucius turned to Bella, "Pack the supplies on the back of the horse and keep him and yourself well hidden. Do not move about or make a sound. You'll be safe here until I return. I'll visit a dealer in animals to get you a mount."*

Lucius carefully studied the camp of the trader before showing himself and so found the guard sitting on the ground with his back against a wall, fast asleep. Being ever on the lookout for a chance to ply his trade as a master thief, Lucius crept past the man to reach the picket line. He quietly saddled the gentlest of the mares, and led her away without waking the guard.

Much of the night was spent before he returned to the wadi in Kidron where Bella waited. She lay curled against one of the packs of supplies, sleeping. He loaded a few of the supplies behind the mare's saddle and helped Bella mount. Packing the rest of the goods on his on horse he motioned for her to follow and jumped into his saddle to ride north.

They started out so late that daylight caught them when they had traveled less than an hour. They found a place to hide in a jumble of rocks not far from the Roman Road. Lucius knew traveling during the day was simply too dangerous. He and Bella took turns throughout the long hours, one sleeping and one guarding the camp, with cold food to eat.

Bella minded this hardship little for to her, any change from the life she led in Jerusalem was an improvement. Her days in the house of prostitution were a poor lot. The old mistress who purchased her from her father when she was barely a woman operated her house for the soldiers of the Insula, and required Bella to do the most menial chores. She was much older than most of the women in the house and unattractive. Few customers asked for her services unless they were low in funds or extremely drunk.

After several nights of cautious travel, hiding in remote places by day, Lucius and the woman reached a little known box canyon in the rugged mountains west of Mount Gilboa.

In the early light of their first day in the hideout, Lucius constructed a brush fence across the opening of the canyon's mouth.

*Once the fence was completed he set the horses free to graze. He also set snares for the ever-present coney to provide them with fresh meat, and Bella set up their camp.*

*After eating his meal and drinking several measures of wine, Lucius raised his voice and began again to rave over Barabbas' gall. He stormed about, cursing in his disbelief that the man would have the nerve to exile him. He threatened how he would repay him for such mistreatment.*

*Burning with anger, he paced up and down before the fire and ranted of the great robberies a new band of his own would soon commit. He raved and shouted into the night air, swearing his band would be so feared that no merchant would dare to use the Damascus road, nor would the Legate be able to apprehend them, for he would be their leader, and he would outwit the Roman at every turn.*

*Finally tiring, he sought the cedar bough bed Bella prepared for him and tried to sleep. Excitement caused by his emotional tirade kept him sleepless. He vented his rage on the woman and lay with her. She felt pleasure in the violence of the act, thinking it prompted by desire for her.*

*Sleep came much later when Lucius, finally exhausted from his ranting, dropped off. He dreamed of the glorious future he would enjoy as the greatest leader of a robber band the Empire had ever known—a leader so powerful he need have no fear of any Roman Legate and his soldiers.*

# The Malefactors

## Chapter 16

*The Legate sat at a table in the commander's quarters of the Insula. He chewed the tip of a stylus, trying to think what to write in a report to Rome. He planned to make a copy of this report for the Procurator. He had come to believe the man should know how he felt about him and understand his suspicions. He could not help but worry that he could give no account of progress toward the capture and arrest of the highwaymen, particularly in the case brought by the Cyrenian, Simon. He could not help but feel discouraged. After working most of a year, he made no progress. Even the Arab he hired to watch Barabbas could find out nothing.*

*It was difficult for him to explain, even to himself, his suspicions of Barabbas, but the feeling persisted that the man was connected in some way with the robberies. He idled in the wine shops and claimed an income from his flocks and herds in Galilee. This claim aroused the Roman's interest. He also received reports that in the past, the man had frequent business with the Procurator.*

*When Marcellus checked the tax lists of the Province he failed to identify Barabbas as an owner of any taxable property, neither land nor animals. His doubts of the man increased. Without other evidence, he could not arrest him, so he hired the*

*Arab to observe his movements, hoping to learn something that would help make a true case against the man.*

*The reports the Arab offered were upsetting. He needed to find out why Barabbas talked to Sylvanius, the Procurator's scribe so often. Why also, did Barabbas visit Pilate? Marcellus could find no acceptable reason. The man went to the palace two days before the last major robbery and went again only two days afterward. There was no real evidence of wrong doing though, only activity that seemed unusual. It began to look impossible to find anything tangible that would connect the man's visits to Pilate's audience room and the robbery. But still—there was the timing. Combined with everything else, it looked doubly suspicious.*

*Marcellus' hate for Pilate became almost unbearable to him. His suspicions increased in proportion, for he learned that the big robberies only occurred during weeks when Pilate sent him away from the city on special duty. It seemed that he was always out on some unnecessary mission, far away from the place where a merchant's caravan came under attack.*

*He continued to worry over the report. A few minutes later, a courier came through the office door. It was the man he sent to Caesarea earlier to find some information on the merchant slain near Jezreel. He reported finding out that the merchant was a Syrian, returning to Damascus with a cargo of ivory statues, a variety of spices, perfumes and medicines from Egypt. Marcellus shook his head in disgust. The courier's information offered him little help in determining what happened.*

*He immediately sent another man to Damascus armed with the information the first man reported. He gave this man instructions to search about the city for someone seeking a lost kinsman.*

Surely someone is looking for the man by this time. No one of his stature lives and dies without someone knowing something about them, not even in this forsaken place.

*Marcellus believed in his heart this effort would be a waste, but it was all that could be done. To his surprise however, this courier soon returned accompanied by a Syrian who sought a lost brother, a trader who had gone to Egypt to buy supplies for his customers. His descriptions of the lost merchant and the list of merchandise his brother sought matched so near the description of the dead man and the tax lists from Caesarea that Marcellus ordered the man's body exhumed so he could be identified.*

*The soldiers who opened the grave complained greatly, for the man had been dead for many days. It was a gruesome job, but although the body was much damaged, the Syrian identified it as that of his brother. The man was re-buried with proper honors in a stone crypt the Syrian purchased to honor his kinsman.*

*Marcellus took a squad of picked men and spent several days in the bazaars of Jerusalem questioning merchants. He hoped to identify some of the merchandise from the robbery, but they found nothing. Discouraged, he decided the only thing he could do was keep watching and wait for something to happen--something that would help him find out who was involved in the robberies.*

*Marcellus did feel that conditions for travelers were greatly improved due to the many patrols on the province's highways. Only a few minor thefts were reported to his office after the slaying of the Syrian merchants and the members of his caravan. Without new information, he was forced to turn his mind to everyday duties and hope the spate of robberies was over.*

*Rising early as usual, Marcellus breakfasted on fruit, bread and a thin, raw wine. A guard stepped through the doorway* and stopped before his table to salute. Returning his greeting, Marcellus rose from his meal and ordered him to report.

"I was standing guard at the Damascus gate," The man explained, rather breathlessly, "it was less than a half-hour gone. This big red horse came trotting up to us. He was riderless, though well saddled. He appeared extremely tired to me. He was lathered and covered in sweat. We noticed the poor beast had a slash on his hindquarters. I thought the mark looked much like a sword cut. The leader of the guard ordered me to bring the horse here and report the incident to you."

Leaving his breakfast, Marcellus followed the guard out to the courtyard, to inspect the horse and its saddle. The bridle bore silver bosses as decoration where the leather crossed.

He called the man in charge of the stables and ordered him to feed and care for the horse, pointing out the cut that needed tending. He knew he must question everyone possible for information about anyone missing from his usual haunts or of any unusual activity by Barabbas.

Marcellus returned to his desk to finish his paper work. A few hours later a man dressed as a merchant came to his quarters. He reported the failure of his father to return from Damascus. Marcellus asked the man to describe his father's mount. He perfectly described the red gelding the guard brought in earlier in the day.

Leading him to the stable, he showed the man the horse. The man confirmed that it was his father's mount and asked, "Did anyone find the two pack mules he had with him?"

"My men found only the horse I'm afraid, but come back to my office and write their description down for me. Include your direction and if we can find the mules or find out anything about your father we will notify you."

Less than an hour after the man left, Marcellus rode in front of a patrol as they passed through the Damascus gate. The soldiers were well armed and led several heavily laden pack horses. He led the men north on the Roman Road, their horses at a brisk trot. When they reached the first section of the road bordered by enough rocks and trees to offer cover for highwaymen to operate, he ordered two soldiers to take up a position on either side of the road. They were to watch for any tracks that could possibly be part of an attack.

When darkness fell the patrol made a dry camp alongside the road. They rose again at first light the next morning to continue the search. They spent three full days scouring the area near the roadway with no success. Even more discouraged and bitterly disappointed, Marcellus led the patrol back to the Insula on the afternoon of the fourth day.

The young man came to Marcellus again to inquire after his father's fate and about the lost goods. He said his father's partner reported to him his father's trip was made to secure a supply of small silver statues of Aphrodite—especially beautiful ones made in Corinth and sold by the Mekels of Damascus. He planned to bring back as many of them as the two mules could pack, for they would sell briskly to the many non-Jewish visitors to the Holy City during the upcoming Passover.

Marcellus and his picked patrol spent many days in the market places of the city vainly watching for a merchant selling the statues. Although he and his men found nothing and were bitterly disappointed, he believed it was only a matter of time before his diligence would reveal who was behind the crime.

***

Before light on the day the merchant on the red horse disappeared into the gray dawn Lucius, well rested and well armed, pulled aside a section of a crude brush and pole fence and led his horse through. Once the animal cleared the gate, he turned and replaced it so the entrance became almost invisible. Mounting, he rode along the winding paths through the rugged hills west of Gilboa until he came to a brush and rock covered hill overlooking the Roman Road between Jerusalem and Damascus.

He dismounted and concealed his horse in the small valley behind the hill. Climbing to the top, he stationed himself at a vantagepoint where he could see travelers on the road long before they reached the curve below him.

Lucius repeated this exercise daily for several weeks, and until now, had seen only large well-guarded caravans. He was about ready to give up and seek another band to join. He actually had learned to fear his own impatience. Several times the rich cargo of one of the caravans almost lured him into attacking alone.

That morning the air was warmer than usual. He roused suddenly from dozing and saw a lone rider traveling toward Jerusalem at a brisk pace. The man led two heavily laden pack mules. "Surely this is the chance I have awaited so long," He said aloud. Running to his horse, he leaped into the saddle and raced around the rock. Positioning himself close to the road, he impatiently awaited the approach of the traveler.

Leaning forward so he could see better, Lucius searched the road both north and south for signs of a patrol. When the traveler came abreast of his hiding place, he burst out of the covert and attacked him. A mighty blow with the sharp scimitar killed the man instantly.

The horse screamed as the tip of the weapon sliced its hindquarters on the left side. Crazed with pain and fear, the animal backed out of Lucius reach and galloped away so fast it was impossible for him to catch the reins.

Lucius went cold with fear as he watched the horse disappear around the curve toward Jerusalem. He knew the horse was living evidence of the robbery. He led the mules out of sight of the road and tied them with his own horse. Going back to the road, he retrieved the body of the merchant and buried it under a great pile of rocks.

He took enough time to brush out every track with a leafy bough, carefully hiding all evidence of the robbery. Satisfied with his work, he returned to his horse, remounted and gathered up the reins of the two mules. Urging his horse to a brisk walk, he set out again for his hidden valley.

Dragging the heavy packs to the campfire Lucius opened them and dumped each one out on a blanket. The site of the large number of statues of Aphrodite, exquisitely fashioned in silver, elated him. He and Bella crowed and cheered over their good fortune, the danger of the red horse forgotten.

"This is the very best thing I could have found. If it proves too dangerous to sell the statues, I can still melt them down and make the silver into rough bars. I can always find a buyer for them."

Bars of silver would be impossible to identify. Lucius was determined to avoid melting the statues down if possible. Intact they were much more valuable than the raw silver could ever be. Carefully re-packing the treasures, Bella helped him hide the heavy packs deep under a rock fall.

When the excitement was over, Lucius felt nervous and fearful again, each time he thought of the escape of the horse. He rose early the next morning and set out to dispose of the pack mules, leading them west, closer to Jerusalem, where a Philistine trader in animals operated. He searched the Roman road for patrols before he crossed, and hurriedly disappeared into the rough foothills on the far side.

Riding around Merged, he hurried across the wide plain to the brush-covered banks of the Crocodile River. He crossed the river at a little used ford on an old, abandoned roadway and circled around so he approached the trader's place by way of its back entrance.

Just as he entered the gate, a man with one eye covered by a black patch stepped into his path, catching his horses' bridle in one hand.

"Good Sir. Please wait here in this little clearing. I will bring my master to you. It is best that animals such as these are not shown in the sales yard where strangers might happen by and notice them."

Lucius waited impatiently. Time dragged. He dismounted to get a drink of cold water from the well, then paced up and down. Thoughts of future successes raced through his mind until he was nearly blinded by pictures of his vividly imagined good fortune. His dreams robbed him of the ability to understand the danger he ran even in dealing with a trader in animals who enjoyed a flexible reputation.

Lost in thought, he started violently when the trader suddenly stood beside him. The man asked, "What have you here, my friend?"

Lucius was so startled he could only stammer, "I came to offer you two fine mules I would like to sell."

The trader looked the mules over carefully, pulling their ears, lifting their feet, and inspecting their teeth. Finally he turned to Lucius, "I can only give you six hundred dinarus for the pair."

"Why man, that is simple robbery."

"How came you by the mules, my friend? If there were no reason to hide these fine mules you would come by the front road to my poor establishment.

"Since it is obvious I must hide these animals until they can be driven to Tyre to sell. That is all I am willing to pay.

"I am forced to take particular care with such stock as this these last months. The Romans seem to have the idea I might deal in stolen animals. They very nearly embarrassed me on several occasions, and I have no wish to end up on a cross. I've learned to be extremely careful and resort to many tricks to make such stock as this impossible to identify."

Realizing the uselessness of argument and the necessity of disposing of the mules for his own safety, Lucius accepted the man's offer of six hundred dinarus with ill grace. Tucking the coins into his belt, he set out to return to his hiding place. When he reached the Damascus road, he stopped again to gaze up and down to make sure he could cross unseen. Near where he crossed earlier, he noticed the tracks of a group of iron-shod horses. The tracks were fresh. He knew such a large group of riders could well be soldiers, and they probably were. He chuckled when he thought, "It's possible my long wait for the trader saved me from running into a Roman patrol.

Unable to stay idle, Lucius rode out again early the next morning, and again climbed to his perch over the highway to watch for another victim. Late in the afternoon he spotted the patrol. It moved slowly, searching carefully on each side of the road. Much amused at the soldiers casting backward and forward for tracks, he chuckled as he watched.

A feeling of pride in his craft, instead of thankfulness for his forethought in covering the tracks he made during the robbery, filled Lucius' mind. When the soldiers moved far enough along the road so there was no chance of them hearing his movements, he left the lookout spot, knowing it would be foolhardy for him to attempt a robbery on the Damascus road for the coming weeks.

Lucius made plans to find a good lookout to watch the Megiddo-Bethshean roads. As he lounged beside the fire and waited for Bella to prepare his evening meal, it dawned on him that the Legate and his patrol would be able to locate his headquarters by simple deduction if he should rob anyone on the east-west highway.

The activity of the patrols forced Lucius into idleness, and idleness forever led him into some sort of trouble. Bored almost to distraction, he began riding out to explore the most remote reaches of his surroundings. He made a trip to Samaria, and on the way back, he passed near Mount Ebal and stumbled onto a remote valley. The small dell narrowed into well-hidden entrances on either end, and opened at the center into an ample, well-watered meadow for his animals.

Near one of the high, sheer walls of the canyon, a tiny mountain stream fed a large pool of ice-cold, continously moving water. Fish swam in the pool, and the overflow went underground, hiding evidence of its existence outside the valley. It was a much better hideout than his present one.

Lucius hurried back to camp. As he loosened his horses' bridle so the animal could graze, he shouted over his shoulder to Bella, "Get up, you useless drab. Stir yourself and help me prepare to move camp. I've found a much better place to live. It is so well hidden no one will ever find us. You pack up everything here and I will start moving the silver statues."

All the work and physical movement of packing, loading and transferring the camp to a different location kept Lucius calm and occupied for several days. He was content even through the time it took him to construct a rough shelter for he and Bella to sleep *under should bad weather come. The first night they rested beside the campfire in their new location, he began his rant again, bitterly cursing his fate in having to hide in the mountains, alone and unappreciated.*

*He had no band to lead—no men to order about, none to wait on him. There was nothing to make him feel his importance. There was no one but Bella to appreciate his wit or admire his craft. He cursed Barabbas for sending him into exile and Argubus for delivering his orders.*

*Finally, he all but shrieked vile curses on the head of the new leader of the legion, the Legate known as Marcellus, the one who made it impossible for him to show his fellow highwaymen his prowess.*

\*\*\*

*When he returned to the city after searching for the site of the latest robbery, Marcellus felt the sharpest edge of frustration. He searched the entire highway from Jerusalem to Damascus without finding a trace of anything amiss. He and his men found neither tracks nor mules nor statues nor witnesses. There was no evidence of the robbery. Every track had disappeared.*

*Nothing he or his men found would help him develop a case. Searching the shops and bazaars of Jerusalem failed to uncover a single one of the silver statues.*

*Somehow he knew—he could not doubt—that this case must and would eventually be solved, and he would be the one to solve it. A favorable solution would determine the course of his whole future in the Empire's service. He shuddered to think of the consequences of failure.*

*Marcellus busied himself signing requests for leave by members of his legion. He approved orders for food supplies and the endless other needs any army generates. One morning, hearing a step in the corridor, he looked up to see his Arab spy rushing through the door. The man approached his writing desk and held out his left hand. Without speaking, Marcellus placed a coin in his palm.*

*As soon as he secreted the coin in his robe, the Arab began to speak, "The man I*

*watch — the one called Barabbas, has done nothing unusual during your absence, your honor, but old Argubus, the charlatan who calls himself a prophet, begins to act strangely of late."*

*"What has he done you deem strange?"*

*"Several days of late, he left the city quite early in the morning. He goes out by the Joppa gate and stays out all day, entering the city again just before the night closing of the gate. He neither carries nor brings ought with him.*

*"I have asked several idlers what he does out in that barren desert and the answers vary. Some say the man is demented. Others say he is a prophet and talks to the Jewish God Yahweh. Still others say he is a spy for some obscure liberation movement. I know not what he is, but his furtive movements are suspicious."*

*"Go back to your post and keep watch on the movements of Barabbas," the Legate said, waving the man away.*

*Marcellus sat at his desk, staring through the window as he puzzled over this new problem.* What in the world could that old devil—perhaps prophet—probably faker—be up to?

*Standing suddenly, he clapped his hands to summon the guard who stood outside his door. When the man entered, he handed him a fat purse. "Here are some coins, go to the bazaar and purchase a robe, turban and sandals, nothing unusual. Go to the chemist shop at the end of David Street and buy some locust*

224

bark for making brown stain. Send someone else in here to me from the guardroom as you leave, I have further orders."

When the second soldier entered, Marcellus gave him orders to lounge about the inns and bazaars. There he was to spread the word that the Legate planned to leave the city for several days—that he would attend a meeting in Caesarea.

Early the next morning, before the city's gates were opened, a tall Arab approached the soldiers who guarded the Joppa gate. "I would leave your fair city, sir. Please open the gate."

The guard stood tall and blocked his way. He asked in a loud, harsh voice, "Have you a pass signed by the Legate?"

"I have not."

"Then stand aside and await the regular opening of the gate like other people, 'tis but a short wait."

The Arab leaned against a corner of the battlement and stood quietly, waiting. When it was full light, the guards opened the gate. Without saying anything more, the man passed through the opening and walked rapidly out of sight around the first bend in the road.

The soldier guarding the gate watched him go with a puzzled frown on his face. The man's actions were unusual. As soon as he completed his watch, he hurried to the Insula to report the incident to the Legate. When he reached Marcellus' quarters he found that the Legate was gone. Vesperian, his slave, referred him to Drusus, the troop's second in command.

When he explained his errand, Drusus asked, "Why do you think this strange? The man was probably in some hurry to reach the seaport."

"It was the looks of the man that were strange, sir.

"What makes you say this?"

"For one thing, he was much too tall for an ordinary Arab. Although he was dark of face as they always are, his features were of one of us. Also, I noticed he did not squat to wait as the Arabs invariably do. He stood with his arms crossed and leaned against a battlement just as you or I would wait. All this I have said and his erect way of walking belied the Arab in him."

"How was he dressed?"

"In the manner of an Arab. He wore a gray robe, hide sandals, a turban and the crooked sword they all carry. Oh—there was one more thing. Everything he wore appeared new."

"If your suspicions were so strong, why didn't you arrest him—bring him here for questioning?"

The soldier's cheeks began to turn red. "He gave me no real reason to arrest him, sir."

"Since when do the Emperor's soldiers need "real" reasons to make an arrest when they are suspicious of someone?" Drusus asked, smiling a little.

The soldier held his head high and looked away from Drusus without answering. After a moment Drusus dismissed the man. He carefully made a note of the incident thinking, "I can't see any importance in it, but I will include it in this report to the Legate on his return."

Marcellus concealed himself in a large jumble of fallen rock to await the coming of Argubus. He planned to follow him and get his answer to the riddle of the man's daily trips. He chuckled to himself several times when he thought of talking to one of his guards and then standing right in front of him for almost fifteen minutes without being recognized. Surely old Argubus would never recognize him.

Argubus hurried through the city streets. He seethed with anger. Rueben had delayed him with questions of potential robbery *victims for Barabbas. For the first time in years he would not be the first through the gates. Leaving the city early kept him safe. Any who might want to follow him, to find where he went so often, would not come to the gate early enough to see him leave.*

*He looked carefully about as he hurried through the gate. He passed the second turn in the road and turned back to see if anyone followed, keeping himself well hidden in some tall reeds. As he watched, a tall man dressed as an Arab stepped out of a covert near the road and started to walk in his direction. Fearing the man would try to follow him to where he hid his treasure, Argubus turned and immediately set out to lose him in the rocks and bushes near the road.*

*Each time Argubus thought he had lost the man, the Arab came steadily on, slowly but carefully unraveling the old man's winding about and backtracking. He was without doubt an expert tracker. Upset, Argubus became desperate to escape the follower. He greatly feared capture, knowing many would not hesitate to torture him to learn the hiding place of his gold.*

*He had spent twenty years in the hills on this side of the city, and knew every trail, bush, and rock. Many tried to follow him. Some were curious idlers. Others were robbers like himself, but most were representatives of some authority within the city. Every one of them held suspicions of him. Never before was anyone able to hang so tenaciously to his trail.*

What manner of man is this who follows my track like a hound and clings like a bur? He unravels my every trick. I still know one special trick that will get rid of him. I hate it, but it has never failed me.

*Trotting so fast he nearly fell over his own feet at times, Argubus crossed a shale-covered valley and reached the edge of a narrow gorge. Poised on the rim, he turned to drop over the edge* and climb backward down its steep side. About one third of the way down he reached a narrow shelf no wider than the length of his forearm. Lying flat, he slid feet first into a small cave in the sandstone wall.

There was barely room for him to pull his head completely inside the cave. Worming his way backward until his feet struck solid rock, he completely hid himself.

The oppressiveness of the tight pocket gave him a momentary feeling of panic. He closed his eyes as tight as he could and tensed his whole body, knowing any movement would result in his capture by whoever the person was who clung to his trail.

Marcellus peered cautiously over the brink of the narrow gorge. He lay flat, peering over the edge, to study the entire ragged bottom. He could see no trace of the old man, not a track, or a disturbed stone, nothing. Finally, he swung his legs around and started descending the rock face.

He stopped often as he descended the cliff and peered into the numerous caves and pockets eroded into its side. When he reached the bottom, he hurried to the far end of the gorge where the bottom flattened into a plain.

There was no sign of the man. That area offered no hiding places.

Disgusted, he returned to the wall, muttering to himself. "The wily old beggar has hidden himself in this gorge somewhere. Why can't I find him?"

Shading his eyes from the glare of the sun with one hand, he examined every cave he could see. There was no sign of the man and no trace of his passing. The entrance of the cave Argubus lay in was so small it never occurred to Marcellus that anyone could hide in it. He walked up and down beside the wall, searching for any possible hiding place, cursing under his breath.

*Finally, he turned his back to the wall and sat down to rest. He took a water skin and a hand full of dates from the bag slung over his right shoulder. After eating his meager meal, Marcellus climbed back to the cliff top and started the long walk back to the city. He never realized the old man was small enough to get into the little cave.*

By the Gods, that old faker outwitted me. All my plans, and nothing to show for it but the waste of a full day.

*Long shadows crept up the cliff side opposite Argubus. He peered from the cave, but could see no one. Almost sick from steeling himself to stay still within the narrow space, he dragged himself out onto the ledge. He felt stiff and sore from lying still for so many hours and his hands trembled from the strain. His hips and shoulders ached almost unbearably as he trudged back to the city. As he approached the gate, the call of the soldier, warning that the time of closing was near, caused him to break into a hurried shuffle so he could pass through to the safety of the city.*

*Fearing the tall Arab still watched him Argubus spent several days without leaving the city. Marcellus commissioned a member of his patrol to watch the old man. The soldier's reports made him wonder even more why the old man left the city so often. Why he found it useful to slip through the gate so early.*

*Staying in his quarters to make good on his announced absence, Marcellus tried to reason out the many problems presented by the highwaymen. No matter how hard he thought, he could not arrive at any reasonable answers.*

*He finally concluded it was valueless for him to worry and study over the problem. He could only wait for some chance opportunity to capture the highwaymen or failing that, simply wait for his sure recall to Rome in disgrace—whichever fate the Gods decided to bring him first.*

*One of the highwaymen or one of their leaders would eventually make a mistake. He would be ready when that happened. Until then he could only make himself content by doing what he could to keep order in the city and patrol the roads.*

# Chapter 17

*The constantly moving, incessantly working life of a farmer contented Josias. He repaired the broken when he could, and sometimes when they were beyond his ability to repair, made anew the tools needed to operate a farm. He spent days in the wadi and the numerous small valleys lying between the farm and the plateau of Beth-Car, searching for willow shoots to weave baskets and make animal traps. The unremitting activity kept from his mind the unrest of old and stopped him from thinking of this new and upsetting problem of understanding Jesus of Nazareth.*

*He and Sarah sat for many hours as she taught him the knack of weaving the willow shoots into something useful. It took so long for him to learn, and he was often so clumsy, that at times she became quite impatient at his ineptness. When he finally mastered the art, he and Joel made several clever traps that allowed him to catch so many of the quail and coney that were plentiful in the coverts and fence rows of the farm, the women finally ordered him to stop catching them. They said they were tired of their taste and tired of smoking and drying their meat.*

*The joy and fulfillment of his love for Sarah and the companionship of her parents amazed Josias. The many new activities made him feel almost happy. His busy life, full of hard work out in the open air, even enabled him to sleep well at night, something long impossible for him. The tranquility of a simple, everyday life was a nearly magical thing he never before knew.*

*He walked with the old dog near Beth-Car one morning, wrestling with memories, worrying about the future.* Suppose I am arrested for my crimes. Sarah, Joel, and Salome would be so terribly hurt and shamed. My new friends in Ramah would be shocked. They would certainly feel I cheated them by pretending to be something I am not.

I must write an order on the Mekal family to Sarah. I'll sign over to her the money they hold for me. I'll also give her the bargain ring. If I do this now, she will be provided for if I am arrested. I'll tell her the story of finding the treasure as well, so she will never worry if the goods were stolen.

*Feeling almost sick with worry and remorse, Josias sat on a stone and dropped his head into his hands as he tried to remember the prayers of his mother. He suddenly felt so filled with fear that he wanted to ask God in a prayer that Sarah be spared ever learning of his evil past.*

*One morning late in the winter, Josias set out to look at the few traps still set for game. The air smelled of spring. The moss growing on the wadi banks seemed a little greener. Buds swelled on bushes growing in sheltered places. A coney, clumsy and large with young, dropped from where she fed to an outcrop of rock and landed almost at Josias' feet.*

*For the first time, Josias knew the thrill of spring. The feeling of being a part of the renewal so well known to those who live close to nature. He wondered at its effect on him. When he finished gathering his traps he hurried back to the house to ask Joel a question.*

*"When do we plant the house garden, sir?"*

*"Nisan, the month that heralds spring, is but a few days away, my son. If the sun is warm again tomorrow there's no reason we can't begin preparing the soil for the garden. We can do that much at least."*

*Morning found both men busy turning rows to plant leeks, mustard and mixed greens. They planted saffron for its flowers. The women used the golden blossoms to make dye and as an incense for the house. They added its delicately piquant flavoring to salads and charlocks. Josias worked in the garden with great gusto, the novelty making the labor a game for him.*

*Joel leaned on his hoe at the end of the garden and watched him work. When Josias, stooping low, finished dropping the tiny mustard seed in the row, he covered them with a sprinkle of soil and patted them in place.*

*When he straightened his back and joined Joel, he was surprised when he asked, "When are Salome and I to expect a grandson, Josias?"*

*Josias face suddenly felt warm. He smiled as he said, "I vow I know nothing of grandsons, sir, but I shall inquire of my good wife this night."*

*When the time of Passover drew near, Sarah asked Josias to accompany her and Joel to Jerusalem for the observance. Josias felt a deep uneasiness. He really did not want to go to the city. He knew it wasn't safe for him. Few ever saw him with Barabbas, or knew him as a leader of the highwaymen, but it still was not safe. Some inward fear kept telling him to avoid the risk, tell her no, but Sarah's urgency finally persuaded him. It seemed impossible for him to tell her his real reason for not wanting to go, and he could not think of any plausible excuse to refuse her.*

*His uneasiness persisted and several times he almost abandoned the trip to turn back, but the beaming smiles on Sarah's face and her assurance that all would be well convinced him to continue. He wondered if any members of the band still dwelt in Jerusalem, if Barabbas still made the city his headquarters, or if the Romans had finally caught the master highwayman.*

\*\*\*

*Barabbas, ever extravagant, was in dire straits for money again. His need caused him to visit Pilate seeking a victim for robbery to replenish his purse. When he broached the subject, the Procurator became exceedingly angry and stuck out his chin to rave at Barabbas.*

*"Are you not aware of the Legate and the vigor he is exerting to prosecute his assigned duty? He not only keeps patrols chasing here and there on every road in the province, I discovered that there are several paid spies operating in the city and they all report to him. If that were not enough to bear, the man disguises himself as an Arab and goes out to follow those he suspects himself.*

*"You don't expect me to risk sending him on a false errand while you commit a robbery and suffer the consequences when he implicates me, do you? What manner of fool do you take me for?*

*"Leave my presence Barabbas. Leave quickly and be sure you are not seen near this building. The Legate has spies everywhere."*

*Barabbas left the Insula by way of the trademens' entrance and hurried to the north gate, pretending to be a farmer leaving the Insula after delivering his goods to the kitchen. Walking quickly, he traversed the road outside the city wall to the Damascus gate and passed through, determined to find Argubus.*

*He found the old prophet sitting idling beside the inner wall, close by the gate. He still did not leave the city, as was his wont, for he feared to go to the place of his treasure since the tall Arab nearly caught him.*

*Barabbas sat down beside him and whispered, "I have need of funds, Argubus—I must have funds. Do you know of a likely victim for a robbery?"*

*The old man sat still for a long time. He stared at the crowds along the street as though deep in thought. He finally began to speak softly, "Bella, the harlot who follows Lucius, came into the city just before the closing of the gates last evening. She carried a heavy pack, and left it with the merchant Zerubbabel. This morning as the gates opened, she left the city. She carried a pack stuffed with all manner of food supplies. I saw a heavy bag of coins tied to her belt as well. I believe the pack she brought in and left with Zerubbabel must have been of great value."*

*"How is it you happen to know she sold whatever she carried in to the merchant Zerubbabel?"*

*"It occurred to me that she wore a strange, sort of sneaky look about her when she entered the gate, so I followed and watched her from afar. She went a roundabout way, but stopped at no other place until she reached his bazaar."*

*"Why do you tell me this?" Barabbas spoke harshly. "Lucius would never part with the smallest piece of his gold and I dare not try to take it from him, even if I knew where he was. That unspeakable vermin has no loyalty. He would go to the cross himself to gain revenge."*

*"I had no thought of you robbing Lucius, my friend, but Zerubbabel. His slave confided in me that the goods he brought from the woman were statues of silver and quite valuable. He also said Zerubbabel knew them to be contraband and hid them in the old tunnels under the temple.*

"Why can't you and I go to the temple and steal those statues this night? We can sell them to the merchants of the caravans entering the city so it will appear they bring the statues in with them, can we not?"

"If I agree and we do this, where could I hide the statues in safety until we can rid ourselves of them?" Barabbas asked softly.

Argubus bent his head closer to Barabbas' shoulder to whisper. "What of the meeting room under the wall? The hidden place where we used to meet the band and make plans for a raid."

"I fear Zerubbabel knows of that room. I don't know if he ever goes there, but he could by chance find them and then he would know our involvement in the theft. He could make a deal of trouble for both of us."

Argubus turned to look into Barabbas eyes. "Do you not have a separate room of your own at the inn now? What of simply hiding the statues among your clothes? Surely no one would suspect a sensible man like yourself of keeping things of great value such as those in such a place?"

For want of a better plan, and desperate for funds, Barabbas agreed.

The two men set the time of their meeting for that very night. Barabbas returned to the inn and spent the remainder of the day scouring his brain, trying to devise a better plan than using his own room for hiding the statues if they were successful in getting them.

The more he thought about the statues lying hidden in his room the more he worried. After hours of thought, he could not improve on the plan, so he quieted his doubts with the thought that Argubus might be right, no sane man would hide valuable treasure in so poor a place as his bedroom—certainly not stolen treasure.

*No one would ever suspect he, Barabbas, would do such a foolish thing.*

*He met the old prophet in the gloom of darkness in the second hour of the new day. "Here are the two fat candles you asked me to bring. I hope you are quick in lighting them."*

*"Never mind me. I've gotten along for many, many years, I should be able to light a candle."*

*Without another word Argubus led the way across the temple grounds, motioning for Barabbas to follow. Both men moved on silent feet. The old man suddenly stopped in front of a huge pile of waste stone that lay behind the new temple Herod ordered built to glorify his name.*

*He pushed aside several of the stones to clear the way and skirted the edge of the rubble. The area behind the pile of stone revealed a walkway strewn with more broken stone and other building debris. Many of the paving blocks were broken and most were overgrown with grass and weeds.*

*They followed the walkway for a few steps as Argubus counted softly. He stopped finally, to turn and hold up one hand in a signal for Barabbas to stop. The bandit chief watched as the old man knelt in the weeds to slide his right hand into a crevice in the stone wall. He strained as he pulled up on an iron lever. The lever creaked in protest as it slowly moved.*

*Amazed, Barabbas watched as a part of the pathway slid back out of sight into the stone wall.*

*As the piece of paving disappeared, it revealed a short flight of stairs. Hardly hesitating, Argubus stepped inside the opening, leading the way down and waving for Barabbas to follow. When they reached the dank and musty smelling floor at the foot of the stairs, Argubus knelt to pull another lever secreted under the bottom step. The platform cover closed above them, leaving them in stygian darkness.*

*"Now I see why you said I should bring two candles. It'll probably take two to find our way about in this black dungeon." Barabbas shuddered as he spoke in an ordinary voice.*

*"Keep your voice down. Others may know of this tunnel."*

*Holding one lighted candle high, Argubus turned to lead the way along the tunnel. Barabbas could hear the old man whispering under his breath as he counted his steps.*

*After a seeming eternity, he stopped. Holding the candle high in one hand, he motioned for Barabbas to climb up on the rough stone wall and push against a certain stone. The block lay loosely in the wall. One push moved it slightly to the left. Barabbas turned to look down at Argubus.*

*"Push it farther over to your left, Barabbas. It opens into the secret room. The one I told you about. This is the room where Zerubbabel stores goods he knows may be sought by the authorities or their rightful owners. He hides them in there until he feels it is safe for him to sell them."*

*After he pushed the stone as far to the left as it would go, Barabbas climbed through the opening. Holding on to the edge of the stone, he let himself down to the floor. It was almost impossible to use his eyes in the dimness, but he felt along the top of the boxes, jars and bags piled around the room until he found a rough goatskin that felt as if it was full of the small statues. He reached one hand inside to check.*

*Once he was sure he held the right goatskin, Barabbas hoisted the heavy silver onto his shoulder. Making his way back to the wall, he climbed back up to hand the skin through the opening to Argubus.*

Turning, he reached back to the top of a wooden box and grabbed a small jeweled casket he coveted, tucking it into the front of his robe. He took care not to let the box clank against the stone as he climbed out of the room and dropped back down in the passageway beside Argubus.

"Wait Barabbas, you must climb back up and restore the stone. I would not wish others to learn how I find my way into Zerubbabel's secret storeroom. I would rather the good merchant blame his own men for the pilfering when choice items disappear from his store."

Impatiently, Barabbas placed the skin of silver statues back on the floor and climbed up the wall to wrestle the stone firmly back into place. When he finally succeeded in closing the opening, he dropped to the floor of the tunnel and grabbing the goatskin, hurried to follow Argubus back to the stairs.

Greatly relieved to be back in the open again where they could breathe properly, both men quickly retraced their steps through the temple grounds and left the way they entered. They parted without speaking. Barabbas returned to the inn and went in by the back door, hoping no one would notice his burden. Moving stealthily, he hurried to his room. Once there, he hid the skin in a bundle of discarded clothes and stuffed the bundle under a bench at the foot of his bed.

The next morning, Josef the innkeeper commented to several early customers that he thought it was passing strange that Barabbas arose so late to demand his breakfast. Several speculated that he since he was not around the night before to join in the gaming, he must surely be ill.

Ahab, Marcellus the Legate's spy, overheard the innkeeper's comments and knew there was a possibility something interesting happened during the night. At first he thought to hang around and listen, perhaps to find out more, but remembering his orders, he almost ran to the Legates quarters to tell him what he heard. As a result of his report, Marcellus hired another spy to watch Barabbas at night.

Barabbas told himself at first that Argubus helped him steal the statutes because of their long friendship. After long thought however, he could not help but feel a little uneasy when the old man refused to accept a proper share of the valuable statues.

Ignoring the advice of Argubus to go out from the city with the statues and sell them to incoming caravans, Barabbas arose the next day to visit the bazaars of the Greek Merchants of David Street. He sold each of them in turn a few of the statues. He moved slowly up and down, stopping to chat with each man, completely unaware of the Legate's spy following him. The newly hired man and the Arab reported to Marcellus early the next morning.

"Arab, are you absolutely certain the silver statues were offered for sale to the public immediately after Barabbas visited the merchants?"

"It is as I have said, Sir. I and Isha, this man who stands here beside me, both observed this."

"There is no need then for me to bother questioning the merchants. I know well enough that each will have a ready story explaining where the statues were bought. They will tell me how they kept them these many months in anticipation of the crowds of buyers that will visit the city during the Passover. You men meet me this night at the entrance of David Street. I have a plan that will allow us to investigate this matter further."

Barabbas sat in the corner of the inn's great room, eating his evening meal. He smiled in satisfaction as he fingered his fat purse. He was completely unaware that the Legate and three of his legionnaires entered the inn by the same back entrance he often used *at exactly that time. The soldiers slipped quietly up the stairs. They forced the door of Barabbas' room and searched until they found the hidden goatskin with the remaining silver statues. Marcellus carried the goatskin with the statues to his quarters and locked them in his chest. They would be used as evidence of Barabbas' guilt in the attack and disappearance of the merchant.*

*Later that night, after Barabbas sought his bed much the worse for drink, he was rudely awakened by four legionnaires. The men forced his door, entered his room without ceremony, and dragged him from his bed. Tying his wrists and holding him by each arm, they rushed him to the Praetorian jail. They refused to wait even for him to put a comb to his hair or don a cloak against the cold. Hustling him through the well-lighted front area of the building, they roughly threw him into a small dark cell, slammed the barred door shut and locked it.*

*Late that very night, long past midnight, the scribe Sylvanius bribed the jail guard to let him enter the cell and talk to the prisoner. "Barabbas, my lord the Procurator instructed me to caution you not to reveal anything of his involvement with you and your activities to the Legate." Sylvanius whispered, watching Barabbas' face.*

*"He sends word that you are not to worry over your safety. He has a plan to free you. You are to hide your feelings when you appear before him. Make no response, no matter what you hear. You are not to speak or make any gesture toward him, even should he sentence you to the cross."*

*Barabbas did not answer, but stared at the scribe's back as he left the cell.* I wonder if I can trust the word of the Procurator. Could such a man ever live up to his word? I am perfectly sure that the only thing that would make

Pilate help me would be fear of what he would suffer should I decide to talk.

*He paced up and down the small cell, his mind full of all the things that could go wrong.*

Suppose Pilate is lying. He might be just lying to keeping me quiet until he can bribe a guard to come in here one night and slip a knife between my ribs. He could probably deny anything I say and get away with it. Especially if I am crucified and there is no one else to testify against the cursed Roman.

If I could get word to Argubus, he could go and find Lucius. By my sword, I'm losing my reason. It wouldn't do me any good to find Lucius. He is undoubtedly as stingy with his loyalty as he is with his gold.

\*\*\*

*Lucius was completely miserable. He found life in the remote valley with only the placid and ignorant Bella for company extremely dull. Physically he fared well. His quarters were warm and comfortable and he had few worries. The valley provided good grass for the horses. With Bella's help he wove cedar branches into a wall across the opening of a tiny cave to form a snug place for them to hide should they ever need it. Their shelter held plenty of food, which Bella prepared at his whim.*

*But there was gold in his belt and an itch for activity in his belly. He called down the wrath of the Gods, any who might hear, on the memory of Jerusalem, of Barabbas and of the cursed Roman Legate, that Marcellus.*

I know who to blame, he fumed. It's the fault of Barabbas and that new Legate that I am forced to hide in the hills like a craven fox. They cause me to spend my days with no real companionship and nothing to occupy my mind or my hands.

Today I'd like to travel into the mountains near the Joppa road to try to find the old faker Argubus' hidden gold. I often noticed the old man sneaking about. I even know the very cave he visits when the old fool thinks no one is watching him. If I could find his hoard the woman and I could travel to some distant city where no one knows me—where I'd be safe.

*Barabbas and Josias were often on his mind. He was filled with a burning desire to show both men he was a greater highwayman than either of them could ever be.*

*Finally, Lucius could stand the idleness any longer. Full of the unrelenting desire to show his former companions how great he was, he saddled his horse and set out for the Damascus Road.*

*Following a hidden route, he soon climbed to his favorite lookout and settled down to watch for a likely victim among the many merchants traveling to the city for the Passover. His passion for action and itch for fame and riches pushed out of his consciousness the knowledge that Marcellus the Legate and his patrols watched the roadways leading to the city at all hours of the day and night, determined to stop the attacks on caravans.*

*Marcellus spent considerable time on the Roman Road from Jerusalem to Damascus. He was determined to investigate every place it seemed possible a robber would set up an ambush. Dividing his force into small patrols to cover more ground, he marked several places he believed would be perfect for a highwayman's purposes and set one of his men to watch each of them.*

*Unknown to Lucius, several soldiers of a small patrol lay hidden near his chosen vantagepoint. The men heard his horse as he approached and watched him climb to his post. Foolishly he dismounted, tied his horse in a small patch of grass near the rocks, and immediately climbed to his lookout spot. No thought occurred to him that anyone could be about, especially not soldiers.*

*Once he reached the lookout place, Lucius did not bother to investigate his surroundings thoroughly. If he had made even a cursory check of the area, he'd have seen the tracks of the patrol's horses—tracks left only a few moments before he arrived. He seated himself to watch the road. Almost immediately a lone traveler rounded the bend and headed his way. The man was alone and led a heavily laden packhorse.*

*Breathless with excitement and a feeling of triumph at his good fortune, Lucius scurried down the side of the boulder. Untying his horse, he mounted and drew his scimitar. Holding the sword straight down beside his right leg, he rode into the bushes near the roadway, leaning forward in his saddle to peer out of the bushes, watching the horseman approach.*

*When the unsuspecting merchant drew abreast of Lucius, he charged into the road screaming "Death thou thieving merchant." The merchant dropped the lead rein of his packhorse and wheeled his horse away from the screaming horseman. He almost rode into the horses of the Roman patrol. The soldiers avoided the merchant's horse to charge down on Lucius.*

*Unable to change his headlong course, Lucius attempted to escape into the brush on the far side of the road. Anticipating he would try such a move, the leader of the patrol struck Lucius a heavy blow on his head with the side of a pike, knocking him out of the saddle to sprawl in the dust beside the road.*

*As he regained consciousness, Lucius felt the movement of a horse under him. His head hurt as if it would split. Moaning, he forced his eyes open. The first things he saw were two horsemen* riding ahead and others to each side of him. He was tied on his own horse with his hands bound together in front of him. Another rope passed through the one holding his wrists and looped around the horse's neck. Worse yet, a rope running under the horses' belly tied his ankles together. One of the soldiers led his horse, holding the reins in his left hand. He could hear a loud voice going on and on. He finally realized it was the leader of the soldiers arguing with the merchant.

The man waved his arms and yelled at the top of his voice. "I do not wish to follow you or to testify before the Procurator. You and your soldiers saw what this miserable, murdering thief tried to do to me. Why must you have me to testify? I have business to tend, and I am in a great hurry."

"I care not for your hurry or your business either, merchant." The soldier's voice rang out, his tone as cold as ice.

"Understand me. You will accompany us to Jerusalem with the prisoner and bear witness against him. You merchants scream eternally of robbers and protection, then scream even louder of the inconveniences imposed on you when asked to testify against them. Catch up your packhorse and hurry about it. It will be near dark when we get back to the city. I will not listen to another word of your foolishness."

Turning his back on the man, Drusus, leader of the patrol, mounted his horse. Riding around the soldiers who guarded Lucius, he took up a position facing the patrol. Without another word, the merchant dropped his head and quickly caught up the lead on his packhorse and led him close to the group of soldiers where he felt safe.

Drusus ordered two men to take the front line, placed the bound thief second with two of his men behind him. He followed the formation, riding close beside the horse of the disgruntled merchant, determined to keep the prisoner and his intended victim under his eye.

He meant to successfully deliver the prisoner to the Legate. He had no stomach for the storm he knew he would face if the bandit were to escape his grasp before he turned him over.

When the patrol reached the courtyard of the Praetorium, Drusus himself untied the rope from around the horses' neck and ordered one of the guards to release Lucius' feet. Yanking hard on the rope, Drusus pulled Lucius from the horse. His legs were stiff from being tied and he fell heavily on the stone pavement. Yelling defiance at the Roman, he jumped to his feet and lunged at the patrol leader.

Catching the thief by his right arm, Drusus motioned for another soldier to hold his left. Lucius could do nothing to resist their strength. The soldiers marched the shouting and cursing man into the Legate's quarters.

Marcellus lips parted in a cold smile that might have frightened a sensible man. He stood up from his desk and walked close to Lucius to inspect him.

"What is your name?"

"I am called Lucius the Hawk."

"Lucius what?"

"Lucius. That is all. I was once called Barsubus, but now Lucius is all the name I possess and all the name I need."

"Where do you live?"

"Caesarea."

"Why did you attack this merchant? He accuses you of attempted murder and robbery."

"The man lies. I only attempted to recover my own goods this lowest of low vermin stole from me this day."

*The merchant ran forward screaming, holding his fist high as if he would strike the bound man.*

*Holding out his left hand, Marcellus turned to the merchant. "Stop Sir. Stop, or you shall also find yourself bound and being questioned."*

*Ignoring the man's outraged expression and indignant sputtering the Legate turned back to Lucius and asked, "What were your goods?"*

*Without hesitation Lucius said, "Spices."*

*A soldier was sent to the storehouse to investigate the merchant's packs. The guards continued to hold Lucius' arms as they waited. Marcellus paced back and forth. The man returned quickly.*

*"The packs contain only black antimony and small flasks of perfume."*

*Returning to face his captive, Marcellus reached out to pull a pendant on a gold chain from the thief's neck. It was the diamond-studded crescent stolen from the person of the slain Syrian merchant. The man's brother described the piece of jewelry for him many months before.*

*"I believe we should take this scum to the prison. Make sure he is secure, and keep him separate from the other prisoners. He may be a great help to us. I will visit him later tonight. I believe he will want to talk to me by that time. "*

*Marcellus stood thus, holding the pendant in one hand and staring down at the bandit until he finally lowered his eyes. Drusus and the other soldier, still holding their prisoner's arms, led and dragged him across the courtyard to the prison and threw him into a cell. He flopped down on the pile of straw in one corner and cursed the legate and every one else he could name, including God.*

# The Malefactors

# Chapter18

*The next morning, the scribe Sylvanius came to the quarters of the Legate, his servant walking before him. Bowing deep, he returned Marcellus formal greeting. Without taking the seat Marcellus politely offered him, Sylvanius announced in a cold supercilious voice, "I was sent here by the Procurator to inform you that he would hold court on the morrow to dispose of the final business before the Passover."*

*As soon as the words left his mouth, the man turned on his heel and left the building. His servant stole a glance at the Legate as he followed. Marcellus seemed to ignore the Sylvanius' contemptuous manner. He sat with his chin resting on his hand, wondering why he received this message in such a manner.*

What is that slippery snake of a Procurator planning to do?

*Sylvanius made a visit to the inner rooms of the temple the same morning. He sought the high priest Caiaphas. When he found the man he announced in a loud voice, "Final court day before the Passover is tomorrow. Be there early if you have business before the Procurator."*

*Caiaphas spent the rest of the day wondering what the Procurator could be planning. Over and over he muttered to himself, "What could that greedy Roman plan to do? By all that's holy—what is he up to?"*

*He sat in his chair with a large goblet of wine in his right hand, cursing Pilate and his games in whispers and mutterings.*

*At the proper hour the next morning, Pilate swept into the audience room, seated himself, arranged his robes and announced the court open. Marcellus and four guards led Barabbas into the room. After he read aloud the charges against Barabbas, Pilate informed the court in a loud voice that anyone convicted of robbing another who enjoyed the good fortune to be given the Empire's protection, was automatically sentenced to die on the cross.*

*The Legate stepped forward to give evidence of his soldiers' findings against Barabbas and Lucius. Lucius confessed that he killed and robbed the Syrian of the silver statues—the same ones found in Barabbas' possession. This confession, added to Lucius's statement that Barabbas was his robber chief, seemed evidence enough to all who listened to gain a sentence of the cross for Barabbas.*

*Without looking his way, and with no change in his tone of voice, Pilate quickly sentenced Barabbas to death. Still holding his head away, as if Barabbas were not in the room, he ordered, "Do not execute this man until the last day of the Passover. On that day the city will be full of these cursed Jews. I will give them an example of Rome's justice and show them what traitors to Rome may expect."*

*Lucius was brought forward next, two guards again gripping each of his arms to drag him before the Procurator's chair. He never ceased his shouting and cursing. Holding his head high he demanded of Pilate.*

*"You arrested the leader and me, the chief captain. What then of the lesser captain—the one known as Josias? What will you do about Argubus the spy and other men of the band? Why, I can name them all, and I surely will if you will release me for helping you. Why is it you have arrested only two men?"*

*Pilate said nothing. He stared down at the screaming man with a disgusted sneer on his lips. The Legate asked Vesperian to carefully record the names Lucius screamed over and over. Smiling, he planned to check on them later and take another step in clearing the province of highwaymen.*

*With the capture of Barabbas, Marcellus felt he was at last making some progress toward ridding the province of the worst of its thieves. This list of names would help him finish the job. He also knew that Lucius' screaming the names of his confederates would not make any difference in the robber's sentence. His death was inevitable. He would be to be nailed to the cross and left to die.*

*The Syrian trader of animals, the one whose brother Lucius killed, was in the holy city. He approached Pilate when Lucius was tried and begged the opportunity to speak. He identified the gold and diamond pendant Marcellus removed from the neck of the thief as the one always worn by his murdered brother. His word convicted Lucius.*

*Almost mad with anger and fear, Lucius boasted at the top of his voice of the many robberies committed by his band. He screamed the names of other men who participated in the robberies.*

*Finally, he carefully described a large golden-bearded Jew—a Jew he called Josias. He referred to the robber captain Josias many times in his rambling, screaming of the vengeance he— Lucius the Hawk, would savor if only that man could be captured and crucified beside Barabbas, his master.*

251

*Pilate smiled as he sentenced Lucius to crucifixion. "I know nothing of this one you call Josias, thief. I can see that you truly hate the man and wish him ill, but you sir, will be the one to enjoy the privilege of hanging beside Barabbas."*

*When the court was over, Marcellus returned to his quarters and summoned Drusus, his second in command. "Order out ten men and brand the convicted men with a cross on each shoulder to mark them as thieves."*

*Lucius uttered a high, piercing shriek when the white-hot iron pressed into his shoulder. The sound of his screams rang in his ears and the ears of all that heard.*

*His heart ached with the pain of his shame as his shoulder burned from the brand. Ill with hurt, within and without, he finally fell silent.*

*When the soldier approached his cell with the hot iron and motioned for Barabbas to turn his shoulder so he could reach him, he closed his eyes and clenched his teeth against the pain. Somehow, he managed to silence the scream that pushed against his lips, straining his jaws so hard they would ache for days.*

*Barabbas settled on a straw pallet in the corner of his cell. He was nervous, something kept telling him he could not trust the procurator.*

No matter how hard I tried I couldn't catch Pilate's eye during the trial. The man deliberately kept his head turned away—and I have to rely on him to get me out of here.

*Days passed and he received no message. Many times as the execution date drew near, he vowed to send for the Legate and expose Pilate. Twice he even called the guard to his cell door, but changed his mind when he saw the man's face and asked for fresh water or some other trifling thing instead. He finally decided that the best thing he could do was wait.*

I will wait until they carry me out in the street and march me to the hill for execution. There'll be crowds in the streets. Then it will be easy to expose Pilate for the traitor he is. I wonder where the other men are, if they're in Jerusalem. If they are, I fear there'll be a grim harvest of crosses on Golgotha on execution day.

I wonder why Lucius was so adamant that the authorities know Josias in particular—why he seemed to deliberately urge the soldiers seek him. Was he still fuming over Josias success with the kidnapping of that merchant—that Simon whose family paid so well for his safe return?

\*\*\*

*Simon the Cyrenian arrived in Jerusalem for the observance of the Passover on the very day of the trial of Lucius and Barabbas. As usual, he assembled a stock of goods for trade several months earlier. Loading his treasures on mules, he traveled to Alexandria, notwithstanding the rainy season.*

*His wise choice of merchandise and shrewd trading with the merchants of that city earned him such a great profit he was able to afford extra guards to protect him as he traveled the roads to Jerusalem.*

*Simon held a great respect for the prowess of the robbers that roamed the hills of Judea. He received lessons at their hands in the past and had no wish to learn more of them.*

*He traveled with two Greek slaves, given to him by the Mekels of Damascus to protect his person. In addition, he hired six trained mercenaries to protect his train. With such strength he had no fear of making the trip.*

The quality and rarity of Simon's goods caused a great scramble among the merchants of Jerusalem. Each wanted a good supply of goods for resale during the Passover. The city would be full of people.

Simon sold so much at such good prices, he decided to sell his animals and forego the long trip to Damascus and Antioch. He would return directly to Cyrene after the observance.

He attended the large animal sale that was always held near the sheep gate of the city. There he disposed of all his animals, including his riding camel, planning to buy swift horses for him and his Greek slaves to ride on their return to Cyrene.

When the sale was over, he returned to the city and deposited a large quantity of gold with the city's largest and most trusted merchant, Zechariah, a man who was called the leader of David Street. With all of his business complete, Simon went to the Praetorium and sought audience with the Legate.

Ushered into the Legates office, he too refused to sit. Standing before Marcellus desk, he demanded, "Have you made any progress toward the discovery and capture of the thieves who robbed me and held me for ransom these two years past?"

"We are not fully certain, good merchant. There are two men convicted and awaiting execution, however. Come with me, if you please. Let us see if you recognize either of them."

Marcellus threw his cloak around his shoulders and led Simon over to the military headquarters, across the courtyard and into the prison house where Barabbas and Lucius were held. As soon as they approached the cells the merchant stepped forward to point at Lucius. "This is the very one who held me prisoner while I waited for the ransom to be paid."

Swearing, he turned to point at Barabbas. "This is amazing, it is a wonder that you have him. But where is the big *one, the one who over-ran my guards and took me prisoner? He is not here. You must make them tell you how to find that man. I believe he was the most dangerous one of them all."*

*Lucius rushed across the cell to grip the bars with both hands. His eyes glowed with evil, his voice was almost a hiss.*

*"The man you speak of is Josias of Bethany. That's the man I told you about, Roman. The tall man with the golden beard—the one who stands as if he would rule the world."*

# The Malefactors

## Chapter 19

*Mattathah was determined to make the trip to Jerusalem for the observance of Passover. She grew lonely. She feared to try to mix with her neighbors. They all knew Josias' reputation as a highwayman—Josias, her beloved son.*

My life becomes nothing but a succession of grievous hurts. My father's death was the first blow. Then the early death of Ammon, my beloved husband-- that day all but killed me. How my heart still aches for him.

In these, my later years, I lived to see my only son, my golden Josias, scorn the honorable trade I taught him to become a leader of highwaymen. I tried so hard to raise the boy to be a devout follower of the God of Israel.

Life is so cruel and hard to understand.

*A small happiness crept into her heart as she made preparation to leave for the holy city. The few happy times she knew of late were in communion with God, when she attended the small Synagogue of Bethany. There she still met a few faithful friends. Friends who still brought all their scribes work to her. With this* she eked out a living, combining that small income with the fruits of her carefully tended garden.

Throughout the long years since he left home, Josias sent her gold coins. They came by messenger, several times every year. She put all the purses into a stout chest, unopened. She could never bring herself to touch his ill-gotten gold. She knew she would not—not ever—even if she should starve.

One day she sat in her garden, her heart aching with loneliness. She heard a knock at the gate and rushed to open it. Her neighbor from across the road stood there. He told a strange story of a man called Lazarus, a wealthy citizen of Bethany.

"This Lazarus died." The man said, "The women washed his body and he lay in his sepulcher for four days. On the evening of that fourth day he was raised from the dead by Jesus of Nazareth. The prophet—Jesus of Nazareth, the one acclaimed by many of the faithful as the promised one."

"Can this be true?" Mattathah asked, clasping her hand over her mouth in amazement, she shook her head. "How do you know this is true?"

"It is not just a tale, Mattathah, I promise you. Many witnessed this miracle. The people are all excited. They say the prophet will go to Jerusalem during the Passover to call down the wrath of God against the Roman tyrants. Some say the man will set himself up as King of the Jews."

Puzzled and not sure what to believe, Mattathah stared into the man's face as though she could read truth or lie in his expression. "I thank you for telling me this, good neighbor. I am to visit Jerusalem for the Passover. Perhaps I shall see or hear something more there. If I do I will be sure to tell you when I return."

*Mattathah spent the rest of the day in a whirl of excitement. She tried to complete her cleaning and pack for her trip and went over and over the message her neighbor brought her. It became hard for her to keep her mind on her work. She stopped several times to stare out of the window, thinking.*

I will see this promised one when I reach the holy city. I will also find old friends to visit in Jerusalem. Mayhap I'll be able to forget my sadness for a few days. It is even possible I'll see my Josias. He's probably there.

*The afternoon before she planned to leave for Jerusalem, Mattathah hurried into the garden for a last look at her vegetables. She shut the broody hen into a coop with her first chicks. When she was assured all would be well for the few days she would be gone, she started back to the house.*

*When she turned to face the road, she saw a company of Legionnaires march by, headed toward Jerusalem. She knew it was customary throughout the kingdom for each city's centurion to send a part of his soldiers to the Holy City to help keep order during the Passover.*

*Immediately after the body of troops passed, Mary the sister of Lazarus, came hurrying across the road toward her gate.*

*Never before had this woman of Bethany's foremost family visited her humble house. Mattathah almost cried out in amazement. She could remember receiving only a few curt nods from Mary when they passed each other going in or out of the Synagogue. The woman never stopped to greet her.*

*"Good Mother," Mary called out, "Jesus, our Lord, is a guest in our house for a feast this evening. My sister and older brother, knowing of the great grief of thy life, bid me come and ask thee to join us. Our Lord hath comforted many and they believe he will comfort thee."*

Overcome at the woman's words, Mattathah dropped her head into her hands and wept.

Mary touched her shoulder with a soft hand and said, "Weep not, Mother. Come to him and he will bring thee comfort and joy."

Barely able to speak Mattathah raised her head to look at Mary. "I shall come, my daughter. I shall come. It is good of thee and thy family to want me."

When Mary turned away to return to her house, Mattathah went to sit on a bench behind her house. Tears ran down her cheeks, yet she smiled.

It was a long time since anyone bothered to even hail her, much less want her, the mother of a famous thief, to come and dine at his or her house. She felt certain she was hated by all but a few old friends who were indifferent to such things. She had felt that way for many years. The kindness of Mary pierced an armor she built long ago to protect herself from this hatred and indifference.

Finally purged of her weeping, she poured water into her hands and washed her face, to repair as much as possible the ravages of her tears. Removing her apron, Mattathah set out for the home of Lazarus, still not completely sure if she dreamed the visit and the invitation.

As she neared the house of Lazarus she saw many of the people of Bethany gathered in the street before its gates. Although extremely self-conscious, she pushed her way through the crowd until she stood at the gate.

She was greeted by Mary herself, invited in and introduced to Martha and Lazarus, her brother and sister. They greeted her cordially and took her arms to escort her to a place at one of several tables set up in the cool of their garden.

*Mattathah looked about, astonished to see many of the leading women of the city gathered around her table. Beyond them, she could see a man sitting at the next table. Although dark of hair and eyes instead of golden, he bore an astonishing resemblance to Ammon, her long dead husband and to Josias, her son.*

*It was a shock, and almost unbelievable to her. The resemblance seemed uncanny. This man was not so large of stature as her husband and son, and his hair, beard and skin were much darker, but he spoke as Ammon spoke, with the soft, lilting speech of a Galilean.*

*She was unable to stop herself from staring. The man turned and looked her way. His eyes were the grayish-green shade people called hazel, exactly the color of the eyes of her husband and son. She saw something all together different in this man's eyes, however. They did not hold the hard glint of skepticism she remembered seeing in the eyes of Ammon and those of their son. This man's eyes were kind.*

*When the meal was ready, Martha stood at the head of the table where the women were gathered and asked, "Master, wilt thou bless our food?*

*Jesus pushed back his stool and stood erect, looked around the garden. All fell silent.*

*After a moment he lowered his head to speak, "Our Father, who watches over us from Heaven, we are thankful for this day—its trials which strengthen us—its pleasure which brings us joy, and thy great blessings. Bless this house, our generous hosts and all those who have come. Bless the eating of the food, may it strengthen us to better do thy will. Deserving not, we pray thy grace will continue with us. We humbly thank thee our God, Amen."*

*Mattathah felt she had never before heard so quiet and assuring a voice—none more pleasant. It seemed to assure her that*

*God was there with them—that God loved this man and heard his voice when he asked the blessing. "Surely this man must be either the messiah or some other great man of God," she thought.*

*She felt as a child, when her father told her of the great men of God, and knew a deep assurance that she sat in the presence of one equally great.*

*When the meal was eaten and the time of leaving at hand, the guests tried to push through the great crowd gathered before the gates of the house. It seemed impossible to pass through the press of them. All of those gathered begged in loud voices for Jesus to tell of his Father's kingdom. The compelling personality of Jesus, which so affected Mattathah when he blessed the feast, caused her to stay to hear his voice. The multitude called out and called out again for him to preach until he held his hands in the air for quiet and began to speak.*

*In a quiet voice that silenced and calmed the unruly crowd, Jesus talked of the Kingdom of God. He told them of the great beauty of its flowers, its grasses, trees and streams. He described the satisfying work to be done there and the many pleasant hours to be spent discoursing one with another. Many of the people who heard believed on him.*

*Among the people who believed was Mattathah. When all was over and she returned home, she realized her bitter loneliness had disappeared. The ache in her heart was gone.*

*She felt all but overwhelmed by the first true feeling of peace she had known in years. She knew that peace was a gift of Jesus, the Master.*

*The same night, Jesus told the twelve that he must go up to Jerusalem the next day, for the time was near that he must die. All who heard him speak thus were distraught and begged him to* leave at once to travel to a far off land that he might escape the Jews.

He chided them with saying that if a seed was to grow it must first die in order to sprout new life. They understood not, but he said no more. He feared they could not bear it if he told them his mission was to die and arise on the third day.

At that moment, in Jerusalem, Caiaphas the high priest comforted the Pharisees with a plan he devised. He assured the ones who feared the man called Jesus would betray them to the Romans that they were safe. He admonished them to calm themselves, cease such fearful whining—Jesus would die. He would die soon, instead of leading a rumored revolt of the people.

Early the day following, Jesus and the twelve set out afoot from Bethany on the road to Jerusalem. He knew the time of Glorification was near. Mattathah followed closely. After a few miles, she saw ahead of her a golden-haired man accompanied by a beautiful girl. Both were well mounted, he on a bay horse and the girl on a fine, slick-looking black mule. The man seemed familiar. Hurrying her steps, she drew closer so she could see his face.

When she drew near she recognized her son—her Josias. Her feelings were mixed. She was happy to see him. She missed him sorely, yet she was hesitant to make herself known, thinking him still a robber. Before she could slip back into the crowd however, Josias turned and saw her face. He dismounted and ran to her, catching her up in his arms.

"My son, my beloved son," Mattathah cried, tears streaming down her cheeks.

Josias was near to crying as well. He led his mother to where Sarah stood beside her mule, holding the reins of her husband's horse.

*"Mother, this is my wife, Sarah. She convinced me to accompany her here for the Passover."*

*The two women embraced. Tears traced down their cheeks. The mother cried from joy and the wife from sympathy for the distraught mother. Mattathah shook her head and looked about her again completely astonished, wondering if all she saw could be possible.*

Could her wild and reckless Josias be married to this beautiful girl and working as a farmer instead of riding the hills to rob and murder innocent travelers?

Could he have learned to believe in Jesus? Would that move him to give up his life of robbery forever? Surely this was a miracle wrought by this newfound Messiah.

*Jesus and the multitude stopped to rest beside the road in Kidron's Valley before entering the Holy City. As they rested, a young woman came from a house beside the way. She held a golden rope tied around the neck of a white ass and pushed her way through the crowd to where Jesus stood.*

*She smiled and handed the hope to Simon Peter and speaking softly, her words fulfilling the Scripture of old as she said, "I bring this colt for the Master to ride, for the way is long and he looks weary." Those of his followers who knew the ancient words looked at each other and nodded.*

*Mounted on the small white mule, Jesus approached the gates of the city that led from the Woman's Court across Kidron to the Roman-Galilee Road. A great multitude ran before him shouting, "Hosanna, the King has come."*

*The people threw fronds of palm trees for the ass to tread upon. Because they praised him and believed him king, Jesus held his hands high, and blessed the multitude. When they were come into the market place, he dismounted and climbing atop a stone, that all could see his face, he began to preach.*

*When the teaching was finished, Jesus sent John and James, two of the twelve who were sons of Zebedee, to a certain man's house that they might arrange for him and his disciples to sit down in his upper room for the feast of the beginning of Passover.*

*As they left his side, Judas Iscariot, one of the twelve, also slipped away.*

# The Malefactors

# Chapter 20

*Judas Iscariot, the son of Simon Cariot of the tribe of Judah, often acted strangely. He was the last chosen by Jesus and the eldest of the twelve. He seemed always alone. He was ever so, even when he was a child. He forever played alone, going into the hills to walk slowly beside a wadi or sitting without moving or making a sound, watching the sky. Sometimes he appeared lonely, at other times he seemed only disdainful of all.*

*Judas was born near Bar-Sheba, but left that village when quite young. His father disappeared soon after his birth and his mother returned to her people in Moab's Mountains, carrying the tiny boy in her arms. As he grew older, the necessity of helping his mother earn a living caused him to seek in many places any work he was capable of doing.*

*He helped an old man herd sheep in the remote mountains for several years and while he was there, he learned the scribe's trade and the counting of money from the shepherd. The man proved to be quite adept at these crafts, but he preferred the lonely life of a herder to striving in the bustle of the city.*

*When Judas entered his teens, another strong influence entered his life. One day as he searched for two lost sheep, he came upon a man known as Archalous. This man was a rabid, fanatic*

*Herodian. He was idle at the moment, so he took time to make friends with the youngster and soon became a great influence in his life. As a Herodian, he was part of a group of fanatics who favored the overthrow of Rome's dominance over Judea. The group plotted and worked and schemed, trying to find a way to make Herod or one of his kinsmen their king.*

*Many of the Herodians wanted to set up Antipater, the Tetrarch of Galilee as their king, for he was a son of Herod the Great. Most of them were full of an avid lust for power, completely unaware of their utter lack of the attributes necessary to use power should they acquire it. The entire party lacked the strength, ability, influence and wealth necessary to support their dreams.*

*The wild ravings of Archalous, some against the Roman occupiers, some against the Jews and against all progressive people of means, eventually wrought a profound effect on Judas. As he grew up, he developed a deep hatred and resentment of authority and any of its representatives. His only true interest was in the betterment of his own lot.*

*He came to believe he would be most successful in this by working with the Herodians. Therefore, with no qualms of consciousness, he set about doing all things necessary to help their return to power.*

*This desire of Judas to be influential in his own right, caused him to seek membership in the party. The first requirement was that a new member act to prove his dedication and loyalty to the group by committing some crime against Rome's civil law.*

*Obviously, this could be accomplished easiest through robbing one of its citizens. To do this, Judas allied himself with other Herodians who practiced the robber's trade on the many caravans who crossed the great desert to obtain salt from the drying yards south of Masada.*

*Judas and his cohort carried out a succession of raids that proved highly profitable. Not only were they able to sell the goods and supplies they took from the caravans for good returns, they sold the animals they captured to the nomadic Arabs who lived in the desert east of Moab.*

*When the proceeds of the raids were divided, Judas felt himself wealthy. Never before had so much money touched his hands. His ambition helped him to progress rapidly in the party. He was soon rewarded with the appointment of Treasurer. This office was most gratifying for Judas. He felt highly important when he doled out money to one sent to commit some crime against the hated Romans or the Jews. Both were guilty in the eyes of Judas and all Herodians, guilty of sinning against God's law—the Romans for daring to rule God's chosen people and the Jews for condoning the hated rule.*

*As the years passed, Judas grew stronger in the party. One day, some of the members became aware that a large group of Galileans followed Jesus of Nazareth. The man took the place of John, the desert preacher known as the Baptist. After much discussion and argument, the Herodians deemed it wise to align themselves with this man and his followers.*

*Through Jesus and his followers, the leaders believed they would gain enough strength for the overthrow of the Romans. They assumed that if the addition of the mob's strength to theirs could make it possible to defeat Rome it would not be difficult to replace this lowly prophet with Antipater.*

*They chose Antipater because he was a descendent of Herod the Great, surely a man who would make a great leader. Judas was selected to find a way to infiltrate the Galileans.*

*When Judas came to Galilee and followed Jesus, there were only ten disciples. He was present with the others when James, the son of Alpheas, known as the lesser, was chosen. It was then that Judas first conceived the idea of becoming one of Jesus' disciples. He never knew then that God ordained that he would be the Christ's betrayer.*

*Jesus taught at Capernaum. One day he went into the mountains to escape the pressure of a large multitude following him. At the Horns of Hattin, there in the wilderness, he preached the sermon of the Beatitudes. When he finished preaching that day, he chose Judas as a disciple.*

*The magnetic personality of Jesus and the utter fairness of his teachings almost persuaded Judas to turn from his plan of betrayal. The presence of other Herodians and the strength of their influence kept him from abandoning his avowed mission. Not many days passed before Judas became keeper of the monies donated to the disciples by the Master's wealthier converts. He guarded each coin as though it was his very own.*

*When James and John went away from the others to prepare the feast of the Passover, Judas followed them through several streets. After they were well away from the other disciples and there was no danger of his being seen, he slipped into the crowd. As soon as he was sure no one followed and knew his errand, he rushed to find Caiaphas, the High Priest.*

*"Rabbi Caiaphas, I come again from the Herodians to talk of a plan to relieve the suffering Levites. The man called Jesus of Nazareth—the one the Galileans think is the messiah is in Jerusalem for the Passover. Many in the crowds are calling him the King of the Jews. They fully expect he will somehow overthrow the rule of the Romans and set himself up as king.*

*"The plan I bring to you is this. All of the Herodians gathered here have sworn to assist in defeating the accursed*

Romans. We will then proclaim Antipater King instead of this simple prophet."

"This is a prime plan, Judas Iscariot," Caiaphas said, looking at Judas admiringly. "Go thee and set in motion all phases of your plan throughout Judea and I myself will see to Jerusalem."

Judas believed Caiaphas true, never realizing the craftiness of the man. As soon as he rid himself of the betrayer, the High Priest went to his father-in-law Ananias, to tell him of the plans of the Herodians and those of his own followers.

"It is not the throne we must worry over, Caiaphas," Ananias began. "It is the priests. The heresy of this Nazarene will convince the people they no longer need the services of the priests and cause them to be cast out of the temples. Another worry is this, if this man leads the people to a revolt and fails, the Emperor will carry out his long time threat of disbursement. He will scatter the Jews over many lands.

"I have little liking for either result." Angry, Ananias almost spat the words. "To avoid suspicion, I advise you to let the Herodians gather as they will--the same for the followers of Jesus. We will devise a plan to have this prophet killed. That way we can spoil the plans of both parties and so continue as we are. All is not perfect, I realize, but we are comfortable.

"Think, Caiaphas, think." Ananias shouted, pounding on the arm of his chair. "You must agree that no system could be better than the one we now have. The Romans protect us and do not interfere with our religious law enough to worry anyone. The tithe of the temple and profit of the money changing and sale of sacrificial animals supports us. The Procurator, Pontius Pilate fears us. How can we hope to better our lot? Encourage the Herodians in their plans and inform the priests to stay in the temple court against our need of them."

*As Caiaphas walked toward the temple he thought over all that Ananias said. He knew that the wife of Pilate, Claudia, forced the Roman to steal from the Temple treasury to build the great aqueduct at Caesarea and the fountains in the gardens of the Insula here in Jerusalem. After that first theft, Ananias was able to bend Pilate to his will. The man lived under the threat of Ananias supplying the Emperor Tiberius the truth of his theft. That would cause no less than Pilate's recall to Rome and then his official banishment. It is very likely it would cost him his life.*

*Word was sent out and many priests gathered in the temple courts as Ananias advised. The old man wanted them nearby to keep the Herodians and followers of Jesus from gaining control, should the Roman's be defeated. The numbers of the rabble was so great they were always in the majority.*

*Throughout his tenure as Procurator, Pilate constantly baited the Jews. He flaunted Caesar's image and that of the eagle. He forced Jewish men to labor on the Sabbath. On more than one occasion, he confiscated temple funds. He did whatever he could to anger them. The Jews in turn made every effort to torment Pilate. They rioted for no reason, threw stones at passing legionnaires and continuously protested something to Pilate. An endless number protested directly to Caesar Tiberius. On top of everything else, they found endless ways to evade paying taxes.*

*Yet withal, the greatest troubles either side knew were brought to them when Jesus scourged the moneychangers and chased them from the temple. The priests all ran howling to Caiaphas. He in turn went to Ananias who sent him before Pilate to complain of the Empire not keeping order in the city.*

*The Legate Gordias was forced to keep soldiers patrolling night and day to quell riots in cities and villages. Finally he was killed during an uprising. Emperor Tiberius received an endless flow of complaints and Pilate refused to return to Caesarea, fearful of traveling during the unrest.*

*Ananias sought to avoid a recurrence of this miserable time. He ordered the priests to keep control of the majority of the temple courts at all times. His scheming was not over, for he knew he must devise a means of forcing Pilate to order the execution of this Galilean heretic.*

*After Judas proposed his plan for betrayal to Caiaphas, he returned to his place among the disciples in time to share the Passover supper with Jesus and the eleven others. As he came into the room, one of the men asked of him where he had been for the last hours.*

*"I have been striving to repair the condition of our purse." Judas answered. "Am I not forced to provide for the wants of all?"*

*When the meal and the observance of the first feast of Passover were complete, Jesus and the twelve returned to Bethany.*

# The Malefactors

# Chapter 21

*On the second day of Passover, many believers set out from Bethany to follow Jesus and his disciples to Jerusalem. Among the teeming crowds were Josias, his wife and his mother. When they found the temple courts unmanageably crowded, many of the faithful left to call on relatives or walk about the town and see the sights, planning to return to attend other services later in the day.*

*After hearing the service in the temple, Josias escorted Sarah and Mattathah along the streets to show them the beauty of Herod's Temple. They also visited the Insula and its beautiful gardens, the Towers of Antonia and the Praetorium.*

*As they came near to the sheep gate, a tall Centurion, accompanied by six soldiers, stepped into their path and demanded, "Are you the man known as Josias of Bethany?"*

*Unnerved, Josias could only stare at the man.*

*The Centurion raised his voice and demanded, "Are you the one known as Josias?"*

*Josias finally found his voice and answered, "I am."*

*Drusus turned to his soldiers and ordered, "Seize this man. Take him to the prison."*

*Two soldiers stepped forward, took Josias by either arm and set out for the prison, all but dragging him between them.*

*Drusus the Centurion followed, offering the astonished women no explanation. Filled with dread, they followed. The guard stopped them at the prison gate. Sarah pleaded, "But sir, please. They have taken my husband—I must find out why."*

*The soldier pointed to the Insula. "Go there—to the audience room of the Procurator. When the scribe asks your business you can explain what happened to your man. Perhaps he can help you. I cannot."*

*When the soldiers arrived at the prison with Josias they waited outside the door, still holding him between them, while Drusus entered the quarters of the Legate. "Come then, bring the man to the cell of Lucius." Marcellus said, leaving his desk to follow Drusus.*

*When they arrived at the cells, Lucius again moved to the front of his cell and held the bars with both hands. He grinned evilly at the sight of Josias held harmless by the strong hands of the two soldiers.*

*"Is this the man you keep describing?" Marcellus demanded.*

*"Yes he is, he's the one. He served as the leader of Barabbas' second band—the one that operated along the Caesarea road. He's the one who captured the merchant we held for ransom."*

*Marcellus turned to the cell of Barabbas, shouting. "Get on your feet, man. Come over here and look at this prisoner. Was this man in league with you? Is he the one known as Josias your second in command?"*

*"I never laid eyes on this man before," Barabbas stared at Marcellus and fairly growled his answer—never turning his head in Josias' direction.*

*"He lies. He is a foul liar. They have made some plan between them. That one may be planning to help Barabbas*

escape—that's probably the reason he is in Jerusalem." Lucius shouted, "Send for the merchant—the one we held for ransom. He'll swear I tell you the truth."

Marcellus looked up into Josias eyes. "What do you say for yourself man, are you a highwayman? Are you this man's second in command as this prisoner says? Answer me—answer me, I say."

Josias stared back at the Roman. After a moment he said, "I am a follower of Jesus of Nazareth."

"Ha—a follower of Jesus indeed." Lucius burst out. "If you follow the man it must be you intend to rob him."

"Jail this man until we find the Cyrenian. He will speak the truth." Marcellus said to the guards as he turned to leave the prison.

On the morning of the third day, Marcellus persuaded Pilate to reopen his court to try a special case. Josias was dragged before the procurator, his arms tied behind him. The Legate accused him of robbing caravans.

Pilate looked down from his chair. "Are you guilty of robbing merchants and travelers as the Legate charges?"

"I am a follower of Jesus of Nazareth," Josias said. This was the only answer he would give, repeating it several times.

"What say you to this, Legate?"

"Procurator, the one called Lucius, the man you ordered crucified for the Syrian's death, accuses this man of robbery. He says he led a band for the thief Barabbas. He also says this man is the one who robbed and held for ransom the Cyrenian that Caesar has troubled us so much about. He is here to testify against the man."

"Is this Cyrenian not a Jew also?" Pilate all but sneered.

"He is, but he is considered a man of honor and is a citizen of Rome."

At a nod from Pilate, Sylvanius called out, "Simon of Cyrene, citizen of Rome. Come you forward and give testimony for the Empire."

The merchant rose from his seat and stepped forward. He swore allegiance to the Empire and turned to face Pilate.

"Merchant, can you identify this man?"

"I can, your honor. He is the leader of those who slew my guards, took my animals and goods and received the ransom for my release. It was almost a year after my release that I saw him traveling on the Damascus Road. Do you remember taking his description when I came before you to complain, Procurator?"

"Yes, I believe I do remember." Turning to Sylvanius Pilate said, "Get me the record of this man's complaint."

When the record of the complaint was found, the recorded description fitted Josias without question.

"What of the money from the goods and ransom, thief? Where is it?" Pilate demanded.

Josias stared at the floor, refusing to answer.

Simon stepped forward to say, "This man received only a portion of the money, Pilate. There was a leader over him. It was to that man the ransom was finally paid."

"Would you recognize this leader if you saw him?"

"The man's face was covered when I was taken before him, your honor, but I swear to you, never will I forget his voice."

Pilate sat silent for a few moments. A light seemed to shine from his eyes as he stared over the audience room. Turning to Sylvanius he ordered, "Have Barabbas brought to this court immediately."

When Drusus left to bring Barabbas from the prison, Pilate turned to Simon. "Come past me here Sir, and hide behind this green curtain. Keep silent and listen as I question this man."

Drusus soon returned, shoving a bound Barabbas before him.

Pilate looked down from his seat, "Barabbas. Do you know this prisoner?"

"No your honor. I do not. I have never before seen this man until he was arrested and brought to the prison yesterday." Barabbas' voice was harsh and loud. "I was asked this question then and I answered it the same way."

"You are quite sure you speak the truth?"

"Yes, I speak the truth." Barabbas answered with an oath. Staring into Pilates' eyes he demanded, "What will it gain me to lie now? Have you not sentenced me to die on the cross and had me cruelly branded as a thief?"

Pilate turned his head to motion for Drusus to take Barabbas away. He leaned forward and whispered to Sylvanius to bring Simon from behind the curtain.

"Well merchant? Did you recognize the man's voice?"

"I did indeed. That was the voice of the man I was taken before the night of my capture. There is no doubt in my mind."

"I thought as much." He turned to Marcellus. "Let this one die with the other two."

Sarah and Mattathah spent the day in the great audience room the day before, hoping for an opportunity to speak, but being ignored by Sylvanius. They returned early this morning, in time to see Josias condemned. They approached the Legate to ask to see Josias, but he waved them away, striding past them without speaking. The two women clung to each other, bewildered over the speedy succession of events and grieved beyond consolation.

*Marcellus ordered Drusus to forgo the customary branding of the third malefactor. He could not explain to himself why he did this. He finally decided it was that he believed this prisoner could not be all bad. He appeared to be just a wild, impetuous youth who had somehow come under the influence of the wrong people.*

*Josias could not define his own feelings. He always expected to be caught and punished for his many evil deeds. For many years he believed it inevitable. This though—this timing was terrible.*

If only they had caught me before I met Sarah. That I should bring this shame on the Master or on Sarah my beloved wife and her family is hard to bear. I have betrayed all those who trusted me. This is the worst. It will surely kill my poor mother.

*His heart aching, he dropped to the stone floor and buried his face in his hands, tormented by his thoughts.* Why have I included he who calls himself Master in those I worry about? Why do I cringe at the thought of bringing shame on him? Why did I twice answer that I was a follower of Jesus of Nazareth when the Procurator accused me?

I am sure this weak Galilean could not possibly be the promised king. What matters all that to me anyway? I have only a few days left of this life. This is a bitter cup I must drink. Oh my Sarah—my beloved wife.

*Sarah watched as the soldiers led Josias from the room. His head drooped almost to his chest and his hair fell forward, almost hiding his face. He saw only the floor. He never knew the women stood there, witnessing his shame. When he passed through the doorway and out of sight, Sarah began to sob aloud.*

*Mattathah took the bewildered girl into her arms. "Oh, my poor child. I feared this might happen. Did you not know before* now that my son is a notorious highwayman and robber of merchants and caravans?"

"Oh, do not say such foolish things. My Josias a highwayman and robber?" She almost laughed aloud, shaking her head as she stated emphatically, "I will not believe such lies. My Josias is too kind—it cannot be—my father—every one in Ramah loved him for his gentle nature."

When she stopped the rush of words Sarah stared at her husband's mother. The truth was in her eyes. Finally accepting, she cried aloud, wiping her tears with her hands. When her tears were spent, she was as one dumbfounded.

After a few moments, Mattathah realized she was not in an understandable state of grief, or unconscious from it, but as one in a state of severe shock. Mattathah petted her and whispered consolingly for hours before she could persuade Sarah to leave the Praetorium grounds and return to her home in Bethany.

Worried that she might be arrested and fearful that Sarah had suffered some irreparable damage in her grief, Mattathah spent many hours trying to console the girl. She resorted to telling her of her family. She told how her father was so proud when she was born, so late in his life. How he named her Mattathah, meaning a gift of God in the old Hebrew tongue.

She told the girl of Josias' father Ammon—of her great love for him and the almost unbearable grief she suffered when he was killed. She told how her father died soon after Ammon, leaving her to fend for herself, raising her young son alone. She described the helplessness she felt when her Josias turned to a life of crime and confessed that she felt even God turned against her.

Her words made no change. Sarah was grief stricken beyond Mattathah's understanding. As she had grown older, Mattathah became inured to grief—she experienced little else in *her life. Sarah grew up the much-petted only child of loving parents and the adored bride of the husband of her choice. During small periods of time when Sarah lay asleep and she dared leave the girl, Mattathah was troubled by tumultuous thoughts.*

What will happen? What will be the outcome of Josias' arrest? Oh my God no—no—I know the truth in my heart—I know what will happen. The Romans will execute him on the cross. That is their custom. They will execute him on the cross before the entire population. It would take a miracle to save him.

The Nazarene—Jesus could save him. He has performed many miracles. But I know that will never happen. I know he could prevent Josias death, but he will not. God's way with me has always been that I must suffer the earthly consequences of my sins although I may be forgiven the spiritual ones. I must follow God's plan. I must accept his will to sit at a table laden with the consequences of my sins, though they are long forgiven. Thus it has always been for such as me.

*Mattathah comforted herself with the knowledge that she could only care for the girl as best she could, pray for her beloved son, and await whatever might come.*

# Chapter 22

On the second morning, when Jesus finished his communion with the Father, he returned to his followers. They waited patiently beside the Galilee Road on the Mount of Olives. Without speaking, he walked down from the mount into Kidron and stopped before a barren fig tree.

He pointed the tree out to the multitude and said, "If a man does not work for good, he too is barren and both should die."

To the amazement of all, the tree began to wither and die before their eyes. Many whispered as they watched and spoke of this. Minutes passed—and Jesus walked on, with the people following.

As Jesus and his followers entered the Golden Gate, many priests scurried through the temple courts warning the moneychangers and sellers of sacrificial animals of his coming. Many feared he would again raise a whip and chase them from the holy place.

Caiaphas, when warned of Jesus' coming, sent many Pharisees and priests to reckon with the man. He hoped to prove him guilty of some heresy. Jesus answered many of the priest's questions with a question of his own. Most of these they dared not answer.

*Some of their questions Jesus answered with parables, using that of the lost son who returned to his father, the wicked husbandman and the King's son, to render unto Caesar that which is Caesar's and unto God that which is God's and many others. The weight and logic of his answers proved the priests naught but tempters, trying to find a way to trap him.*

*Failing in their purpose, the Jewish leaders went away, for they dared not arrest Jesus in fear of the reaction of the multitude of people following him. They left him, marveling that he could not be trapped in the maze of Jewish law.*

*After the Pharisees and priests left, Jesus and his followers crossed the Women's Court and came to the outer porch of the temple. Here the priest-merchants sat laughing and talking idly as they plied their wares. Upon seeing the Nazarene enter their guilt drove them to rush about, grab up their money tables and run away, driving their animals before them.*

*The moneychangers carried the guilt of shortchanging those who were unaware of exchange values. The vendors of animals often sold to the unwary, trusting souls, animals they knew the priests would turn away as blemished and not fit to sacrifice. They would then buy the animal back for only a portion of its cost and later they would sell it to another worshiper. All would gather at the end of each day to divide their profits. The knowledge of their perfidy and the accusing eyes of the strange Galilean were more than they could face.*

*When all left the temple except the disciples and the people who believed on him, Jesus discoursed of the Pharisees. He told how they bid others to obey the laws of Moses, but kept it not themselves. He explained how they sought for themselves the best and gave in return the least. To those who heard his voice he counseled that to be served, one must first serve. That to be first, one must begin by* being last—to give orders, one must first obey—to be paid, one must first pay.

He raised his voice as he charged, "there is only one Master. One Christ, and one God, the Father of mankind."

All these things he said unto them, afterward leading all those who believed into the temple yard beside the great fountain. Here he pointed to the beauty of the temple and its magnificent ornaments. He prophesied that someday there would not be one of the great stones left in place, that God would cause the temple's destruction to pay for Judea's sins.

When he finished speaking of the temple, the people followed him again as he walked toward the Mount of Olives. As Jesus passed through the Golden Gate, one of the lesser priests ran forward screaming "blasphemer." He cast a stone that dropped near the Master's feet.

Standing in the shade of an olive tree at the summit of the mount, Jesus was asked by James, the son of Alphaeus, one of his disciples, when these wonders he spoke of would occur. Turning to the man, Jesus answered, "Only God the Father knows when these prophecies will be fulfilled."

He charged them to ever be ready. For, he said, no man knew when, "Only God knew of his coming and going."

Jesus told the multitude gathered of the coming destruction of Jerusalem and the utter devastation sin would bring. He told them it would be far better if all died before that day than suffer the terrors to come. Again he told them of the greatness of God's Kingdom, comparing it to the widow's mite and the parables of the virgins and talents.

While he yet spoke to the faithful, Judas Iscariot, condemned of God, left the Master's presence and went into the city seeking another audience with Caiaphas, the high priest. Judas thought Caiaphas was in accord with the Herodian's plan to overthrow the Romans and make the Nazarene king so they could later overthrow him in favor of the Herodians. In that certainty, he plotted with the Levite to identify Jesus with a kiss, when the soldiers came to escort him into the city to lead the revolt.

The betrayer hurried as he returned to the disciples, unaware that Caiaphas intended Jesus to be crucified along with the other prisoners of the Romans. The high priest Caiaphas could demand of Pilate that he suffer this, for had the Galilean not said to all that he was king, setting himself above Caesar?

Pilate was also in the midst of deep intrigue. The time drew near when Barabbas was to die and he must devise some plan to circumvent this lest the robber tell all and implicate him in his depredations. Surely there was some way to free Barabbas. If Marcellus were less zealous in his assignments a bag of gold should suffice, but no, the man could not be reached that way. As he sat brooding over his problem, Sylvanius entered the room.

"Sylvanius, you were wily enough to get me into this fearful state, tell me a way out."

"You blame me, Sir? You blame me for the acts of that betrayer—of that low-born swine of a Lucius?"

Pilate did not answer, but turned away. Sylvanius sat pondering the question. He knew full well that if Barabbas revealed Pilate's involvement in his activities to the legate, Pilate in turn would not hesitate to implicate Sylvanius as his accomplice. Like Pilate, he was in no way desirous of suffering the cross.

After a while it came to Sylvanius that the Jews held some foolish ideas about forgiveness. They practiced some primitive superstition about casting out all debts every seven years and a ritual of freeing a prisoner on the Passover. That was it. He would have several of the temple priests who owed him favors, demand of

Pilate the release of Barabbas in accordance with the ancient custom.

After thinking the plan through several times, Sylvanius explained it to Pilate. "This is what we can do, to free the man without any possibility of the Legate understanding what we really want."

"By the gods, Sylvanius, you have it—you actually have it." Pilate slapped his knee and laughed aloud. "This relieves my mind more than my escape from the Gauls at Treves did those many years ago. Hurry to the prison and tell Barabbas of this plan before he decides to talk to someone of our involvement in his robberies. Make sure no one overhears you."

Sylvanius wrapped his cloak around his shoulders and scurried from the audience room, almost running across the vast courtyard toward Barabbas' cell. He was not alone in the darkness. Judas also moved about the city, his head well covered and held low so his face could not be seen.

When Judas arrived back at the mount he found the others gone. He hurriedly returned to the city, hoping to overtake them. He did not know that Jesus told the others that he would be betrayed to his death and be resurrected. He had no idea that the disciples waited for their master to point out his betrayer by giving him a sop. He did not hear Jesus tell the disciples that they should not grieve over his death, explaining that only by his death could mankind be redeemed.

Jesus and his disciples gathered with him in the upper room. He took up a loaf of bread, blessed it, broke it and gave to all to eat. The wine he also blessed, giving thanks to the Father for his bounty. Afterward, he sipped of the wine and passed the cup around the table that all might join him. He charged each disciple to see that this act be repeated regularly, in remembrance of him.

*When the cup returned to his hand, he placed it before him. Taking up a loaf of bread he broke off a piece and dipped it into a dish of honey. Without a word, he turned and handed Judas the sop.*

*Smiling, happy that Jesus so favored him—Judas looked into the Master's eyes as he held out his right hand to receive the bread and honey. He remained unaware of the looks of loathing and hatred on the faces of the eleven other men gathered around the table.*

*Jesus announced that he would return to Gethsemane for prayer. As they left the house where they ate supper, Judas hurried away again. He rushed through the city streets to Caiaphas with news of where the Nazarene could be found.*

*The others followed Jesus. On their way to the garden, the master foretold of Peter's denials of him. The fisherman protested violently, almost screaming in his anger, then falling silent, to sulk.*

*Jesus prayed with the disciples first, then instructed them to stay where they were and await his return, for he wished to commune alone in the darkness.*

*It was late when he returned, and Judas Iscariot was again with the rest of the disciples. As Jesus came out of the garden, a large group of temple guards approached him. The betrayer gave his signal and the guards rushed forward to seize the Nazarene by either arm.*

*Simon Peter, in great, turbulent anger, seized a guard's sword and swinging it high, cut an ear from one of the men who held the Master's arms. Jesus remonstrated with Peter and announced to all that he would go peacefully with the guards.*

*Of the twelve who followed the soldiers and their master into the city, all were grievously worried over his fate except the one. He was assured of the Master's safety by no less than Caiaphas, the high priest. Judas watched calmly as the guards led Jesus away, not to the prison, no. Judas believed he would be taken to a place of comfort in the temple and cared for by the servants of the priests.*

# The Malefactors

# Chapter 23

*In the cells of the prison, Josias and Barabbas were much wearied of Lucius' voice. For many days he bragged at the top of his voice naming himself the greatest robber of all. He shouted and yelled continously, arguing that he was the best and wiliest fighter and the strongest man in all Judea.*

*Ranting throughout day and night, over and over he raised his voice to exclaim how the great Barabbas and Josias the favored one, would be no better than he—Lucius, a slave—when they all hung from crosses on the hill at Golgotha.*

*He marched from one end of his cell to the other, laughing and bragging at the top of his voice, insisting it would be worth forfeiting his life to see the two men condemned thus. As he ranted, he claimed it repaid the two of them for the years that they dared to treat him as a lessor person.*

*Josias concluded the man raved in an effort to cover up his fear of the approaching end. He said nothing, but spent his time thinking. Barabbas held his head in his hands and cursed Lucius as a nuisance.*

*The shame Josias felt was far greater than his fear. For years, he resigned himself to the possibility of being found out, captured by the authorities and punished for the many times and* many ways he defied Rome's law. His great regret was that he was not been caught before he found a worthwhile life with his beloved Sarah.

The shame he would face when hanged naked on the cross before the entire population was great, but that would be much smaller than the shame he would feel when Sarah and his mother looked up to see him hanging there. A wild feeling of urgency to escape this fate surged through his chest and almost panicked him, but he closed his eyes, dropped his head back against the wall and finally calmed, gaining control of his emotions.

Barabbas knew no feelings of shame, but was pressed by a great and growing worry over his predicament. Pilate's promise to protect him still rang in his ears, but it was no longer reassuring to him. The final day grew near and he still heard nothing—nothing at all. Thoughts of the cross—of hanging naked, nailed to the cross—haunted him.

Many times he was tempted to send for the Legate and tell him of Pilate's involvement in his depredations, but each time he did not. He held out a small sliver of hope that Pilate would eventually concoct some plan to see him free at the last moment. Besides, he knew that if he told the Legate everything it still would not save his life.

He fretted so much, day in and day out, that he was almost unable to keep himself silent. He grew furious at the sound of Lucius' wild ranting. It seemed to never cease. His only consoling thoughts were of the many pleasures his violent life gave him. Yet at times he was swept by a terrible wave of despair, for he knew the cross would be a high price to pay for any pleasures.

\*\*\*

Angry and full of fear at the sound of the curses and threats the people of Jerusalem hurled at them, the temple guards hurried, pulling Jesus along with them to the palace of Caiaphas for his trial. When the Nazarene was ushered into the audience room his only companion was John, the disciple he most loved. Simon Peter stayed without, never entering the temple, fulfilling Jesus' prophecy that the fisherman would deny the master before the crowing of the cock.

Jesus stood in the chamber for many hours. The guards lounged about. Finally, the Sanhedrin gathered for his trial. Following the testimony of a horde of false witnesses, the judges condemned Jesus for his blasphemy.

Caiaphas felt grievously wronged that Roman law forbade him to personally sentence the Nazarene to death. It was a bitter pill. But he knew he had only to send the man before Pilate and he would be sent to the cross.

The expression on the Procurator's face and harshness of his voice demonstrated the extent of his anger at being called to the hearing room at so early an hour. He rudely interrupted Caiaphas' testimony and ordered the temple guards to carry Jesus before Antipater, the Tetrarch of Galilee sneering at Caiaphas as he asked, "is the man not of that province?"

But Antipater cared nothing for matters of state. He sought only wealth and pleasure. He refused to even hear the case, much less make a decision and ordered the guards to take Jesus back again before Pilate.

Sylvanius, thinking of his own welfare, went to Pilate and suggested that he remind the Jews of their customary act of manumission on this, their holiest day. He whispered to Pilate that in so doing he could appear to favor freeing Jesus, then he, Sylvanius could demand Barabbas' freedom when the priests clamored for Jesus' blood. If he did this, Pilate could keep his promise to the *robber leader—a promise that would allow he and Sylvanius to escape implication in any wrongdoing.*

*Pilate stood and announced to the crowd. "I see no wrong in the man." The crowd roared. Motioning for quiet, Pilate continued speaking, "Free him according to the custom of your Passover, I urge you."*

*Prompted by Caiaphas, the priests screamed repeatedly, "Crucify the blasphemer. Crucify the blasphemer."*

*There began a great shouting throughout the hall. There were those who were urged by Sylvanius loud voice saying over and over, "Free Barabbas. Free Barabbas."*

*Others who were urged on by Caiaphas and the other priests, continued to call out, "Crucify the Nazarene, Crucify the blasphemer."*

*Pilate called for a servant to bring him a bowl of water. He waved his hands and then ceremoniously dipped them both in the water, at the same time. "I see no guilt in this man and wash my hands of the whole affair. Nevertheless, we can do nothing less than write orders to the Legate to crucify this Jesus of Nazareth and release the highwayman called Barabbas as this crowd demands."*

*Pilate, fearful of serious objections from Marcellus the Legate over this strange turn of events, sent a message ordering the Legate to be relieved of the duty of overseeing the execution. He ordered him to take a patrol outside the city walls to keep order among those who raced animals. To manage as well the crowds who attended the races and were loud and profane as they wagered on their favorites.*

*Happy to escape the grisly task of overseeing the planned crucifixions, the unsuspecting Marcellus appointed Sextus Tullus, the Centurion of Masada, who was in the city to help keep order during the Passover, to carry out the executions. He then hurried to leave the city, riding at the head of his patrol, unaware of Sylvanius and Pilate's maneuvering.*

*Sylvanius arrived at the Praetorium just as Marcellus and his patrol left. Fear of the honest soldier caused him to remain quiet about the change in events. He sought out Tullus, the commander who was to relieve Marcellus. He found him in the courtyard adjoining the parade area busy assembling his patrol. Waiting until he heard the sound of Marcellus's patrol leaving the area, Sylvanius approached Tullus.*

*"You are ordered by the Procurator to take your patrol and carry out the executions."*

*"Why this last minute change? I thought the Legate himself was supposed to have this duty."*

*Sylvanius lowered his eyes and looked away. "I am only a scribe. I know only to obey the orders as given me by the Procurator. I do not question his decisions."*

*When the patrol left to receive the Nazarene from the temple guards, Sylvanius went to the bars of Barabbas cell and whispered, "Your friend Pilate has gained your freedom. Your life is to be spared under the old law of the grace of the first day of the Passover. Pilate orders also that once you are free, you must leave the city before darkness this day and never return."*

*Barabbas wanted to laugh and shout aloud in his joy and relief, but he held his peace. He knew if anyone else found out about his release, something or someone might warn the soldiers. They would never allow him to leave. He may have escaped the cross, but he would never escape their swords.*

*Meanwhile, Pilate returned to the palace sitting room to relax. He took a cup of rich wine and lay on the soft cushions of his favorite couch, listening to the softly whispering waters of his fountain. He stretched out on the couch as he had many times before after his many verbal bouts with his subjects--bouts that were completely unsavory to him. This time he found he could not relax. He could not even sleep. Open or closed, his eyes saw only the accusing expression in the piercing eyes of the Nazarene.*

*"Curse the man." He said aloud. "He is nothing—only another one of those damned Jew fanatics."*

*Throughout the trial, every time the man caught his eye, Pilate remembered feeling that he and all others in the chamber were on trial before the man, instead of they trying him. Now, he could not get the haunting look of the man out of his mind.*

*"Curse him," he complained to the empty room as he turned his cup up and emptied it. "Curse all Jews, and curse Tiberius for sending me to so desolate a place to deal with these strange fanatics."*

*Passing along the hallway, Claudia heard the angry note in her husband's voice, curious, she entered the room to ask, "Is it that you are not feeling well Pontius?"*

*Pilate did not answer. He turned his head to face the wall and ignored her. After a few moments, she shrugged and left the room.*

*Pontius Pilate, the Procurator of Judea sat brooding many days. He became so fearful of everyone that he allowed only Sylvanius and Claudia to enter his chambers and refused to leave them. He never left his rooms after the day he allowed the Nazarene to be condemned.*

*One evening Sylvanius brought him word of Marcellus' recall to Rome and the appointment of Quintus to replace him. It was the last time Pilate allowed Sylvanius admission to his rooms. Only Claudia was allowed to enter his quarters and she complained bitterly of her duty.*

*Months later, Claudia came to Pilate with a message from Quintus. He said a group of Samaritans worshipped their God against Pilate's express orders. They worshipped the one called Yahweh. Pilate sent word back to the Legate to take a patrol to Mount Garizim and slay all that worshipped there.*

*The Legate obeyed his orders. The Jewish people screamed loudly, for Rome had promised them religious liberty. Many wrote letters to the Emperor. They even sent emissaries to Rome in protest. Tiberius recalled Pilate for this act.*

# The Malefactors

# Chapter 24

*Jesus stood on the parade ground before the prison. Part of the patrol stood nearby, guarding him. The other soldiers led the three convicted robbers from the depths of the dungeons. Tullus ordered the blacksmith to strike off the chains that bound Barabbas ankles and the ones that held his hands behind his back.*

*When he saw what the guards were doing Lucius began to scream invective mixed with the vilest of curses. Finally one of the legionnaires struck him with the side of his pike as he harshly ordered him to be quiet. Josias reacted with amazement. His heart filled with grief to see Jesus put in Barabbas' place for the execution. He could only stare at the bowed head of the Master.*

*As soon as his arms and legs were freed, Barabbas ran from the parade ground. Keeping to the back streets, he scurried through the city to his old hangout in the wine shop on David Street. He had no money, but finding his old room empty; he threw himself down on a pile of rags. He lay thus for hours, completely exhausted. His body relaxed from the tension of the past week and the wild exhilaration he felt over regaining his freedom.*

*He rested into the night before he walked to the stair and called a serving girl from the bar. He ordered her to fetch Argubus to him and returned to the room to wait. When the old man* arrived, he dispatched him to prepare food to revive him and bring him certain packs hidden in the old meeting room within the city wall. When Argubus returned he sent him to purchase and pack sufficient travel rations to sustain him when he fled the city.

Without regret, Barabbas fled the city of Jerusalem in the night. Weeks later, after traveling many nights while avoiding people, stealing food to augment his sparse funds and walking endless miles, he arrived at Caesarea. Determined to go far enough away from Judea so he could never meet any that knew his face, he took passage on a small ship bound for Tyre.

The ship was unable to go directly across the wide, turbulent waters of the Mediterranean because of its small size. It made its way carefully around the coast near shore. When they came abreast of the hills north of Mount Carmel, where the rugged mountains of Lebanon jut out into the sea, a pirate ship shot out from behind a promontory and attacked. It was only a matter of minutes before the pirates overcame the crew, capturing the ship and its passengers.

Any members of the crew who were too badly wounded to work were summarily dispatched and their bodies cast overboard. Two Jewish merchants made ransom bargains with the pirates, immediately changing themselves from prisoners to honored guests.

The pirate chief preemptory ordered Barabbas to surrender the expensive hand-woven robe he wore. When he removed it, the man could saw the crosses branded on his shoulders—the mark of a thief.

"So, you escaped the Roman cross, did you?" The pirate leader grinned as he pointed to the barely healed scars.

"No." Barabbas insisted angrily. "I was pardoned by demand of the priests of Jerusalem. "

*The pirate leader laughed aloud. Finally sobering he continued to grin at Barabbas as he said, "I am most amused. Since you are such an important man, we will chain you to the end seat of the galley. An oar should amuse you until the priests again demand your freedom."*

*Barabbas paled. His heart seemed to fall at his feet. With the help of Pilate he escaped his fate in Jerusalem, but ran head-on to one much worse. He knew the iron collar that chained a man to his seat at the end of a lead oar on the galley would be as sure a death, if much slower, as the cross.*

*** 

*After Barabbas left the parade ground, Tullus order Josias, Lucius and Jesus to shoulder the crosses lying on the stones close by the prison walls. The crosses were recently cut from living trees, extremely heavy and difficult to carry. Lifting the weight of the cross was especially difficult for Jesus. Although ordinarily quite strong, he had been without food or rest since the morning before.*

*Portions of the guard preceded the prisoners and the rest followed as they marched into Jerusalem's main north-south street. This street would come to be called the Via Delorosa, or the way of sadness, by those who loved the Nazarene.*

*The long, humiliating march began. Holding the crosspieces on their shoulders, the heavily laden men made their way between great throngs of the devout on their way to the temple. Other crowds of people tried to make their way to the other side of the city and Golgotha, the hill of the skull.*

*Josias saw Jesus stumble under the weight of the heavy cross. He knew why they cut new crosses from living wood for each crucifixion. Using newly cut wood would make it easier to drive in the great iron spikes they used to attach the condemned ones' hands and feet to the cross. As he watched the Nazarene, he felt an almost overwhelming urge to drop his own burden and help the man shoulder the heavy beam, but knew he could not.*

*He moved forward, the edge of the heavy beam cut into his shoulders, and asked himself over and over--w*hy is it that I want so badly to help this man? I have never felt so toward anyone before.

*Simon the merchant hurried along the street toward the Temple. He did not want to miss the new cantor as he sang the Psalms of deliverance for Passover. He was much annoyed as he pushed through the crowds to be forced to stand aside and await the passing of a patrol guarding condemned criminals.*

*Glancing at the prisoners, he met Jesus' eyes. The man's expression was full of agony. He stumbled, bent low beneath the heavy cross. Simon never before experienced so strong a feeling of compassion. All his life he lived as a devout Jew. He believed the teachings of Moses and the Prophets. He knew the laws and remembered an eye for an eye and a tooth for a tooth. He observed the law and journeyed to the temple each feast day. This feeling was new and strange.*

*Jesus saw Simon's bewilderment and mentally forgave him his sins. Moved by something he could not understand, Simon reached out his hand and stepped forward to help the Master.*

*Tallus shouted, "If you would help the criminal, shoulder the cross, for he is too weak to carry it to the hill. If you cannot help then move away so we can proceed."*

*Pressing the crowds to the side of the street, the patrol hurried the condemned men and Simon toward Golgotha. Instead of the customary cries of derision, laughter and mockery there was an eerie silence. Instead of hurling filth at the men, as was always and forever the custom, this crowd stood back. Some met the*

*Master's eyes and were awed. Other appeared to be stunned. Still others bowed their heads and hid their faces, overcome with grief.*

*Josias looked about him and felt a thrill of excitement. Often in the past he was one of a crowd who shouted in derision and threw all manner of waste at the condemned men as they struggled along the street dragging the heavy crosses. To see the long established custom so changed was almost unbelievable to him.*

*At one of the turnings in the narrow way, a group of Jesus' disciples and several devout women who followed him stood hard beside the wall to allow passage of the condemned and their guards. Josias thought them the saddest, most dejected group he had ever seen.*

It is well that they feel as dejected as they look. This is a terrible thing. To crucify this man, who has always done only good, is a truly terrible thing. Surely the Romans are mad. If only I were free and had my scimitar, these dogs of Caesar's would soon be cut down and the Master released.

*Fuming in anger, Josias never thought of his impending end. The heavy cross lay across his shoulders unheeded. He marched along, thinking only of the soldiers taking Jesus to the cross.*

*On Golgotha's brow, Tullus ordered Simon to throw down Jesus' cross before the center of the three deep holes prepared for this hour. Each of the malefactors did the same, Josias on the right of center, and Lucius on the left.*

*Four of the legionnaires positioned Jesus atop the cross. One of them held each of his hands outstretched on the crossbeam that gave Rome's vicious implement of death its name. A fifth guard fitted the point of a hammered iron spike to the palm of Jesus' right hand. He raised his head and nodded to another who hit the spike a terrible blow with a large maul, driving it through*

*Jesus' hand and into the wood beneath. Two additional blows made sure the spike was secure.*

*In the crowd around the hill the prisoners heard great cries of elation and derision mixed with the sound of animal ferocity from the Levites. Those sounds were soon lost in the swell of sound created by the groans and gasps of compassion from the people who believed in the Master.*

*One man, who recently became a believer, charged barehanded into the soldiers. One of the guards knocked him unconscious with a staff. He lay quiet and unknowing beside the Nazarene while the grisly task of nailing his hands and feet to the cross continued.*

*Josias cringed with pain at each blow of the maul. He felt as though each blow was struck against his own flesh instead of that of this strange man many now called the Christ.*

*When Jesus' hands and feet were firmly nailed in place, four of the guards picked up the cross by its short piece and pushed and pulled until it stood erect, and the long end dropped into the hole. The Nazarene's face twisted in anguish when he felt the terrible pain that racked his hands and feet when the full weight of his body jerked against the rough iron spikes.*

*Lucius was next. Each guard required additional help to hold the screaming wretch in place for the nailing. After they finished and stood the cross that held Lucius in its place, the Legionnaires turned to Josias.*

*The time of reckoning arrived. Josias turned his face toward that of the Master and mentally pleaded for strength. He felt a great desire to muster the courage to face his just due without screaming as Lucius had done. The first blow was so great a shock that his mind wavered into semi-consciousness. He did not think clearly again until after his cross stood erect at the Master's right hand.*

*The realization that he hung there, nailed to the cross, soon to die an inglorious death, caused Josias to tremble with a great terror. It was almost too much for him to control. He reminded himself to be proud that he did not scream when the nails cut into his flesh as Lucius did, and this punishment, although harsh and cruel, was only just punishment for his many crimes. He finally managed to calm himself and turn again to the Master for strength.*

*"The Master." He mumbled to himself, shaking his head, "Ha—why do I say that? Why have I called him the Master?"*

*He heard or perhaps he only felt his words, but he knew they meant he had accepted Jesus as his Savior. With this knowledge, a great surge of compassion and peace swept over him.*

# The Malefactors

# Chapter 25

*In the early morning of the holiest day of Passover, Sarah rose from her bed and readied herself for the long trip to Jerusalem to see Josias. Mattathah made great efforts to dissuade the girl from her plans, fearing what she would find, but to no effect.*

*Sarah would only say, "I must see my beloved."*

*Unable to change the girl's mind, Mattathah donned dress suitable for the trip and the two women set out together, joining many others of Bethany on the way to the Holy City.*

*A soldier recognized them from their previous visits to the prison and directed them to Golgotha, or the place of the skull. Mattathah tried in her most persuasive manner to dissuade Sarah from her intent to see her husband, but she would not be dissuaded and set out through the crowded city for the hill.*

*A long way south of Golgotha they came upon a throng of those who came to witness the executions. Many who believed on him were there and when they discovered who the women were, helped them press through the crowds so they might be nearer to their loved one.*

*It took a long time for the women to climb close enough to recognize the faces of the condemned men. At the sight of the Christ and her beloved Josias hanging beside him, both men naked and bloody, in great misery from the pull of the nails that held them fast to the cross, Sarah let out a choked scream and turned to bury her face in Mattathah's bosom. Josias' mother comforted her as best she could, although she too was heartbroken.*

*As the wife and mother stood, crushed by grief, they heard Lucius rail. "If thou are the Christ, save thyself and us with thee."*

*Josias heard him and lifted his head. Forcing his eyes to open, he looked toward Lucius and said, "Dost not thou fear God? We receive that which is our just due, for we have robbed and murdered, but the Master has done nothing—nothing, yet he hangs between us."*

*He turned his face to Jesus, "Lord, I pray thee, remember me when thou comest into thy kingdom."*

*His voice soft, Jesus said, "Verily, I say unto thee, this day thou shall be with me in Paradise."*

*A look of peace came to the face of Josias, the condemned robber. Lucius screamed louder.*

*As the crowd left the place of agony, great ominous clouds gathered over the hill amidst long, crackling, darting streaks of lightening and unnaturally loud peals of thunder. People scurried for shelter. Some screamed in fright. All were fearful of so violent an exhibition of the power of the elements. Many prophesied of evils to come, but few knew the fear that overcame the priests when the veil of the altar was rent within their holiest sanctuary.*

*As Mattathah comforted the stricken girl, she felt her grief might be easier for she had heard the Master's promise to Josias. Somehow, Sarah concluded that her husband gave his life in an abortive attempt to save the Master's. This belief would make her grief bearable.*

*Sarah's grief was eased even more when John, whom Jesus loved, with the help of several other disciples carried the body of*

*Josias to Bethany. With help from Lazarus they buried him in the garden of graves beside the resting place of his father. Mattathah attempted to thank them and John said to her, "The Master forgave him. Those the Master loved, we love."*

The End

# Anne Haw Holt

Anne Haw Holt, writing as A. H. Holt, is a Virginian transplanted to a 1910 "Cracker" cottage in Monticello, Florida. She attended PVCC in Charlottesville, Va. and received her BA from Mary Baldwin in Staunton, VA in 1989. She holds a MA and Ph.D. in History from Florida State University in Tallahassee, Florida.

Anne is an accomplished storyteller and photographer. She writes fiction, poetry, and non-fiction on writing, history, parenting and Frontier Florida. Dr. Holt writes grants and teaches writing, grant writing, writing and leadership.

Other Books by Anne Haw Holt

Fiction

High Plains Fort
Ten in Texas
Silver Creek
Blanco Sol
Riding Fence
Kendrick
Blood Redemption


Nonfiction

Grant Writing Step by Step
From Writer to Author
Beautiful Places:
Monticello & Jefferson County Florida

Thank You